Jorge   and swaggered
down tne room towards the front of the
bar.

'Hey, Antonio,' he called cheerfully, 'I
thought *I* was the one who couldn't hold
my drink. You should see yourselves
now!'

Rodriguez, D'asser and Eloi swung
round.

Simultaneously the soldier across the street
saw the movement – and perhaps the glint
of Jorge's glass – in the *canteena's* shaded
interior. He threw the 66mm rocket
launcher to his shoulder. He paused for
only a fraction of a second to sight it, and
squeezed the black rubber-covered
activator tit on top of the tube.

There was a flash at the muzzle of the
disposable glass fibre tube. The rocket flew
with unerring accuracy across the still,
dusty road and through the open doors of
the bar.

A millisecond later, it exploded.

Also by Chris Dempster

CONTRACT!
HIT!
FIREPOWER (with Dave Tomkins)

and published by Corgi Books

Havoc!

Chris Dempster

CORGI BOOKS

HAVOC!

A CORGI BOOK 0 552 12642 X

First publication in Great Britain

PRINTING HISTORY
Corgi edition published 1986

This book is set in 10/11 pt Baskerville

Corgi Books are published by Transworld Publishers Ltd.,
61-63 Uxbridge Road, Ealing, London W5 5SA, in
Australia by Transworld Publishers (Aust.) Pty. Ltd.,
26 Harley Crescent, Condell Park, NSW 2200, and in New
Zealand by Transworld Publishers (N.Z.) Ltd., Cnr.
Moselle and Waipareira Avenues, Henderson, Auckland.

Made and printed in Great Britain by
Hunt Barnard Printing Ltd., Aylesbury, Bucks.

They go to fight
In farflung lands
In steaming jungles
In tropical sands.

Not for honour,
Glory, recognition or fame,
But for money, excitement
And the love of 'The Game'.

And if they should die
By the bullet or sword,
'Tis a far better way
Than some 'terminal ward'.

The rallying cry
They all seek to appease
Is the wild clear call
Of the 'Flying Geese'.

Havoc!

1

'Cowards die many times before their deaths.'
William Shakespeare

Williams pressed his tense, sweating body against the parched, iron-hard ground, as if willing it to open up and give him refuge. He strained to remain totally immobile, but the panic surged through his body, turning his breathing into a series of ragged, painful gasps. His eyes were clamped tightly shut, but he could not close his terror-fuelled imagination. The enemy were out there, their eyes glinting over their gun sights. He pictured them smirking, extracting every ounce of enjoyment from their cat-and-mouse game with their cornered prey.

A burst of machine-gun fire ripped through the hot, heavy African silence. Another followed, overlapping with the first. The bullets chewed chunks from the hard ground. Some of the dirt sprayed over him from both sides: the bastards knew exactly where he was. The next bursts would be only a few feet apart. Then they would concentrate on precisely the same spot: himself.

A mortar bomb fell close by. Williams shuddered involuntarily. He prayed with the complete faith of despair that they hadn't seen the slight movements. His only hope of surviving was if they thought he was already dead.

It was getting harder to breath. He took tiny gulps of air, minimizing the chance of them seeing his chest movements. But his racing blood demanded oxygen: suddenly the pain of constriction within his aching lungs grew too agonizing to

9

bear. Panic welled up into a huge, irresistible torrent which flooded into his mind and expelled the vestiges of reason and sanity.

Williams jerked bolt upright and let out a great howl of sheer terror. His eyes were still shut; he covered them with his hands to make doubly sure that he would only feel death, not see it as well. As he waited, the sweat ran together in a river and cascaded down the middle of his chest.

But when it came, the end was neither a machine-gun bullet nor a mortar bomb. His wife Sandy was shaking him. Williams' screams had woken her a few seconds earlier. She used the same tactics to soothe him as she did with their young son after a nightmare.

'There now, darling,' she whispered gently. 'It's all right. It wasn't real. It's all over . . .'.

But Williams was a man, not a four-year-old boy. His nightmares were real; they needed more than a few caresses to make them retreat. He squeezed Sandy's shoulder and got out of bed, his hand fumbling for the cigarettes and matches on the bedside table. He sucked in a lungful of smoke, revelling in the cool night air which swirled through his thin pyjamas. Out *there* it had always been hot and muggy; he had hungered for the cold of an English night.

He sat in the darkened room for nearly an hour. He smoked six cigarettes. Sandy's breathing soon slowed into the familiar rhythm of sleep. Williams could hear the children turning restlessly in their sleep in the next room. It was all right, he told himself: he was *here*, and he would never have to go back. At last he got back into bed, curled up under the duvet and allowed the tide of exhaustion to roll over him.

A few hours later the remorseless monotone of the radio alarm cut its way into his sleeping mind. He was dreaming again, but this time the dream was gentle and vaguely pleasant. For thirty seconds he struggled to remain with the dream in the no man's land between sleep and consciousness. But that insidious alarm could not be ignored.

Williams slid out his hand from the warmth of the duvet

10

and fumbled awkwardly with the small plastic knobs on the facia of the alarm. Why the hell did the manufacturers have to make them so tricky? The LEDs on the facia glowed malevolently at him, the seconds winking inexorably away. At last he found the button which controlled the alarm.

The sound died. Williams rolled back into the bed, luxuriating in the warmth all the more because he was now wide awake and knew he had to leave it. Sandy, who made a later start than he did, slept on. He ran his hand along the plump hip which was angled towards him and reluctantly edged from under the bedclothes.

The cold caught him unawares and he shivered violently. He grabbed his towelling dressing gown from the chair and shrugged into it. The summer was finally banished for another year: he made a mental note to adjust the timing device and the thermostat on the central heating; he had no intention of waking up to a cold house on the frosty mornings which lay ahead.

Sandy was snoring softly in the big double bed. Williams picked up his clothes and tiptoed out of the room. He knew from bitter experience that if he woke her too early she would be in a foul mood for the rest of the day.

He closed the bedroom door quietly behind him and went into the bathroom. The harsh strip lighting and cold water on his face unpleasantly but effectively purged the last traces of sleep.

William shaved with care, easing the razor over his thin, angular face. A man in his position could not afford to have unsightly red blotches or wisps of cotton wool on his face; the customers wouldn't like it. He wished — as he did every morning — that he could grow a beard and dispense, once and for all, with the singularly uncomfortable task of shaving; but old habits died hard, and besides Sandy hated the feeling of bristles on his face.

The final part of his bathroom routine involved a five minute stint with the exerciser. At first he kept his eyes on that small red indicator, vainly trying to push it past his achievement on the previous day. Then his gaze drifted up

11

to the mirror over the basin. He was six foot two and thirty-two years old; his blond hair had no hint of grey; he carried no excess weight; he should be in the prime of his physical condition. That was the trouble: he should look like Charles Atlas; instead he looked like the weed who got sand kicked in his face. His scrawny shoulders strained against the exerciser. He gave it another futile, vicious wrench.

His thoughts moved on to the day ahead. Today could be important for the future, and the prospect made him apprehensive. He abandoned the exerciser two minutes before schedule; the time could be more usefully spent on brushing his clothes.

Twenty minutes later, Williams slipped out of his front door, gently pulling it closed behind him. He glanced up at the curtained bedroom windows of the modern semi-detached house. It was too cold to linger. He walked briskly through the early morning gloom into the neat, horseshoe-shaped cul-de-sac. On every side were houses identical to his own, differing only in the details of their paintwork, the lay-out of their gardens and the quality of their net curtains.

The Ford was parked at the kerb, its black paintwork and chrome trimmings gleaming dully in the half-light. Williams walked around it, checking that its immaculate appearance had not been marred by bird-droppings. Williams hated birds. This time the car had been spared: Williams gave a small, self-satisfied smile.

He caught a glimpse of himself in the wing mirror as he passed it on his tour of inspection. His smile broadened: he glanced down at his crisply-pressed grey flannel suit and the highly-buffed black leather shoes; his hand automatically checked the set of his unblemished white collar and small neat knot of his black tie. That was one thing the army taught you: how to look after your appearance. He looked what he was, Williams thought: a chauffeur who was accustomed to work only for the very best employers, and whose appearance was modelled on that of the better class of undertaker.

He unlocked the car and got behind the wheel. The big,

smooth engine fired at once. Peter Williams rubbed his hands as he waited for the engine to warm up. Only then would he permit himself to push the slide controls of the heater on to boost. He pulled down the sun visor over the windscreen and checked his appearance once more in the vanity mirror concealed behind it. The college boy hairstyle needed no attention, but there was a speck of dandruff on his jacket collar; he quickly brushed it off. Clients could be extraordinarily touchy about personal hygiene.

Williams expertly reversed the black Ford out of the cul-de-sac. He drove sedately down the long, tree-lined avenue beyond. At this hour of the morning there were few other cars. He passed a milkman and a newspaperboy, both heavily wrapped up against the cold.

The grass at the centre of the big roundabout which switched Maidenhead traffic on to the M4 was white with hoarfrost. Minutes later, Williams was driving east towards London on the six-lane motorway.

He could have pushed the powerful car up to its limit on the near-empty road, but he preferred to cruise at a steady sixty m.p.h. The respect that Peter Williams showed to his car was due to more than the mere fact that he owned it. The Ford also represented a second mortgage on his Maidenhead home, a point which Sandy regularly mentioned with bitterness in her voice. But, most importantly, it was the foundation on which Williams' firm was built: the Ford was his hope for the future.

He pulled into the centre lane to overtake an articulated lorry, taking a mild pleasure from the firm movements of his hands on the controls — *his* controls. It hadn't always been like this. Sometimes he had felt he had no future to look forward to at all. For three years Williams had been employed by a private car hire firm. He had spent long, gruelling hours behind the wheel of one of their cars. His earnings were regular and secure — and unlikely to show a significant increase in real terms until the end of his working life. Williams' discontent increased as he watched the company expanding rapidly and raking in immense profits.

He decided that the profits he earned for them could just as well be for him. But Williams was a cautious man: before he struck out on his own, he observed the workings of the company and cultivated personal relationships with a choice selection of his employer's clients. Once he had established the right contacts for future contracts he approached his bank for a loan to buy his own limo.

Only then did Peter Williams resign from his car-hire firm. Africa had taught him the folly of acting rashly. It was not a lesson he was likely to forget in a hurry.

The purring luxury of this big Ford, Williams thought, was an achievement. It was going to be the first of many. He allowed his mind to wander back to earlier stages in his career, taking pleasure in the contrast between then and now. He hadn't always been a chauffeur: his work record was a hotch-potch of poorly-paid jobs, most of which he had held only for a few months. The one exception was his six-year stint in the army.

He had served in the Royal Corps of Signals, training as a wireless operator; he had learned what he had to know and no more. His six years had been totally uneventful. At the time he had thought he was wasting his life in the forces — but now he wasn't so sure. Without that training he wouldn't have gone to Africa.

But when he left the army it seemed that no one wanted to capitalize on his skill with VHF radios. The one opening was the Merchant Navy — and the thought of spending the rest of his working days closeted in the private hell of a radio shack on the high seas failed to appeal to him. He was out of work and nearly broke when he saw that advertisement in one of the national daily newspapers: men with military skills were 'wanted for interesting work abroad'.

They wanted mercenaries; and they were paying enough to make Williams want to be one. They wanted him to go to fight against the Communists in Angola, a little African country he had hardly heard of. Williams was perfectly happy to oblige — he would have fought anyone if the money was right and the odds were on his side.

14

But the realities of combat in a war-torn, poverty-stricken African country were different from how Williams had imagined them. What was going on bore no resemblance to British Army manoeuvres against an exotic backdrop. He spent only two weeks in Angola, in the terrified condition of a man who has finally realized that nightmares can and do come true. He kept as far as possible away from the fighting. Fate finally answered his prayers: he was manning the radio in a Land Rover when the vehicle accidentally overturned. Williams' leg was broken and he spent the next three weeks recuperating in a hotel in neighbouring Zaire. The other mercenaries who were convalescing there avoided him: they could sense with the infallible instinct of fighting soldiers that he was there under false pretences.

Wiliams' fears increased as he recovered from his injury. But fate decided to answer his prayers a second time: by the time he was fit for duty, the mercenary effort was spent. Much to his relief, the survivors were summarily repatriated.

When the mercenaries flew into Heathrow airport they found the press had turned out in force to meet them. Their activities had created a furore in Britain. Williams, back in the safety of his home territory, was not slow to spot an opportunity for gain. He made a comfortable sum of money by selling his inside story to the media. His exclusive releases were full of lurid details and were not reticent about Williams' own extraordinary heroism. The fact that practically everything he said was untrue or exaggerated beyond recognition bothered neither Williams nor those who bought his story.

The other mercenaries took a different view.

The media money paid for the deposit on the three bedroom semi in Maidenhead; Sandy had always dreamed of living there. But Williams' short stay in Africa had other, more profound effects on his life. Previously he had been a mediocrity — he had even recognized it himself. He had few friends; people only asked him to parties to make up the numbers.

Since his stories and his photograph had appeared in the press, however, all this had changed. Williams pretended to be blasé about his experiences, real and imagined, but he was very much aware that they made him mysteriously attractive to others. Many people admired a soldier of fortune; and most respected him.

Williams often said to Sandy that his trip to Angola had been the turning point in their lives. Without it, it was unlikely they would have had their own house and their own business.

Sandy always agreed it had been a turning point, but not for the same reason. She had been woken too often in the early hours of the morning by the hoarse, terrified cries of her husband. She had seen the cold sweat running down his rigid, skinny body. The nightmares had started after Angola — that was the real difference.

Since Angola, Peter Williams had spent his dreaming hours waiting for that final bullet or shell.

2

'A new broom is good for three days.'
Italian proverb

As Williams drove over the elevated section of the Great West Road, past the Cunard Hotel, he glanced at the round quartz clock in the wooden trim of the Ford's dash panel. He was going to arrive at his destination with almost half an hour to spare. He had allowed extra time this morning because there was yet another national rail strike to bedevil the lives of commuters. But he was early enough to have avoided most of the extra traffic.

His route took him past the Victoria and Albert Museum and Harrods, down Piccadilly and up Shaftesbury Avenue. Few people were about and fewer shops were open, but he knew of a workers' cafe where you could get strong, sweet tea at any hour of the day or night. He parked outside and spent a quarter of an hour over a mug of tea, staring through the windows at the world outside, distorted by dirt and condensation.

He drove back the same way as he had come. This account customer was a new one, and he felt the familiar tension rising; it was vital to make a good impression, particularly if you were self-employed.

He parked outside the rear entrance of the Ritz, locked the car and went into the foyer. The first few times he had come here, the sumptuous surrounding had overawed him. By now he was used to them: it was just another place where he picked up customers. At least you could usually be sure of a reasonable tip if you met them here.

News of his arrival was telephoned up to his client's room. Williams waited patiently, clutching the cap which was his badge of office in his hands. Sometimes you could wait for hours for a client to condescend to turn up. Williams mentally shrugged: it was okay by him if that was what they wanted; they were paying through the nose for the privilege of treating him like a servant.

'Williams. My name is Alexander Dorian.'

Startled out of his reverie, Williams hastily swung round, composing his bleak features into the servile mask he reserved for clients. The thick carpet had muffled Dorian's approach.

'Good morning, sir. The car is waiting.' As he spoke, Williams unobtrusively examined his new customer. Dorian was a thickset, middle-aged man with broad, impassive features and watchful blue eyes. His neck and shoulders were heavy like a bull's, giving an impression of physical strength. He was well-protected from the cold by a knee-length astrakhan coat with a beaver lamb collar. A black Homburg sat squarely on his head.

Dorian handed Williams the heavy leather document case he was carrying and, with a wordless jerk of his head, indicated that Williams should precede him to the car.

There was money here, the chauffeur thought as he opened the rear door of the Ford. Dorian's crocodile leather shoes were Gucci, matching the document case. His skin had that sleek patina which accompanies high living — and high blood pressure. Williams wondered about his nationality: the man's American-accented English had guttural undertones, suggesting a German, Swiss or maybe Austrian origin.

Dorian settled into the back seat of the car. He removed his Homburg, revealing a mane of well-groomed black hair, shot through with streaks of iron grey. His eyes quickly assessed the interior of the car; he was clearly a man who wanted value for his money.

As Williams slid into the front of the car, Dorian clicked open his document case and pulled out a perfectly typed

18

sheet of paper which he passed over the seats to Williams.

'This is my itinerary for each working day over your hire period of four weeks.' He paused and added: 'I insist upon promptness at all times.'

'Of course, sir.' Williams glanced through the crowded schedule. Each of the appointments had been underlined and included the time and the address. Most of the firms were financial houses of one sort or another, located in the City.

'I am a Swiss,' Dorian answered Williams' unspoken question. 'My bank's business often brings me and my colleagues to London.'

Williams took the hint like a trout snaps up a fly; he didn't need to have it spelled out. If this job went well, it could lead to a great deal more work. But Williams knew from long experience that there would be more to come: that sort of hint was usually a prelude to a request.

Dorian coughed. 'In addition to the itinerary, I shall also require your services most evenings as well. I anticipate that some of my appointments may develop into — ah — social activities.'

The slight stress on the word 'social' was not lost on Williams. He nodded intelligently at his employer.

There was a flicker in Dorian's heavy-lidded eyes. 'I may also desire . . . company on these occasions, and afterwards. A man must relax.'

'I understand, sir. There will be no problem with the itinerary, morning, noon or night, or with the other request.' Williams concealed his delight beneath a blank, obliging expression; the commission he could earn on subsidiary services could be worth almost as much as the driving itself. 'The last item,' he said smoothly, 'will have to be paid for in cash, on a daily basis.'

The Swiss nodded. He terminated the conversation by closing the document case and leaning back against the plush upholstery. Williams clipped the itinerary to a small millboard and eased the big car into the now-congested stream of traffic which moved sluggishly down Piccadilly.

During that first day there was little conversation between the two men. Dorian appeared absorbed, either by his papers or by his thoughts. Williams spoke only when spoken to, as befitted the perfect chauffeur. The grey London drizzle descended incessantly throughout the day. Williams ushered his charge between the car and his appointments beneath a big, black umbrella. At six-thirty they returned to the Ritz.

Dorian glanced up as Williams opened the rear door. 'My evening is free. I should like to relax in pleasant company.'

'Yes sir,' said Williams. 'Do you have any particular preferences?'

The relationship between employer and employee altered considerably in the course of the next week. The main reason for this, at first, was Dorian's insatiable appetite for women — and Williams' ability to supply him with a seemingly-unending stream of fresh girls and fresh locations. Dorian — or rather, his bank — paid heavily for the privilege, but the investment was worth it; Williams seemed to have a passkey to at least half of Greater London.

After a few days, the Swiss began to travel in the front of the car, alongside his driver. Williams still preserved a proper distance between them, always addressing him as 'Sir' or 'Mr Dorian', but the personal climate between the two men rapidly thawed as the weather outside grew colder. Dorian encouraged Williams to talk about himself, enjoying the flow of anecdotes which the chauffeur was happy to provide if it kept the customer happy. Moreover, it was almost a matter of habit for Dorian to encourage others to talk about themselves; much of his phenomenal success as a banking executive stemmed from two related facts — everyone likes to talk about himself, and Dorian was quite prepared to listen. It was astonishing what people would let drop when they were engrossed in their favourite subject.

And Williams was only too happy to oblige. He told

20

Sandy that he could be on to a gold mine with this particular punter: the foreigner had wealth, connections and a healthy taste for extracurricular activities.

Early one evening, Williams was driving Dorian up Haverstock Hill; the Swiss was due to dine in Hampstead with one of his bank's more influential customers. The traffic was heavy, and the Ford spent more time standing still than it did moving. Dorian drummed his fingers against his document case: his host was well-known for the fetish he made of punctuality, and the banker had no wish to be late.

Just before Belsize Park Underground station, a tanker pulled out of a side road directly in their path. Williams was forced to jam on his breaks. The tanker ground up the hill in front of them.

Dorian's face darkened. 'They should not allow such heavy traffic in the residential sections of your capital,' he spat out in his precise, oddly formal English. 'And that man ahead should not be allowed to drive at all.'

'Makes you want to turn to violence, doesn't it, sir?' Williams said with a sideways glance at his passenger. 'I once saw someone chuck a grenade into one of them tankers. Amazing sight. The driver was roasted.'

Dorian glanced quickly at his chauffeur. 'Where was this? You mentioned you had been in the army, but I thought you said your time was uneventful.'

'Ah, this was later on, Mr Dorian.' Williams paused, sensing that he had his employer's interest. 'In Angola.'

Williams had hoped the revelation of his mercenary background would impress the banker, but Dorian's interest in it exceeded all his expectations. His passenger's impatience to be in Hampstead vanished. Dorian immediately began to question him about his experiences with gratifying attention.

The Swiss often reverted to the subject in the next few days. He wanted to know why Williams had become a mercenary, what he had done, and whether he was still in touch with his old comrades.

Williams discussed his mercenary past in great detail and

21

with an elaborate casualness born of long practice. Dorian flattered him by seeming to believe every word he said. They became less like chauffeur and client and more like two friends. Several times they had a drink together. Williams made quite a point of his brief career as a media celebrity, and even showed Dorian some of his newspaper clippings.

Naturally, the chauffeur claimed, he was still in regular touch with his old colleagues; he hinted that he had inside knowledge of the current mercenary scene and, more vaguely, of the secret violence which lay behind the smooth façades of newspaper headlines.

But Williams would have been surprised if he had learned the banker's real opinion of him. Dorian had not got where he was by taking people at their face value. It had struck him from the first that his driver was fundamentally a fawning sycophant: he was scarcely in the usual mould of men of violence.

Williams had no idea how thoroughly Dorian was investigating him. Many of those conversations served as the settings for carefully contrived questions which exposed inconsistencies in the chauffeur's account of his doings. The clippings reinforced the opinion that Dorian already held: that Williams was a braggart.

The porters at big hotels provide an efficient and remarkably wide-ranging variety of services for their guests; those at the Ritz are particularly good. For a suitable remuneration, one of the porters obtained photocopies of the relevant back-issues of the British newspapers in which Williams' disclosures had appeared. Dorian studied them diligently.

In the final analysis the banker's assessment was shrewdly accurate. Williams had certainly been in Angola but his activities there had probably been far less dramatic than he maintained.

But the crucial consideration lay in the present, not the past: what was Williams' position now in the murky world of the modern soldiers of fortune?

Dorian pondered the question, trying to come to a decision.

His future might depend on it. He suspected that, if Williams was still in contact with the men whose names he had bandied about in Fleet Street, that contact would be slight indeed. On the other hand, it was just possible that the chauffeur's claims might have a grain of truth in them: the man might be able to provide the banker with his initial introduction to the closed world of the mercenaries.

Alexander Dorian shivered, but not with fear. Despite himself, he was amazed by the enormity of what he could do — *would* do — with a group of such men.

Their loyalty, he reflected happily, could be bought and paid for; their morals and scruples were not in doubt because they had never been in existence in the first place.

3

'The faults of burglars are the qualities of financiers.'
George Bernard Shaw

Towards the end of his stay in London, Alexander Dorian broke with routine and spent the evening alone in his second-floor suite at the Ritz. To an outside observer it would have seemed that Dorian spent most of his time staring into a heavy crystal glass containing — the bottle's label was clearly visible — twelve-year-old Glenlivet. But the banker's mind was not on malt whisky: he was staring at his past, present and future.

He was aware he had reached a crossroads in his career, though he believed — and — hoped — that few of his colleagues had realized the fact. The board members of the large, multi-national bank which employed him considered his post to be one of the most important in the organization's corporate and executive structure. He was at the head of an immensely lucrative department which handled Third World investments and offered a consultancy service; most of the business he handled emanated from Africa.

The department's importance was implied by its location: it was housed on the first floor of the huge headquarters of the bank, an imposing building largely constructed of marble and dark glass in the expensive heart of Geneva's banking district. It had achieved for its parent organization what very few other Western banking establishments had managed to do: a steady expansion of profits, sustained over a period of twenty years, from investments in Africa. Dorian had set up the department nearly a quarter of a century ago. Since then the department had expanded with the profits it brought in.

Over the past twenty-five years nearly all the African countries had emerged — by one route or another — from beneath the yoke of colonialism. Their former masters had sought to build financial empires on the crumbling foundations of the political ones: they invested huge sums in the new states, creating a climate of constant debt which ensured that the flow of cheap raw material continued uninterrupted to the parent countries. The foreign powers used their own banking institutions to fund the various investments. Throughout the late Sixties and early Seventies they poured billions of dollars, francs and pounds into ambitious hydroelectric schemes, trans-continental highways, capital industrial plant and dozens of similar programmes.

Most of the banks had their fingers badly burned. The present rulers of the former colonies preferred to use a large proportion of the investment for gold-plated bath-tubs, fleets of expensive European motor cars and lavish coronations or investitures.

Dorian's bank invested as well but astonished its competitors by coming out with a consistently healthy profit. Several of those competitors would have paid millions for the Swiss bank's enviable formula for success.

But there was no formula: the secret was very simple. From time immemorial, the bank had had a huge safety deposit section in its vaults. From time to time the anonymous owners of a deposit would either disappear or simply fail to pay for the use of the facility. The bank would make every effort to ascertain the whereabouts of the owner or the existence of a beneficiary. But if these procedures failed, the bank would legitimately assume title of ownership after some years had elapsed.

It was Dorian — then an ambitious young man on the threshold of his career — who had realized that the

25

windfalls which accrued from this form of banking could be pursued as a line of business. He astutely calculated that the greatest potential for it was in Africa, with its volatile politics and the immense wealth of some of its leaders.

The board listened with interest, and decided to give this bright young man a chance to prove himself. He was sent to Leopoldville, in the newly and precariously independent Congo, to advise Prime Minister Patrice Lumumba on his financial affairs.

The African needed little persuasion to see the advantages of a personal numbered account whose existence was only known to the board and himself. Dorian, the obliging young man from Switzerland, showed the grateful Lumumba how to skim off a percentage of the Western aid money, and how to convert innumerable kilos of his country's uncut diamonds into currency; all of the cash naturally found its way into the vaults beneath the Geneva bank.

Dorian's forethought paid off handsomely early in 1961, when Lumumba was assassinated. The young banker personally erased the account entries from the records; and the bank quietly absorbed an estimated $140 million, secure in the knowledge that this action, with all its professional ramifications, was known only to the four members of the board and Dorian himself.

On behalf of the bank Dorian used the money for a series of African speculations. It was their policy to invest only in those countries where they had the full cooperation of the resident dictator. In effect, any investment was always underwritten by the contents of the dictator's personal account in their own vaults; the account's contents, of course, had almost always been skimmed off from the public monies of the country concerned.

Whatever happened, the bank couldn't lose. The world is tightly governed by good, honest banking procedures. Dorian's secret of success was simply a complete reversal of the single rule from which the procedures flowed: honesty was replaced by dishonesty.

By the late Seventies and early Eighties, Dorian's department had grown to be one of the largest in the bank; it was certainly the most profitable; and its investments had the advantage of being completely secure. The department employed a large graduate staff with a background in African politics to monitor the day-to-day situation in Africa; but not one of them was privy to Dorian's unique strategy for success.

Alexander Dorian sailed into Africa like a latterday Livingstone, equipped with the bank's high reputation, his department's information and his own, ever-widening circle of contacts. He brought home not title to foreign lands, but signatures on valuable contracts.

But despite his success, the banker was not at all happy with his position, and had not been for some years. He knew that he was responsible for the bank's vast increase in profits, and that the financial life blood he had drained from the Dark Continent had made possible the extension and diversification of its investments in other fields. By rights he should have been invited on to the board of directors long ago.

But he knew this would never happen; he would never rise further in this organization. The reason for this had never been mentioned explicitly, by the directors, but Dorian knew quite well what it was. They were happy enough to give him *carte blanche* in African affairs, and to pocket the profits he brought back to them; but they secretly despised his methods. Had anyone else been in his position, Dorian might have found the directors' hypocrisy amusing.

As it was, he diverted his anger and his thwarted ambition into the setting up of freelance deals. He was sufficiently shrewd to do this outside the bank's sphere of influence, knowing that he couldn't afford the luxury of cutting his ties with his employers; their organization offered him too many advantages.

Now he was glad of his restraint: if he had left the bank he would now be spending the night in a seedy bed-and-breakfast, not the Ritz. His attempt to construct his own financial power-base had gone disastrously awry. Private

27

enterprise had cost him dear — he had lost nearly all his personal investments and depended for survival on the bank's monthly paycheck and the generous expense account which went with it. He was honest enough to realize that there was a hitherto unsuspected flaw in his financial acumen which only appeared when he was working for himself. He was like a boxer of world class who, when managed by a professional man, rises to the very pinnacle of success. Then the boxer tries to manage himself — and finds that not only is he incapable of management, but that he slips down the ratings as a boxer as well.

Alexander Dorian swore. For the past half-hour, the only sound in that hotel room had been the rumbling of the traffic outside. He finished off his whisky, got to his feet and began to pace up and down. The thick carpet deadened the sound of his feet. As he walked, he unconsciously loosened his tie and unbuttoned his waistcoat. He was fed up with restrictions, both physical and financial. The ambition which consumed his every waking hour had to find an outlet.

If he couldn't find one legitimately — well, there were other methods. He had been employing the latter on behalf of others for most of his working life. Why not employ those methods on behalf of himself?

And Williams could be the key to those methods.

Dorian laughed bitterly. He crossed the room and poured himself some more whisky. It was ironic that his future should be dependent on a man such as Williams. He flung himself back in his chair and began to drum his fingers on the arm, a nervous habit which he found irresistible whenever he was tense or impatient. Just suppose Williams could introduce him to a group of men to whom life was as cheap as a can of beans: what then?

His mind went back to a deal he had set up just before his trip to London, in his role as the bank's representative. It involved the president of a small West African state whose diamond mines were world famous. The First Citizen — as he frequently termed himself in his speeches — naturally

28

had unrestricted access to the vaults of the nationalized company. Every four to six weeks, the president would personally select a quantity of uncut diamonds from the vaults. These would be placed in a sealed container and entrusted to a courier, who naturally had the additional protection of diplomatic status.

From that point onwards, Dorian's arrangements came into force. A car and driver would meet the courier as he flew into Heathrow. The courier was taken to a small, discreet hotel in Knightsbridge. Dorian, anxious to minimize the risk of the theft or loss of the courier's vital brief-case, insisted that the man should not leave the hotel during his overnight stay. With his customary attention to detail, Dorian arranged for the fleshpots of London to be brought to the courier's room, in whatever shape the latter required.

The following morning one of Dorian's employees would collect the tired but happy courier and escort him to Hatton Garden. After a jeweller had appraised and catalogued the stones, the courier took them on to Geneva, where Dorian personally would meet him.

In the ensuing months the bank circumspectly sold the diamonds through a variety of American and European diamond merchants. The profits were lodged in the president's account — minus, of course, a 'handling charge', the amount of which was rather more than the president realized. But the president was delighted — not only with his account but with the progress that the bank's construction company was making on his new palace.

Doran's fingers stopped moving on the arm of his chair. He could feel a tide of excitement pulsing through him. The glass of whisky stood untouched on the table. With fierce concentration he focused his memory on his briefing session with the courier.

He had impressed upon the black man the absolute necessity of keeping the diplomatic bag in his possession at all times, whether in transit or at the hotel. He had quoted instances — and God knew there were enough of them — of hotel safes being robbed with childish ease. At the time

29

Dorian's concern had been for the security of the stones — and therefore of the bank's eventual profit.

Now he realized that his caution could just as well work for himself.

Alexander Dorian laughed. He was still at the crossroads of his career, but at least he had found a signpost. The despair which had haunted him earlier now receded. His mood swung abruptly upwards. The night was young. He no longer wished to spend it alone. Why should he, if the bank would pay for company? He picked up the telephone.

The hotel porter system was really very efficient, he thought, particularly at the Ritz.

Two days later, Williams drove Dorian down to Heathrow. At the airport, the driver carried the banker's luggage to the check-in desk. The VDU showed that passengers were already boarding the Swissair flight to Geneva.

Dorian turned to Williams, extending a hand. 'Goodbye, my friend,' he said with heavy Teutonic cordiality. The younger man winced: Dorian had a grip like a grizzly bear's.

'I hope I'll be seeing you again, Mr Dorian.' Williams surreptitiously massaged his right hand. Out of the corner of his eye, he could see that Dorian was reaching for his wallet.

'Of course.' Dorian had the wallet in his hand now, but he made no move to open it. 'You have some business cards? Many of my colleagues would be interested in the services of a — ah — *reliable* London driver.'

Williams breathed a sigh of relief. For a moment he thought the Swiss had forgotten his earlier promise. He hurriedly produced a handful of cards.

'Just give me a day's notice when you're next coming to London, sir,' Williams assured him. 'I'll be here to meet you.'

Dorian opened his wallet and extracted some banknotes, one by one. Williams watched, trying with only partial success to conceal his eagerness. Twenty, forty, sixty . . . *Christ!*

'There is one other thing,' Dorian said casually, the banknotes still in his hand. 'On my next trip to London, I would like you to arrange an introduction for me. To two mercenaries with international experience. You understand?'

'Oh yes, sir.' Williams nodded violently, mesmerized by the banknotes. 'No problem.'

4

'Big mouthfuls often choke.'
Italian proverb

The tip of Williams' tongue protruded as he concentrated on buffing away the last traces of polish from the bonnet of the Ford. His jacket was off, his shirt sleeves rolled up, and there was a faint sheen of perspiration on his forehead. It was a chilly day, though brilliantly sunny, but the exercise had kept him warm.

He stood back and enjoyed his reward for his hour-long labour with wax and duster: a rich deep shine which would have impressed Henry Ford himself. Like all chauffeurs, Williams spent most of his working hours, when not actually driving, washing and polishing his car. He flicked one last smear of polish from the chrome of the bumper and stowed away the cleaning materials in a leather holdall.

The Ford was in the car park of a South London film studio. Williams crossed over to the nearby toilet and washed his hands. On the way he examined with a professional eye the sheen on the other cars and nodded to a couple of other chauffeurs, both of whom had dusters in their hands. It was no competition, Williams considered: they just hadn't got his touch.

He returned to the car, inserted a Rod Stewart tape in the multi-mode stereo system and lit a cheroot. The brand was more expensive than that he usually smoked; but life had been good to him recently. Over the last three weeks he had had a veritable stream of customers referred to him by

Dorian — so many that he had had to make another trip to see his bank manager. The Williams Car Hire Company now boasted two identical Fords; Williams had taken on his first employee, another driver; and the bookings — both from his old bread-and-butter accounts and from his new foreign clientele — were flooding in.

Williams blew out a luxurious cloud of smoke. You had to expand — it was the only way to go. In a few years he could have a fleet of Fords; in ten years . . .

He wrenched his mind away from rosy visions of the future and considered the problems of the present. Dorian had returned to London yesterday, booking Williams' services for a full four weeks. That was all to the good. The trouble was, Dorian had been very insistent about that introduction to the mercenaries. With the eternal optimism of the coward, Williams had hoped that the banker would forget the awkward request, once he was back in Switzerland.

The skin tightened over Williams' thin, angular face as he remembered, all too vividly, his last meeting with his fellow mercenaries. If it hadn't been for the presence of several of Fleet Street's finest, he wouldn't have got away with his front teeth intact.

A uniformed security guard appeared at the big swing doors of the studio's main entrance, holding them open for Dorian. The big banker shook hands with the pair of executives who had come to see him off and walked briskly down the steps to the car park. Williams was out of the car in a flash and deferentially opened the passenger door.

Dorian settled heavily into his seat. There was a look of satisfaction on his face. 'I would like some — ah — company tonight,' he said absently. 'At the hotel, I think. You will need the evening free to set up my meeting with your — ah — friends.'

Shortly after six, Williams left the Swiss in the tender embraces of two girls and set off on the long crawl through Kensington, in company with thousands of commuters who were trekking homewards to suburban Surrey. It took him nearly an hour to pass Heathrow; he turned off on to the A30, where the traffic was even more congested. It was almost eight o'clock when he reached the tiny but picturesque village of Bagshot.

The lights of a roadside burger-house beckoned him invitingly. He pulled off the road, went inside and ordered a snack and some coffee. He wasn't hungry — fear wasn't much of an appetizer — but any excuse for a delay was good enough for him.

He had two men in mind who fulfilled Dorian's requirements. But he had to think of a ploy to get them to agree to a meeting with the banker. But it was unlikely that he would get anything out of them except a long-promised thrashing. He pushed aside his half-eaten burger with a feeling of revulsion and ripped the cellophane from another packet of cigarettes.

The sound of raised voices caught his attention and he lifted his eyes. On the far side of the room the young Scots girl behind the counter was chiding her leather-jacketed boyfriend.

'Jus' you tell the truth,' she was saying firmly, 'an' none of yer aul nonsense.'

Oh God, Williams thought, *she's right*. Telling the truth was his only hope where men like that were concerned.

Ten minutes later, the gleaming Ford slid to a halt outside a small, redbrick terraced house in Camberley. Williams stared at it from the safety of the car, hoping against hope to see strange faces at the window. He screwed up his courage and got out.

The single wrought iron gate shrieked on its hinges as he opened it. Williams scuttled up to the newly-varnished door and pressed the small brass bellpush. He could hear it ringing deep inside the house.

A movement caught his eye in the bay window beside the door. A massive grey head abruptly twitched aside the curtains. Baleful amber eyes stared at him with a mixture of anger and scorn; the ears were laid back flat against the

34

head; and a low, menacing growl rattled the window-pane.

Williams swallowed nervously. It was only a dog, he told himself: a pet. He rang the bell again and the dog vanished. Seconds later it reappeared on the other side of the door, barking deeply and loudly. Williams backed away. The door was solid enough, but there were glass panels set in its upper half. He could see the brute clearly: it was up on its hind-legs, the claws on its front paws scrabbling against the glass. The door itself acted as a sounding-board, amplifying the frenzied barks and giving them a terrifying resonance. It was a Great Dane, Williams told himself in an attempt to calm his mind with facts. Good God, the bloody animal was taller than he was.

He backed down the garden path and got into the car, making sure the door was locked after him. He lit a cheroot, hoping it would calm him. Only an inch had been smoked when a Transit van passed his parked car. The van slowly turned round at an intersection a little further down the tree-lined street. It returned and stopped immediately behind the Ford.

Williams watched the driver emerge in his door-mounted mirror. He slammed the door and walked slowly up to the Ford. Williams' stomach muscles constricted as the stocky, middle-aged man approached.

Davies. Williams had recognized him as soon as he swung out of the cab. The compact sun-burned man with the battered face had changed little in five years; he even seemed to be wearing the same ex-army camouflage jacket. Perhaps the hairline had receded a little, and the pronounced limp was new. But Williams had no doubt whatsoever that Davies' sudden and violent temper would be precisely the same as he remembered.

Fear, the greatest laxative known to man, was working in Williams' bowels. He resisted with difficulty the temptation to turn the key in the ignition and drive off as fast as he could. But the thought of Dorian effectively blocked off that option. For an instant he wondered if he could conduct negotiations through the car window, rolling it down only a couple of inches.

Instinct forced him to take the only sensible course. He tumbled out of the car and faced Davies with his hand outstretched.

'Hullo, Davies, I've come to see you with a proposition.' The words came stumbling out. 'For cash, of course. Cash upfront.'

Davies looked at the chauffeur for a long moment, ignoring the trembling hand which was held out to him. Without a word he took a crumpled packet of Benson and Hedges from his top pocket. He lit the long cigarette and stared at Williams through the smoke, making no attempt to disguise his contempt.

'I won't say it's good to see you,' he said at last. His blue-grey eyes were shrewd. 'But you wouldn't be here unless it was important. And it had better be important for me as well as you.' He jerked his head. 'Come on. If we have to talk we'll do it inside.'

Williams followed the shorter man into his house. The great dog greeted his master with enthusiasm but at once obeyed when he was sent back to his vigil by the window. Davies wordlessly indicated one of the big sofas and Williams obediently sat down.

For a few minutes he was completely ignored. Davies went through to the kitchen to brew some coffee. Williams glanced nervously at the Great Dane; the dog was staring out into the road. He was uncomfortably aware that just one word from Davies could transform this motionless guard into the savage inhabitant of one of his nightmares. He sat awkwardly on the sofa, kneading his hands on his lap.

Davies came in with the coffee. 'Well?'

'This Swiss bloke has been hiring me lately,' Williams said jerkily. 'A banker — *really* loaded. I don't know why, but he wants to meet a couple of mercenaries. I thought maybe you and Tippett — '

Davies leant forwards. 'So he wants *real* mercenaries?' he said softly.

There was no mistaking the implication. Williams flushed. 'Yeah,' he said uncomfortably. He couldn't keep his eyes off Davies' muscular hands, wrapped around the coffee mug. Those hands belonged to a former middle-weight champion of the British Army. 'Look, Davies, all he wants is for you two to come up to town and have a meal with him. And, whatever happens, I'll make sure you're all right. I'll give you both a hundred quid expense money out of my own pocket.'

'Well, Tippett can't come — he's in a hospital in Limassol right now.' Davies smiled, without humour. 'You can give me his share as well. Beforehand.'

Williams tried to conceal his relief. One mercenary was better than none: Dorian should be satisfied. He broached another subject, hoping to keep Davies talking.

'The limp's new, isn't it? And those two scars on your face? You been abroad lately?'

'Lebanon,' said Davies laconically. 'We nearly got out with a haul worth millions of dollars, but the Israelis got their hands on most of it. I had to spend some time in Limassol too, but they patched me up quicker than Tippett. He'll be back in England soon.'

Williams was secretly fascinated and tried to pump Davies into telling him more. But Davies brushed aside his questions with one of his own.

'When do I meet Dorian?'

'Would tomorrow night suit you?' Williams suggested hesitantly. 'I could come down to Camberley and pick you up.'

Davies said nothing. Williams suddenly grasped what was lacking. He drew out his wallet and passed a bundle of notes to Davies. The older man stuffed them into his jeans without counting them.

'Listen, mate,' Davies said drily, 'for two hundred pounds I'll listen to a proposition on any night of the week.'

5

'He that makest haste to be rich shall not be innocent.'
Bible, Proverbs 28:20

By now Davies had reached the tail end of his convalescence. It was the hard part: he had to rebuild the muscles and ligaments which had been greatly weakened by gunshot wounds in the Lebanon and by the subsequent months of enforced hospitalization in Cyprus.

On the day fixed for his meeting with Dorian, he did not vary his routine, despite the fact that his mind was full of speculation about the evening. As usual he was up early, leaving the house with his dog. He spent half the morning alternately jogging and walking. On his return home he went up to the first floor. He had converted what had been the landing and the second bedroom into a versatile multi-gym. He had welded together a free-standing structure of one-inch box steel, from which depended a complex assortment of pulleys, wheels, wire ropes and weights.

He spent much of the rest of the day here, methodically working the damaged tissues and sinews back into shape. The work-out was followed by another run, walk, run session with the dog. At this point he diverged from routine. His usual practice was to have a meal and then to go down to a local hotel which boasted a disco. He didn't go for pleasure: he worked on the door as a bouncer, wearing a brown velvet jacket and a bow-tie provided by the management.

Instead he waited for Williams, his thoughts running

restlessly ahead to the meeting with the banker. A lot could depend on it. Davies had not let on to Williams how desperate for money he was. The job as a bouncer was the end of the line. The small amount of cash which he had managed to salvage from the Beirut disaster had long since evaporated. Tippett had run out of money in Limassol, and Davies had been forced to sell his old Jaguar — albeit for an abnormally good price — to keep his friend financially afloat. By now he was scraping the bottom of the proverbial barrel. He couldn't afford to ignore Williams' offer.

Williams arrived punctually in the big black car. Davies sat in the front passenger seat, but there was little conversation during the forty minute drive. Traffic was relatively light at that time of the evening. Williams soon realized Davies had no desire to talk to him. He drove fast, with his eyes on the road.

The rendezvous was a club just off Shepherd Market. The smoke-filled interior had been done-up in a luridly fussy style which was no doubt designed to appeal to visitors from the Middle East. It reminded Davies of the inside of a chocolate box.

Williams led the way to a table in the corner. The big Swiss banker got to his feet as they approached.

'Mr Davies,' he said, extending a hand, 'how good of you to come.'

Davies shook hands with Dorian, his eyes automatically assessing the man's physical condition. The Swiss must have been a tough character in his youth, but it looked as though an uninterrupted diet of high living was taking its toll. His solid build and the streaks of grey in his shock of dark hair gave him the look of an overweight badger.

The three of them sat down. Dorian was already provided with glasses and a bottle of whisky. As they drank, Williams' eyes darted uneasily between the other two men. Dorian tried to question his guest about his past activities, but Davies answered in monosyllables; he had no intention of talking about himself in Williams' presence. At last the conversation died. The chauffeur stared into his drink, while the banker and the mercenary let their dyes roam around the crowded room, appraising the female talent on display.

But Dorian was nobody's fool. For some time he had suspected that Williams' 'friends' among the mercenaries were no more than unwilling acquaintances. He could sense the antagonism flickering between the two Englishmen on either side of him.

He turned to Williams. 'You remember those two American girls you found for me last night? One was called Candy, I think.'

The chauffeur nodded.

'I would like to see them again tonight. Would you go and find them for me?'

'But Mr Dorian,' Williams protested. 'They could be anywhere at this time of the evening. It could take me hours.'

'Yes, it might,' the banker blandly agreed. 'Still, that is what I want you to do.'

The words were polite, but there was an unmistakable threat beneath them. Williams — hypersensitive where he himself was concerned — interpreted it immediately: if he wanted to retain this big-spending client and his colleagues, Williams would have to treat his wishes as commands; now that the banker was in direct contact with a mercenary, Williams was no longer necessary to his scheme of life.

The chauffeur left the table, his hunched shoulders betraying the truculence he was trying to conceal. Dorian refilled Davies' glass, noticing that his guest had visibly relaxed.

'Now we can get down to business,' he said with a surprisingly charming smile. 'First, I must enquire whether your — ah — services are available?'

Davies nodded. 'I'm open to offers.' He indicated his leg: 'In another two weeks I'll be a hundred per cent fit.'

'The Lebanon? Williams mentioned that to me.'

Davies shrugged. He had expected that. 'What do you want to talk to me about?'

40

'First let me tell you a story, Mr Davies,' Dorian began. 'I guarantee you will find it of interest. It is about a young man who worked in a bank.'

In a low, oddly-compelling voice, the banker talked almost non-stop for three-quarters of an hour. He described how the young man — whose identity was obvious to Davies, though it was never stated — had built up a new and particularly lucrative form of business for his bank in areas of the Third World, especially Africa. He went into the complex ramifications of the operation in great detail.

Davies listened without saying a word. What the banker told him to some extent dovetailed with his own experiences, in Africa and elsewhere. The size and audacity of the scheme impressed him. To an outsider Davies looked as if he was listening with casual interest, but in reality he was on a mental red-alert: why was Dorian telling him all this?

At length the Swiss came to a halt. He leant back in his chair. 'Well, Mr Davies, do you have any thoughts about what I have been telling you?'

'Only one.' Davies paused before asking the vital question: 'Are you asking me as the bank's representative — or as Alexander Dorian?'

The banker raised his massive eyebrows, realizing his guest had gone straight to the heart of the matter. 'Alexander Dorian,' he said softly.

There was a faint smile on Davies' face. 'I've just been made privy to a very well-kept secret.' He flicked a coil of ash from his cigarette on to the ashtray between them. 'Now you haven't done that just to impress me — though make no mistake, I'm certainly impressed. The way I read it is that you want some of the bank's action for yourself; and that is going to involve breaking somebody, or somebody's law.' Davies ground out his cigarette, staring quizzically at his host all the time. 'That's why you want someone like me. Right?'

Dorian nodded. He was impressed by the mercenary's rapid grasp of the situation; he had expected a brainless man of action, not someone who was capable of swift and

41

accurate analysis. In the short term, he thought, it was all to the good; but it might become a liability later on. A man with a head on his shoulders could cause complications.

No hint of what was going through his mind showed on the banker's face; he was a skilled poker player — the sort who greets every turn of the cards with an unchanging half-smile.

'I have several operations in mind,' Dorian said. He was too wily to reply directly to a direct question. 'All of them should generate a great deal of — ah — mutual profit. The first one I have already planned in detail. It is particularly vital because the proceeds from it will fund later, more ambitious ones. It is London-based and really very simple.'

'What's in it for me?' Davies asked bluntly.

Dorian looked steadily at him. 'Seventy-five thousand pounds in sterling and in cash, immediately on completion.'

Davies was a poker-player too: his expression betrayed nothing of the surprise he felt. The banker was talking about one hell of a lot of money, which meant that the overall profits must be proportionally great. And that in turn implied that the 'more ambitious' operations must be immense. His mouth twitched as the irony of it all struck him: earlier this evening he had been worrying about how he would pay for the van's MOT and the dog's anti-Parva injections.

The banker hitched his chair closer. 'Let me tell you what needs to be done.'

As Davies listened, his enthusiasm declined. True, the money was excellent and the risks were relatively small; but the job itself made him feel slightly dirty.

Just as the banker finished, Williams returned to the club. He was accompanied by a gangling girl with huge brown eyes who appeared to be wearing little more than a blonde wig and a white leather mini-dress and by a well-built black girl with an Afro hair style.

Dorian's face brightened.

Davies pushed back his chair and got to his feet. 'I'll be off

42

now. I'll give you a ring tomorrow and let you know my decision.'

The banker watched the compact figure of the mercenary leave the club. He felt slightly disappointed: he would have liked an answer now. Still, all in all, it had been a good evening's work. He turned to the new arrivals.

'Candy, my dear,' he said welcomingly. 'Or is it Mandy?'

6

'All great ideas are dangerous.'
Oscar Wilde

Dorian returned to the Ritz in the early hours of the morning. He was tired but happy: the evening had been a good one, both for work and pleasure; he had little doubt that Davies would ring him a few hours later, accepting his proposal. What sane man could resist it? And Davies, Dorian was sure, was as sane as they come.

His mood changed abruptly when he found there was a telex waiting for him. It was from his personal aide in Geneva, who had tried to telephone several times while he was out. Though Dorian was based in London for the next few weeks, he had known from the start that he would have to return to Geneva for two days of important meetings, with board members and two influential clients, on the following day. The telex announced that the meeting had been unexpectedly brought forward to today. Dorian would therefore have to fly to Geneva as soon as possible.

Dorian had no option — he couldn't disobey a summons of this magnitude and hope to keep his job. He telephoned Switzerland — dragging his aide out of her bed — and spent nearly an hour trying to shuffle around his timetable. In the end he had to admit defeat: he would have to miss Davies' call.

Fuming with ill-suppressed rage, Dorian made the best of a bad situation. He paid the hotel porter a small fortune to handle his incoming calls on his behalf. He issued instructions to the unfortunate Williams, who drove him down to Heathrow, about what to do if Davies should fail to ring.

Tiredness made him boorish during the day, and several of his colleagues remarked on — and felt the brunt of — his ill-temper. His aide had her head snapped off when she reminded him that he and the senior members of his department were hosting a cocktail party that evening for a group of Third World Africans who used Geneva as their European base.

Dorian went to the party, which was held in one of Geneva's most expensive hotels, with bad grace; but he recognized that he, as head of department, could hardly stay away. He intended to stay there for the shortest possible period of time consistent with politeness. He would plead a backache or a migraine to cover his early departure.

Accompanied by his aide, Dorian made the rounds of the guests, exchanging a few words with each and trying to keep the brittle veneer of his politeness intact. Apart from himself and five colleagues, everyone in the room was black. Most of the faces he knew. When in doubt his extremely efficient aide would perform the introductions.

One guest stood by himself in one corner, nursing a drink and staring blankly at one of the undistinguished water-colours which the hotel management had bought by the square metre to decorate the walls. He was a frail, elderly man with a bony, balding head. He wore a pale blue safari suit with a Mao Tse Tung collar, and a pair of heavy-rimmed tinted glasses which gave him the air of an intellectual. There was something forlorn in his solitude.

'Who's that?' Dorian whispered to his aide.

She wrinkled her nose in faint disapproval. 'Holden Roberto. We had to ask him, but the others treat him like a leper. I hope to God he doesn't stay long.'

There was a sudden flash of interest on Dorian's heavy features. 'Introduce me,' he demanded.

The aide obeyed, concealing the fact she was puzzled. The bank had little to do with — and little to gain

45

from — Holden Roberto. The man was an exiled politician from Angola. He was the leader of the FNLA, the nationalist party which had all but lost the civil war to its communist rivals. Roberto had also lost most of his credibility because he had used European and American mercenaries in a futile last-ditch attempt to stave off defeat. The mercenaries had caused a howl of protest from the Organization of African Unity. As a result Holden had lost one of his most important assets — the support of his brother-in-law who was the president of Angola's neighbour, Zaire. Holden Roberto had been forced to move to a modest villa in Geneva. Even here, his fellow Africans treated him as a social outcast.

Dorian was soon in conversation with Roberto, ignoring the *frisson* of interest which ran round the room, among colleagues and clients alike. It was well-known that Angola was not a country where Western investment of any kind was likely to flourish: it had been impoverished by a long and bloody civil war and was now muffled under the communist blanket.

But Dorian's desire to meet the discredited leader was due to private rather than professional curiosity. After all, Roberto had been a previous employer of Davies; and Dorian hoped to glean some insight into the mercenary's career. After the initial introduction he asked a casual question about Roberto's opinion of mercenaries.

The African shrugged. His eyes were watery behind the tinted glasses, but still shrewd. 'Some were efficient; some were not.' His mouth twitched bitterly. 'I made a mistake to use them. Some of them at least.'

The name of Colonel Callan hung unspoken in the silence between the two men.

'We all make mistakes,' said the banker diplomatically.

'And others make them worse for us,' Roberto replied tartly. 'Some people still say that those mercenaries went to Angola to steal diamonds from the mines there, not to fight. That is rubbish.'

Dorian looked up sharply. He knew, of course, that Angola had been one of the major sources of diamonds in

Africa before the war; he had assumed that the war had interrupted the flow — or at least had made it inaccessible to his bank.

'Diamonds are still produced there?' he asked, keeping his voice casual. 'In bulk?'

'Oh yes.' The African leader put down his glass and picked up a plate of cocktail savouries from a nearby side-table. 'De Blooms still hold the mining concession, you see. A South African firm like that isn't going to let a little thing like a communist takeover come between it and its profits.'

An idea began to stir in Dorian's mind, as yet undefined. He talked with Roberto for another quarter-of-an-hour, always returning to the subject of diamonds. As they talked, Dorian came to certain conclusions about the African: he might be discredited, but he still had local support; though defeated, he was still ambitious — and obviously desperate.

Dorian glanced at his slim, rolled gold watch. 'I must be off, Mr Roberto. I wonder if you'd care to join me for supper tomorrow evening. I would greatly like to continue our conversation. In private.'

Roberto glanced sharply at the Swiss and then looked away. Both of them had instinctively lowered their voices some time ago. 'Believe me,' he said softly, 'I shall look forward to it.'

Dorian put the intervening day to good use. He set his department's team of researchers to work on Angola. By the end of the day they had amassed a quantity of information which confirmed and amplified what he had heard from Holden Roberto. Rather to Dorian's surprise one of the African's claims which had seemed dubious at the time turned out to be true: Roberto still had some sort of guerrilla army in the field, and it was significant enough to cause major problems to the Soviet-backed regime.

The supper was held in the privacy of Dorian's home, a luxurious house in Geneva's most affluent residential quarter. Dorian's housekeeper provided *filets de boeuf en croûte* with a premier grand cru Pomerol; there was no point, Dorian thought, in spoiling the ship for a ha'p'orth of tar. Afterwards he plied his guest with old brandy and searching questions. After the preliminaries were over, the banker brought up what seemed to him to be the crucial point.

'If your support is as extensive as you say — and your troops as effective — why haven't you simply taken the diamonds? You could use the proceeds to buy unlimited *matériel*.'

The politician spread his hands wide. 'You think I haven't thought of that? It could change the whole balance of the war. The problem is that my troops are guerrillas: they are superb in the bush, but they lack the military skills and equipment to take on the regular garrisons of the towns. They can make no impression on well-trained and well-armed men in a defensive position.'

Dorian nodded. 'I see that. But the problem is not insuperable.' He left his chair and unfolded several large scale maps over the oriental carpet. He continued to ask probling questions. The level of the brandy bottle steadily lowered. Holden Roberto's mouth lost that bitter twist which the banker had assumed was a permanent part of his expression. As the questions were answered and the plans developed, Dorian grew more and more like a large and excited schoolboy.

Thirty hours later the two men met again, this time in the first class departure lounge of Geneva's international airport. There was little conversation between them as they boarded the Swiss Caravelle bound for London.

Within minutes of unfastening his seatbelt, Alexander Dorian was fast asleep. He dreamed of huge wooden packing cases stuffed full of diamonds, each the size of an ostrich egg.

7

'A little learning is a dangerous thing.'
Alexander Pope

'One day I shall disembowel Holden Roberto.' The pock-marked man spat ritualistically on the cracked concrete floor. 'Now, what were we saying?'

The words were spoken a thousand miles south of Geneva, on another continent. Neither of the other two occupants of the Nissen hut paid any attention to the remark; they applauded the sentiment behind it, but they had heard it too often before to feel a reply was necessary.

The oldest of the three men leafed through a sheaf of papers and jabbed a grimy forefinger at one of them. The pock-marked man nodded and hunted for his own copy in the folder on his lap.

The third soldier was some way from the others, at the far end of the hut. Rojer Eloi was the youngest of the trio. He was twenty-five, but his fair skin still retained the bloom of adolescence. At present his face was grey with tiredness after an exhausting day. His energies were concentrated on one goal: the liberation of his feet.

Sitting on his bed, he eased the long leather laces from the well-worn brass eyelets of his military-pattern boots. They were calf length with rubber soles, and removing them cost him considerable effort.

One by one, they fell on the concrete with a dull thud. For a long moment Eloi gazed with detachment at the thick grey woollen socks which constituted the last barrier to freedom.

The socks were thick with dirt and sweat; they appeared to be moulded to his feet. He was pleasantly surprised when he found he could still waggle his toes.

The smell drifted up to him: he gagged and started to breath through his mouth. Eloi wondered whether he should keep the socks on — at least they kept the smell local. Eventually, however, curiosity got the better of him: he hadn't seen his feet for two weeks. He bent down and peeled them off. The smell immediately became intensified, reminding Eloi of strong, rotting cheese. He stared clinically at his anaemic-looking toes. He flexed them tentatively, sending fresh waves of the offensive odour, spiralling invisibly, through the hot corrugated iron hut. He sprawled back on the bed, luxuriating in the freedom. He began to daydream, seeing with his mind's eye a low, white-washed cafe, tall misted glasses of ice cold beer and the flashing legs of passing girls.

Rodriguez, the oldest man who had been reading aloud from the piece of paper in his hand, stopped abruptly in mid-sentence.

'*Madre de dios!*' he swore, his large brown eyes watering involuntarily. 'Can you smell that, D'asser?'

The man with the scarred face nodded. His hand was over his mouth and nose, trying to protect them from the stench. Both men silently turned to look for the source of the smell.

Eloi was oblivious to the discomfort of his companions, securely insulated from the outside world by his daydream. But after a few seconds he snapped out of his fantasy of his own accord, aware that he couldn't afford the luxury of wasting time. He got up from the bed and rummaged through his battered Aeroflot flight bag, his back to his comrades. He pulled out a worn, green, military issue towel, flicked it over his muscular olive-skinned shoulder and strode down the length of the hut to the door.

Rodriguez, his hand clamped over his nose, tore open a window. He and D'asser then returned to their studies.

Meanwhile Eloi walked across the baked dirt surface of

the compound to the shower enclosure. It was late afternoon, but the desert sun was still swelteringly hot. The glare emphasized the long, irregular shadows cast by the rows of Nissen huts. Eloi worked the handle of the well-head pump with his eyes half-closed. Eventually the water began to flow in fits and starts out of the rusting iron pipe. It splashed into the antiquated tank of galvanized iron on top of the shower enclosure.

He had become so used to the discomforts of the camp that by now he hardly noticed them. He grinned to himself, remembering the difference between this desolate reality and what he, D'asser and Rodriguez had anticipated. When they had arrived in Tripoli five months ago, their Libyan hosts had assured them that they were going to a virtual paradise, bursting with wild life. They had even been shown pictures of lions with jet-black manes.

It hadn't taken them long to discover the truth. The camp itself was Spartan; most of its buildings and fittings were legacies of World War II. It was one of a cluster of camps in the desert north of Tripoli, in an area which was not only designated as militarily secure, but free from the prying eyes of Western journalists.

The camp was surrounded by a barren wasteland, studded with hard, flintlike stones which cut the feet of the unwary. As for the much-vaunted wildlife, they had only come across three varieties: a small, sadistic yellow scorpion; a tiny but persistent black fly which was attracted to people's eyes as moths are to candles; and Rodriguez had once been bitten by a huge, fawn-coloured spider which was supposed to live on camels — not that they had seen any camels in this wilderness.

None of the three men believed there were any lions here. Quite simply, there was nothing for them to feed on. Back home in Angola, before the civil war, the lions used to raid the herds of domestic cattle; the big cats had to kill nearly every night.

Eloi released the handle of the pump: at last the tank held enough water. He stripped off his olive green shirt and

51

threw it in the bottom of the shower enclosure. After removing the contents of his trouser pockets, he stepped beneath the dented brass shower rose, with a bar of unscented soap in his hand. He kept his trousers on.

The valve beneath the tank was opened by tugging a piece of wire. At first the water was stained a deep blood-red by the oxide of rust flakes in the tank. Gradually the water cleared: its colour thinned to a faded brown like pale gravy. Eloi stood beneath the jet, revelling in the relative cool of the water. After a minute he bent down and began to work up a lather on his soiled green trousers. The trousers, together with his shirt, socks and boots, represented his complete wardrobe.

Twenty minutes later, Eloi stepped out of the tin cubicle and walked back to his Nissen hut. He was completely naked, apart from the solid gold crucifix on a heavy chain around his neck. Seeing the crucifix swinging as he walked reminded him of his grandmother, who had given it to him as a confirmation present. One day, he promised himself, he would fulfil his lifelong ambition and visit her in Portugal. She lived in an apartment of unimaginable sophistication near the square of the Black Horse in Lisbon.

But that dream, he told himself sternly as he entered the hut, belonged far into the future. There were many, far more important things to be done in the present.

The scene inside the hut was unchanged. Rodriguez and D'asser were still sitting on their beds, sweating heavily and studying their sheafs of papers. Eloi carefully arranged the wet clothes over the tubular metal frame of his bed. Then he lit a cigarette, lay down on the thin flock mattress and picked up his own folder of typewritten papers.

The long room had an academic air, like a college dormitory on the night before an examination — which, in a sense, was exactly what it was. But the subject matter which the three men were so earnestly studying was not to be found in the usual college curriculum. The three Angolans were part of a multi-national student body; the course was provided by courtesy of Emir Muamer Ghaddafi, the leader of the Libyan people, for those he considered to be 'freedom fighters'.

The camp was one of several in the Libyan desert. They had been in operation since the late 1960s; their graduates were terrorists from all over the world. Their Libyan training had enabled them to be responsible for the unparalleled wave of death and destruction which had swept through the West in recent years.

The students were not necessarily required to be devout communists. Eloi, D'asser and Rodriguez came from Marxist Angola but many other shades of fanaticism were represented on the same course. There were several quiet Irishmen, a group of Moslem Fundamentalists from Syria, some SWAPO representatives from Namibia, Turks belonging to the Grey Wolves, and over a dozen Latin South Americans of assorted nationality. The camps' Libyan organizers had discovered at an early stage that their students, although they all belonged to the unholy brotherhood of international terrorism, were quite capable of fighting among themselves. One of the camps had been the scene of a massive gun battle between the students in the early 1970s. Since then, the Libyans had taken care to isolate the groups: that was the reason why the three Angolans were alone in a hut designed to hold forty.

The hut remained in a scholarly silence for over an hour. Eloi's shirt and trousers dripped themselves dry. In the intense heat, even the pools of water, caught in small depressions in the uneven concrete floor, evaporated within minutes.

D'asser and Rodriguez tossed aside their folders, got to their feet and stretched. 'Time to eat, boy,' Rodriguez called down the hut to Eloi.

The younger man scrambled up and pulled on his trousers. He was secretly very flattered that the two older men treated him as a comrade. They were older than he was; they came from far wealthier backgrounds; and, most importantly, they were both established military figures in Angola. Eloi quietly hero-worshipped his two compatriots.

He was unaware that his own intuitive grasp of mechanical and electrical principles made up for his inexperience in the eyes of his two friends. He was frequently able to help them with the trickier technical problems in their syllabus.

Rodriguez and D'asser left the hut together. Eloi quickly laced up his boots and ran after them. The three Angolans walked through the lines of huts to the brick-built cookhouse where meals were served twice a day. The ancient and withered Arab who served as the camp's cook-cum-dishwasher spooned a highly-spiced stew on to their tin plates. They returned to their hut and ate with furious concentration. There was no time to be wasted on this, the last night of the five month course. Tomorrow, their instructors — four grim-faced Americans — would test not only the military skills they were supposed to have acquired, but also their command of the English language.

While they ate, the Angolans speculated about the presence of the Americans, as they had done nearly every night. Their instructors were clearly top-grade ex-service personnel. What were they doing, training men whose ultimate goal was to destroy America, the heart of the 'decadent West'? The Angolans would never know that the question could only be answered by certain ex-CIA operatives who still had access to the CIA computer at Langley, and whose services were up for sale to the highest bidder. As a result, the US Government was unknowingly providing tutors for anti-American terrorists.

After the meal there was time for a little more revision before the light faded. Eloi's special subject was the art of the booby-trap. He paid particular attention to the section on aircraft, memorizing in fine detail exactly where to place an explosive charge to maximize its effect; the total disintegration of the aircraft was the only acceptable outcome. He also studied the lethal new binary explosive which the American had provided, paying particular attention to its potential use in an airport departure lounge. He reckoned he would almost certainly get a question on the topic.

Meanwhile, his two companions were testing one another

on the innocuous ingredients of an explosive gel, whose chief constituents were the acid from a car battery, clean cotton rag, petrol and some typing paper.

The gathering dusk soon made reading impossible. Rodriguez yawned.

'Wonder what Jorge is doing now,' he said to D'asser.

His friend's stern, scarred face split into an unexpectedly charming smile. Jorge was Rodriguez's sixteen-year-old brother. Since D'asser's family had been killed, Jorge had become a sort of brother-by-adoption to D'asser.

'Probably he's trying to wheedle a new horse out of your grandfather.' D'asser laughed. 'And he'll get it. The old man dotes on him.'

The two men's thoughts both turned towards home. There was a comfortable silence between them, for they had known one another all their lives. Their fathers — Angolans by birth but Portuguese by extraction — owned neighbouring coffee plantations near Nova Quimbundo in Northern Angola. D'asser and Rodriguez had played together and been to school together. They were both heirs to huge colonial estates, carved out of the virgin jungle a couple of centuries earlier by their forefathers. The families had the same lavish lifestyle, based on a seemingly inexhaustible supply of cheap black labour. Neither family bothered much with local or national politics — there was no need. To all intents and purposes they were the absolute and autonomous rulers over areas the size of many English counties.

Everything had changed for the two families in the late 1960s, when Portugal gave Angola its independence. The civil war broke out and Rodriguez and D'asser — then eighteen — rushed off to the capital, Luanda, to join the army.

It didn't matter which army. Adventure was the lure, as with young men the world over; politics was the business of old men. They joined the communist MPLA and were soon officers in Augustino Neto's army.

At the time the MPLA was in retreat on two fronts: it was

55

sandwiched between two opposing armies, both funded by Western powers. D'asser and Rodriguez were sent to support the UNITA army in the south, which was vainly attempting to block the advance of flying columns of South African 'Troopies'. Within a few weeks the two friends were back in Luanda — this time in the van of the retreating UNITA army. The news was equally bad in the north — the MPLA was being pushed back towards Luanda by the FNLA, the army of Holden Roberto. Rodriguez and D'asser were shocked to learn that their hometown of Nova Quimbundo and its neighbourhood had fallen to the enemy.

In the MPLA's darkest hour, a saviour appeared in the unlikely guise of a one-time peanut farmer from Plaines, Georgia: Jimmy Carter's new US administration decided to withdraw all aid from armies opposed to the Neto regime. Carter, terrified of Angola escalating into another Vietnam, also pressurized the South Africans into withdrawing.

The MPLA — backed to the hilt by Soviet aid, Cuban troops and East German 'advisers' — soon turned defeat into a sweeping victory. Rodriguez and D'asser joined in the fresh offensive, transferring to the northern army because they feared for their families.

The two friends took part in the liberation of Nova Quimbundo. The recapture of the town was easy enough — they simply bracketed it with the Stalin Organs which the Russians had supplied; and Holden Roberto's army was in no condition to put up much of a fight.

The town was deserted and plundered. But a few survivors gradually trickled in from the bush. They showed the MPLA troops the shallow mass graves which contained the majority of the town's population.

Rodriguez and D'asser made straight for their homes. Rodriguez's family — with the exception of his father, who had died of smallpox — had survived. But D'asser found his entire family in a shallow pit, stained rust-red with blood and covered with flies. Holden Roberto's retreating soldiers had dishonoured, dismembered and disembowelled them all.

From this point onwards, the two friends were no longer

fighting for adventure but because, above all, they hated Roberto, his troops and his right-wing backers.

D'asser — hitherto a mild-mannered little man — rapidly built up a reputation as a merciless hunter of the FNLA. His exploits as the leader of a small, elite commando soon became legendary, as did the cruelty he showed to those he captured. He became a notoriously efficient interrogator. At the same time he grew heavily dependent, first on amphetamines, then on harder drugs. The drugs blunted his sensitivity to others' pain still further.

But there was another side to D'asser, which showed itself towards the end of the war when he spent a few days' leave with Rodriguez and his family. Jorge Rodriguez bore a marked resemblance to his own, slaughtered young brother; and D'asser found himself growing as fond of the boy as if he had been his own kin.

Soon afterwards, the war in the north had come to a sudden and bloody end after a last-ditch stand by some Western mercenaries. D'asser and Rodriguez united their two plantations and returned to barracks in Luanda where their unit was now stationed.

The next two years were quiet. Both men — and many of their comrades — began to wonder when their Cuban and East German allies would leave. Their curiosity turned to anxiety as cadres of hardline communists were promoted to key positions in the army. Their anxiety became alarm when they realized that their leader, Neto, had no more control over their former allies than a man has over a growth of terminal cancer. There was a price to be paid for every Soviet bullet, shell and tank, for each Cuban and East German: the wooden yoke of colonial rule had been replaced by the steel one of communism.

A group of young officers staged an abortive coup d'etat. Rodriguez and D'asser, though sympathetic to their cause, were fortunately not implicated. (Ironically enough, the reason for this was that the conspirators considered D'asser to be unreliable because of his dependence on drugs.)

The Soviet-inspired response to the failed coup was

rapid, ruthless and predictable. Its leaders were liquidated and many sympathisers disappeared. The 'doubtfuls' — including Rodriguez and D'asser — were confined to barracks. President Neto died in mysterious circumstances while on a state visit to Moscow. Informed sources knew that he had gone there to present the Russians with an ultimatum to get out of Angola; his fatal illness was not only unexpected but suspiciously well-timed. His successor was quick to reaffirm his allegiance to Russia.

The new president introduced sweeping reforms for the military, the most significant of which was that party membership was now essential. Rodriguez and D'asser — with dependents in the country and nowhere else to go — had no choice: they became party members and attended the compulsory indoctrination classes.

As a result, their lives in Luanda were unpleasant and insecure. The two men jumped at the opportunity to apply for a special course in Libya. Somewhat to their surprise, they were selected.

The course had been long and arduous, but it had given both men a breathing space. As they sat in the gathering dusk in the Nissen hut, their thoughts were running along the same lines. Both of them were thinking of the journey tomorrow, by road and plane, which would take them home. For, despite everything, Angola was home.

A tentative cough brought D'asser and Rodriguez out of their reveries. They looked up to see the shadow of Eloi looming over them.

Eloi held out a piece of paper to each of them. 'Here,' he said hesitantly, 'this is my address in Henrique de Carvalho. I've also written down the address of the best *anteena* . . .'

Rodriguez looked up, smiling lazily. 'We might just run over and see you while we're on leave. Henrique de Carvalho is only about a hundred and sixty kilometres from Nova Quimbundo. How about it, D'asser?'

'We can get drunk together.' It was too dark to see Eloi's face but his delight was evident in his voice. 'The first six bottles will be on me, because of all the help you have given me.'

In practical terms, most of the help had been in the other direction. But Eloi was overjoyed at the thought of fraternizing with two nationally-known heroes in his own town.

'Okay, kid. Perhaps.' D'asser yawned. 'Push off now. I want to sleep.'

8

'In baiting a mousetrap with cheese, always leave room
for the mouse.'

Saki

The doorbell rang just as Davies was dishing up the curry
dinner he had cooked for himself and his Great Dane. The
dog barked. Davies pushed him into the small room behind
the kitchen and diverted his attention with a bowl of Indian-
flavoured Winalot. He looked with regret at his own
steaming plate, wiped his hands and went to answer the
door.

There were two men on the doorstep, dimly illuminated
by the streetlamp. Davies immediately recognized the bulky
shape of Alexander Dorian; another, slimmer man was half-
concealed behind him.

'Good evening, Mr Davies,' Dorian said in his precise
English. 'I hope we do not disturb you. Since you do not
come to me, I must come to you.'

Davies waved the visitors into the front room. It was
several days since he had heard Dorian's proposition, and
already the episode had begun to slip into the past tense.
Despite the money which the Swiss had offered, Davies had
decided that he wasn't interested in the job. It had about as
much appeal as sticking up his local post office.

His forced welcome became suddenly genuine as the second man came forward into the light. Davies immediately
recognized Holden Roberto, his former employer and
comrade-in-arms. He greeted the exiled African leader

warmly, and poured out a couple of large scotches for his guests.

Dorian started to say something, but Davies shook his head. 'Give me five minutes, will you? I was just about to have supper.' If these men had come all the way to Camberley to see him, they could wait a little longer. Davies sensed he was in a strong position.

When the mercenary laid down his fork a few moments later, the banker wasted no time in preliminary chit-chat.

'I ran into your old friend Mr Roberto quite by chance, in Geneva. Our conversation naturally turned to Angola. To our surprise we found that we may have a — ah — mutual interest there. An interest, Mr Davies, which you may share.'

Davies circulated the whisky bottle and leant back. He kept his face expressionless. Lack of encouragement did not daunt Dorian. He proceeded to outline the current military situation in Angola, paying particular attention to the guerrilla war in the north and to Roberto's substantial support in the area. He stressed that the African's information had been corroborated and extended by the findings of his own research department. When he had finished he passed to Davies the thick report which his researchers had compiled.

Davies leafed through it. He was at once impressed by its high quality. Nothing had been taken for granted: all the information had been checked against other sources. Many little-known aspects of the Angolan situation dovetailed with the mercenary's personal knowledge.

As he read on, he noticed that the report had an unstated focus of interest. It provided an in-depth study of the area of northern Angola around the township of Henrique de Carvalho and a considerable amount of material on the diamond-mining concession operated by DeBlooms. His mind swiftly correlated this with the presence of a maverick Swiss banker and a discredited but still formidable Angolan politician. He glanced up at the two men who sat watching him intently on the opposite sofa.

'I think I can save you a lot of time,' Davies said drily.

'You want to know if it's possible for me to go back to Angola, to Henrique de Carvalho, and nick the diamonds.'

The African looked startled, but Dorian nodded slowly. His eyes narrowed momentarily: yet again he wondered whether Davies was too astute for comfort. None of his doubts was betrayed in his voice.

'Precisely,' he purred. 'Obviously, you would have the assistance of Roberto's ground troops. They would lead you there and back. You and as many other mercenaries as you would need. But we have one big problem.'

Here the banker sighed heavily, like a bad actor. In the ensuing pause, Davies lit a long filter-tipped cigarette. He kept his eyes on Dorian but refused to prompt him verbally.

Dorian's face twitched irritably. 'The problem is money,' he said harshly. 'We need a lot of finance — for transporting you and your force, monies for their pay, a considerable capital outlay here in Europe for the equipment you will need . . . I just don't have that kind of money.'

For a moment the three men sat in silence. Davies ignored the Swiss, his mind concentrating on the logistics of such an operation, on the size and composition of the mercenary force which would be needed, and on the weaponry they would require. He turned to Roberto:

'Arms?' He spoke the word flatly, making it sound more of a statement than a question.

The Angolan paused, grappling to fit his thoughts into an unfamiliar language. 'I can give you rifles and ammunition.' His English had a heavy Portuguese accent: the vowels were elongated, silent syllables were spoken, and the 'r's rolled like a choir boy's. 'Also rockets — those American ones you used before. And grenades and some explosives, okay?'

Davies nodded. He turned his attention back to the financial problem which Dorian had outlined. The solution was obvious — and he knew it was in Dorian's mind as well.

The mercenary expelled a long lungful of smoke. 'And you want to raise the capital with the help of the proposition you mentioned the other night.'

'Yes!' The Swiss leant forwards, flushed with enthusiasm.

'It is the perfect solution. So simple. So foolproof.'

The conversation went on for another four hours; they were well into the second bottle of whisky by the time it finished. There was a good deal of horse-trading between Dorian and Davies, with Roberto sitting and sipping quietly on the sidelines. For the initial, London-based piece of the action, Davies would get £75,000. Dorian wanted to delay this payment, but Davies insisted that it should be on the nail — cash on delivery. The Swiss protested that he couldn't lay his hands on that amount of money right away, but Davies was obstinate.

Roberto touched the banker's shoulder at this point, and there was a whispered conversation between the Swiss and the Angolan. At last Dorian looked up and smiled.

'Agreed,' he said to Davies. 'Seventy-five thousand on delivery.'

'Where's the money coming from?' Davies asked suspiciously.

Dorian inclined his head towards Roberto. 'It's a joint effort.'

Davies looked thoughtfully at the African leader. He realized that Roberto needed the diamonds more than any of them. For himself and Dorian, this was just a way of making money; for Roberto, however, it represented the one way he could regain his position and avoid a slow political suicide.

It was after midnight when Davies' visitors left. Both of them found it difficult to walk in a straight line by this time. Roberto, in particular, a fragile figure in his tinted glasses, swayed against the wall when he stood up. Davies offered to ring for a taxi for them.

Dorian shook his head. 'There is no need,' he said. 'We have a car.'

Davies grinned. 'Can you drive it at present?'

The banker shrugged. 'That is Williams' job.' His heavy eyelids drooped. 'I did not bring him in — he would not have been — ah — good for business.'

Davies repressed a smile at the thought of the chauffeur

being outside on such a freezing night, huddled in his Ford. He showed out his visitors and drained the last of the scotch into his glass.

The Angolan angle, he thought, put a very different light on Dorian's original proposition. The latter was still a sordid little job but at least it now had some justification, because it would lead to bigger, better things.

Davies had no objection to ripping off a communist regime like Angola's. It was almost a duty; it might even be a pleasure.

He reminded himself to telex Tippett tomorrow. At last he had some news which should speed up his old friend's convalescence in Limassol.

9

'He who holds the ladder is as bad as the thief.'
German proverb

To all intents and purposes the street was in Kensington, but it was far enough east for its inhabitants to be able to say they lived in Knightsbridge. At this hour, just after the pubs had closed, it was nearly deserted. Few people wanted to be outside in the fine cold drizzle which was given savagery by the gusts of an east wind.

Davies, wearing a long gaberdine raincoat and a flat cap, moved slowly along the pavement, apparently window-shopping. He paused outside an antique shop, and stared fixedly at the goods on display. He looked for all the world like one of London's anonymous faces out for a late night constitutional.

In the window, Davies could see reflected the street behind him and the small tree-lined square which backed on to the opposite side of the road. A few cars passed, their tyres hissing through the puddles. A black Ford turned into the square and pulled up outside the small hotel on the corner.

Williams emerged from the car, opening up his huge umbrella. He held it over a large man, carrying two bags and swathed in an overcoat which increased his bulk still further, who emerged from the rear of the car. He ushered his passenger up the flight of steps which led to the main door of the stucco-fronted hotel.

Davies pulled up the deep collar of the mackintosh with gloved hands and walked away in the opposite direction. He had no need to hesitate — he had walked over his route the day before, and Dorian's instructions had been very detailed. A brisk ten minute walk brought him to the alleyway which ran behind the gardens at the rear of the houses looking out over the square. The door, which was hardly ever used, was unlocked.

The mercenary let himself into the small, rain-sodden back garden. He picked his way round a row of overflowing dustbins and reached the foot of the iron fire-escape which zig-zagged down the back of the hotel. He climbed silently up to the door which communicated with the dimly-lit first-floor corridor. In seconds he had slipped the catch and was inside.

The hotel seemed as quiet as a tomb. The little room stank of disinfectant and was littered with mops and pails. Davies went into the first door on the left. At this time of night, the cleaners' room was deserted. He stood in darkness, with the door slightly ajar, for half an hour.

Beneath him, his ears caught the sound of the lift humming into life. It bumped to a halt at the first floor. Two young women walked confidently down the corridor to a door on the right, halfway down. They knocked and were immediately admitted.

Still Davies waited. There was a false alarm when the lift took someone up to a higher floor. At last — after another twenty minutes — it stopped again at the first floor. The doors hissed open. Davies watched as the night porter emerged, with a tray carefully balanced in his left hand; he pulled across the ash-can to hold open the lift doors.

The porter walked along the corridor to the same door. Davies could make out a bottle of Johnnie Walker Black Label, three glasses and plates piled high with sandwiches on the tray. He knocked — rat-tat, *tat*-tat. A hand appeared, took the tray and reappeared briefly with a tip. Whistling softly, the porter strode back to the lift.

When all was quiet again, Davies took the Walther PK from his pocket and slid the well-oiled mechanism backwards to cock the weapon. He left the cleaners' room, carefully closing the door, and moved along the corridor.

Rat-*tat*, *tat*-tat. It was a precise imitation of the porter's knock. As Davies rapped with one hand, he used the other to pull down the stockinette mask from under the flat cap.

The door half-opened and one of the girls stuck her head round, a question poised on her lips. The question remained unspoken as fear froze her into immobility.

Davies moved with the speed of a striking cobra, the adrenalin pulsing through him. His right arm shot forward and gripped the girl by the throat, abruptly shutting off the great inrush of air as she prepared reflexively to scream. He glanced quickly to either side of him: the corridor was still empty. He frog-marched the terrified girl backwards, still at arms' length, into the suite.

He found himself in a small passage-way. On his left was a door which led, according to Dorian, to the small en-suite shower and toilet cubicle. He pushed the girl onwards into the main room.

A huge pair of black feet protruded over the edge of the bed. Davies put one finger of his gun-hand to his mouth in a gesture of silence. The girl, her eyes wide with fear, nodded violently. He released his strangle-hold on her windpipe and shoved her across the thick carpet, keeping her body — naked except for a pair of briefs — between himself and the black.

His caution was unnecessary. The black was locked in a sexual embrace with the other girl. He was in no position to move anywhere except to and fro in one direction; any other move would emasculate him.

With his free hand, Davies dug out a roll of black sticky tape from his raincoat pocket and tossed it to the unoccupied girl. He moved forward into the black's range of vision. The latter's eyes widened in shock as he saw Davies and the gun in his hand.

'Any noise and you get a bullet in your head,' said Davies quietly. 'That goes for all of you. But if you do just as I say, no one gets hurt.'

The first girl followed Davies' further instructions to the

letter. In a few seconds she taped together her friend and their client so securely that their embrace would be prolonged for longer than either of them could wish. When she had finished, Davies gave her the same treatment. None of the three was able to speak, let alone to move.

Davies ignored his captives. He used a chisel to open the black man's attache case and removed the two aluminium cannisters and the military-pattern Colt Automatic inside. He then squatted down beside his host.

'I wouldn't call the police if I were you, mate,' he said conversationally. 'Might lead to a lot of problems. I don't think your president would be too happy if it became public knowledge that he was bleeding his own country white. Think of the political repercussions. You'll be okay if you keep your mouth shut.'

Davies left the hotel by the way he had come in. No one saw him. He could feel the comforting weight of the cannisters in the pockets of his coat. Two minutes walk brought him to the side street where he had left the big Honda. He had already removed the flat cap and the mask; now he pulled off the mackintosh, revealing the motorcyclist's leathers beneath. His appearance was completely different.

He unchained the bike, removed the crash helmet from its own retaining lock, and strapped the raincoat on to the pillion. He tucked the cannisters into his jacket and kicked the great engine into life.

His route took him from Kensington to Hampstead. He stopped only once, apart from at traffic lights, and that was in a quiet cul-de-sac in St John's Wood. There he opened the cannisters and transferred half-a-dozen of the larger stones into his pockets. A man had to take precautions.

The rain had eased off by the time he reached the rendezvous. It was a small redbrick terraced house in a residential road which led down to the Heath. Davies parked the bike a couple of streets away. Instead of going to the front door he slipped down the passage-way which gave access to the back of the house. He had reconnoitred it earlier in the day when

Dorian had arranged their meeting-place. The passage-way led to a small yard, sandwiched between the kitchen and the fence of the neighbouring house, and giving on to the garden.

The yard was overlooked only by the small sash-window which belonged to the dining-room. Davies took from his back pocket a thin flexible oblong of strong plastic, a little larger than a credit card, inserted it between the upper and lower window-frames and flicked back the catch. He climbed noiselessly into the darkened room beyond.

His boots made no sound on the carpeted floor. He picked his way across the room and gently opened the door. The hall beyond was also in darkness. On one wall a rectangle of light showed that the door of the front room was slightly ajar. He could hear voices: the bass rumble of Dorian and the higher, more staccato chatter of Roberto.

Davies moved closer but found that the door muffled most of their conversation. Disconnected words and phrases filtered out to him.

'. . . Angolan support . . . knows what he's doing . . .' There was a chink of glass on glass and then Dorian's voice continued. '. . . back in Kinshasa . . .'

Roberto broke in: '⁻ . . . foolish to split it three ways . . . my brother-in-law's secret police . . .'

Dorian's booming tones took over: ' . . . will have outlived their usefulness . . . your reputation . . . mercenaries . . . media exposure would . . .'

Davies backed silently away; he had heard enough. His mind slotted together the fragments he had heard. It was as if he had been given the minority of the pieces of a jigsaw puzzle — but he had enough to see what the picture was. Yet again his innate caution had paid off.

He climbed out of the window, closed it behind him and slipped round to the front. He toyed with the idea of making off with the cannisters into the night — there was nothing to stop him. But there was another way to play the hand he had been dealt — more risky, certainly, but also more profitable. There was a half-smile on his lips as he pressed the doorbell.

Dorian let him in, an anxious expression on his face.

Davies pushed by him into the hall. 'Don't worry,' he said laconically. 'No problems.'

The banker sighed with relief. 'I knew you would do it. Come and have a drink and get warm.'

Holden Roberto got to his feet to welcome Davies. The mercenary fished out the cannisters and gave one to each man. He poured himself a substantial slug of whisky and warmed himself by the fire. Roberto and Dorian exclaimed with pleasure like children opening Christmas presents. Davies kept one hand in his pocket, his fingers tracing the cool familiar outline of the butt of the Walther PK.

After a few minutes Davies broke their rejoicing. 'Cash,' he said quietly, 'on delivery.'

Dorian looked up. 'But of course, my dear fellow!' He lumbered over to the table and picked up a heavy-duty Tesco carrier bag which lay on it. 'It's all here.'

Davies checked quickly through the bag's contents. It held nothing but twenty-pound-notes, fresh from the bank. He riffled through each bundle as a matter of form, though he knew that Dorian and Roberto at present needed him too much to want to cheat him. There would be three thousand, seven hundred and fifty brand-new notes here, just as arranged.

It was over an hour before he was able to get away. This was Dorian's first direct attempt at crime (for himself, at least, if not on behalf of his bank). The ease of the operation and the success which had attended it made him almost delirious with pleasure. He fingered the uncut stones constantly and wanted to talk about the future.

He kept clicking his fingers and saying, in his heavy Teutonic accent: 'We shall make these diamonds breed like little rabbits!'

Jesus! Davies thought, *what the hell have I let myself in for?*

The mercenary saw Dorian only one more time before the old year was replaced by the new. The meeting took place four days after Davies had relieved the courier of his cannisters.

The two men met in the plush anonymity of one of the big hotels near Heathrow. They sat in the corner of the vast saloon bar and talked quietly for half an hour. The banker had tamed his exuberance and was once more his controlled and faintly pompous self.

From Davies' point of view the importance of the meeting lay not in the conversation but in the brown Samsonite travel-bag which Dorian gave to him. Since Dorian had succeeded in placing the stones, money was no longer a problem. The bag contained a hundred thousand pounds and the latest satellite maps of northern Angola and the areas immediately on its borders, superimposed upon the Angolan equivalent of the Ordnance Survey maps.

The money was to cover the cost of the recruitment, training, wages and equipping of the force which Davies was to command, plus transportation expenses.

Davies in return gave the Swiss an address where he could be contacted over the next four weeks, together with a list of certain supplies. Dorian and Roberto were in a better position to obtain many of the items which the mercenaries would need, because of their wide range of African contacts. Delivery would be made to the bureau of Roberto's political party in Kinshasa, Zaire.

The banker smoothed back his thick hair. 'It all looks most promising, my friend.' He drained his glass and signalled for another. Davies had noticed that Dorian was drinking more now, and his colour was higher.

'So-so,' the mercenary said non-committally, declining another drink with a shake of his head.

'You do not anticipate any problems over recruiting?'

'No, mate.' Davies grinned. 'I've already sorted out my number two. As for the rest, they'll be queuing up to sign on.'

10

'With age, reputation increases, ability decreases.'
                                        Dag Hammarskjöld

In the event, however, Davies ran into a totally unexpected
problem when recruiting for the Angolan operation. In the
past there had been an abundance of manpower from which
to choose. Many ex-soldiers stayed in and around the garrison towns doing casual labouring jobs while they waited for
a lucrative freelance opportunity to use their military skills
to the full.

But the recent series of defence cuts had changed the
situation dramatically — and, as far as Davies was concerned, for the worse. There were far fewer potential
mercenaries available. Davies trekked round at least a
dozen garrison towns, trawling the pubs and bars for
recruits.

After Christmas — by which time he was considerably
behind schedule — he struck lucky in Aldershot with a lad
named Sanderson. They met when they were simultaneously chucked out of a pub after a brawl between rival
factions of Paras. Sanderson looked absurdly young — his
face was youthfully bright and Davies would have been
surprised if he had to shave more than once a week. But he
was certainly fit, and he had more than pulled his weight
during the fight.

The two of them went on to another pub. Sanderson,
whose Somerset origins still showed in his drawling voice,
had just taken his discharge from the Paras after three years.

After tours of duty in Germany and Northern Ireland, he had become disillusioned with what peacetime soldiering had to offer.

Davies asked him a couple of questions about current affairs, and was agreeably surprised by the lad's intelligence. He might look and sound like a West Country yokel out of a cider advertisement, but he certainly didn't think like one. After Sanderson had brought in the next round, Davies put the vital question to him:

'So what do you want to do now? Become a brickie? Sit in an office?'

The younger man shook his head. 'I used to work in a photographic studio down in Bridgwater. I couldn't go back to that sort of life. As a matter of fact I was thinking of the Foreign Legion. They're in Chad now, and the Shaba province of Zaire: I'd stand a chance of getting into some real action.'

'What would you say,' Davies asked softly, 'if I offered you the certainty of real action? And a damn sight more money than you'd ever get in the Legion?'

Sanderson's enthusiasm for the project seemed to bring luck to Davies' recruiting drive. The young ex-Para was able to put Davies in touch with a couple of his mates who had just returned to civilian life. They in turn knew of others. Inside a week Davies had fifteen recruits, all newly-released from the Army and all barely out of their teens. They made him feel like a premature grandfather.

January was freezing and wet. Halfway through the month Davies set out with his team in a couple of battered Transit vans. He closed up the house in Camberley and put the dog into kennels. There would be no room for them in his life for a while.

They drove down to Dartmoor. Their destination was Blackfriars Farm, just outside Okehampton. The farm belonged to one of Davies' contacts in the mercenary world. The house was uninhabited and nearly derelict. It stood in isolation in the middle of a few weather-torn fields. Davies had often used it for training sessions in the past; his contact welcomed the taxfree income it brought him.

Most of the first day was spent fixing up the house, trying to make it halfways habitable. They nailed plywood to the glass-less window-frames, gathered wood for the open fireplace, and bought supplies in Okehampton. The locals evidently believed they were on some sort of Outward Bound course.

Davies was aware that a training session on Dartmoor in winter was hardly the best way to acclimatize for a job in Africa, but it was a cost-effective way to get his men fit and to sort the wheat from the chaff. He had fifteen recruits; but he was only going to take ten of them with him.

It was bitterly cold out on the moors and Davies was sure that a period of hard work here would soon bring to light any weaknesses.

He was right — but in an unexpected and embarrassing way. His thickening waist and thinning hair should have told him that guile, not example, was the best way with these young harriers. He was old enough to lead from the rear.

His downfall came when he led the youngsters on the first of their five mile jogs across the bleak hills, where the only vegetation seemed to be moss and heather. They hadn't covered much more than a mile when Davies realized that the pace he was setting was far below what his followers considered to be par for the course. He forced himself to increase his pace. Soon enough, old wounds and the habit of smoking began to take their toll.

They came to a fast-running brook, which had to be negotiated. Davies, red-faced and panting, leapt for a large outcrop of slate in the middle of the stream. He missed his footing, fell into the brook and sprained his ankle into the bargain. The chuckling recruits had the pleasure of carrying their soaking, cursing leader back to the farmhouse.

After that, Davies led from the sidelines. As far as his ankle permitted, he lost no opportunity to bring himself to the peak of condition. Just as the swelling disappeared there was a welcome arrival at the farm.

Tippett, Davies' old comrade, turned up on a dark night

spitting with rain. He made doubly certain of his welcome by arriving with four bottles of Glenfiddich under his arm.

Davies' first thought was that Tippett looked remarkably fit for a man just out of a hospital bed. He bore no obvious trace of the horrendous wounds he had acquired in the Lebanon. His six-foot-two frame was as lean and hard as ever; he was deeply suntanned, which made a vivid contrast with his well-groomed but almost white hair. He looked more like James Coburn than ever.

The youngsters retired to their sleeping-bags, leaving the two older men talking well into the night. As the level in the Glenfiddich bottle sank lower, Tippett revealed that his healthy appearance was not entirely due to the good offices of the Limassol hospital. He had spent the last two months working closely with an attractive young Greek physiotherapist; and the narrow hospital bed had been exchanged for a much more comfortable double version in the girl's flat, overlooking the golden beaches of Cyprus.

His arrival made an immediate difference to Davies. The two men had always made good running partners. Tippett took over half of the training responsibilities; and — perhaps more importantly — he was able to contribute intelligently to Davies' plans for the future.

For three weeks they hardened their bodies and sharpened their minds. By the end of this time, the two men agreed that there was no more to be gained from subjecting themselves to the severe discomforts of the January moors. Davies decided that it was time to move their base of operations to Zaire, and begin training with the soldiers of Holden Roberto.

One decision remained to be taken: which of the five youngsters would they leave behind? Davies discussed the matter with Tippett, and then summoned Sanderson to join them.

By force of personality, the lad from Somerset had become a sort of unofficial junior NCO, the natural leader of the youngsters.

Davies didn't beat about the bush: 'Five of you are going

to have to stay. I can only use ten of you at present. Which do you reckon?'

Sanderson pulled his lower lip thoughtfully. He glanced round to check he couldn't be overheard by his comrades at the other end of the huge kitchen.

'Lawton should be one,' he said quietly. 'None of the other blokes like him, and he's a lazy bugger.'

Davies nodded. What Sanderson said confirmed his own opinion. 'Who else?'

The youngster looked awkward. 'I don't know . . . maybe Brown?'

'Why?' Tippett asked.

Sanderson shrugged. 'Just a feeling. He talks too much about what he did in Northern Ireland.'

'You think he's all talk and no action?' Davies put in. He had wondered the same thing himself. That sort of soldier usually turned into a liability when you got into action. He mentally awarded Sanderson a good mark for having spotted it.

But they found it impossible to decide who the other three to be left at home should be. Davies wanted Sanderson with them; Lawton and Brown were staying; that left nine places and twelve men to fill them. As far as Davies was concerned, any of them would do.

In the end he told Sanderson that they should sort it out among themselves. They drew straws to find out who was going. Davies made the three unfortunates feel a little better by giving them a small financial bonus and promising them a phone call in the near future.

Early next morning the party crammed into the two Transit vans with their luggage. Davies dropped off the five lads who weren't going at the railway station. The rest of them took the motorway up to Bristol, forked on to the M4 and moved steadily towards London.

The flight arrangements had already been made. In London the twelve men separated for the sake of discretion. They made their way by a variety of routes to Brussels International Airport. Davies had booked the whole party on to a Sabena flight which left there the following morning.

Ngili Airport, Zaire, came as a shock to ten of the mercenaries. Only Tippett and Davies were prepared for the tropical heat, all the more of a shock because of the freezing northern European winter they had left behind.

Davies led his men out of the huge silver aircraft on to the warm tarmac. They carried only flight-bags, having deliberately kept their luggage to a minimum, for greater flexibility. Davies heaved a secret sigh of relief as he saw Holden Roberto, flanked by a couple of black aides, striding towards them from the terminal building. The status of foreign mercenaries in a strange country was always uncertain, especially at first — even when that country was run by your employer's brother-in-law.

Roberto shook hands briefly but warmly with Davies and Tippett (the latter had fought for the African leader in Angola as well). He ushered them quickly through a side-door of the terminal, avoiding customs and passport formalities.

A dented Volkswagen minibus was waiting for them. The mercenaries were packed inside. Roberto muttered instructions to the driver, a young employee of the Kinshasa FNLA bureau, and told Davies that he would be in touch once the mercenaries had had a chance to settle down.

As Davies watched, the wiry African and his aides climbed into a gleaming air-conditioned Mercedes and drove off rapidly down the highway. Davies climbed into the VW beside the FNLA driver, his mouth twisting wrily as he compared the two vehicles. Whether winning or losing, politicians could be trusted to put themselves first.

Within a few minutes the minibus was passing through the sprawling centre of downtown Kinshasa, high above the mighty cataracts of the River Zaire. But soon they had left the capital behind and were driving south-west through the night.

The mercenaries tried to sleep, worn out after nearly forty-eight hours of travelling. Davies dozed. His seat was more comfortable than that of most of his men, but that was counterbalanced by the fact that he was having to watch the recklessly erratic driving of the young African.

They drove for almost eight hours with only one halt for petrol and calls of nature. Some hours after dawn had broken they passed through a dusty Zairean town. Davies woke Tippett who was squeezed uncomfortably between his friend and the door on the passenger seat.

'We're in Tshikapa,' Davies muttered. 'Roberto said the camp is a few kilometres beyond the town.'

Tippett grunted, running his hand over the stubble on his face. He still looked like James Coburn — but James Coburn with a bad hangover. 'I hope to God they know how to make coffee there.'

Half an hour later they reached their destination. The camp was largely composed of rows of Nissen huts, surrounded by a high fence of rusting barbed wire. It had obviously seen far better days. Vegetation sprouted unchecked through the cracks in the concrete. Like so many African settlements, of whatever kind, it gave the impression of being a rural slum.

A guard in a filthy uniform waved the VW through the gate without leaving his palm-thatched shelter. The minibus rolled to a halt in what had once been a parade ground. One-by-one, the mercenaries stumbled out and stood blinking in the harsh sunlight. All of them were dishevelled, red-eyed from lack of sleep and beginning to wonder what the hell they had let themselves in for. Their driver scuttled away from the minibus.

Davies's eyes narrowed. Several dozen African soldiers had emerged from two of the Nissen huts. All of them were armed. In the still tropical air, he heard a click as someone cocked his weapon.

The mercenaries involuntarily moved into a knot around Davies and Tippett, their eyes flicking nervously towards their sullen, if not actively hostile hosts.

A cock-up? Davies wondered. *Treachery? It doesn't make sense.* Half-a-dozen of the Africans were over by the gate

78

now, their automatic weapons blocking their chance of flight.

Davies swore. He muscled his way through the mercenaries and stood in full view of the Africans, his hands on his hips. If ever he needed a weapon it was now. He would just have to make do with his personality.

11

'Time spent in reconnaissance is never wasted.'
                                        Max Waterman

'Davies!'

The shout echoed across the parade ground, slicing through the tension. Both Africans and mercenaries swung round to find the source of the interruption. A tall black officer stood in the doorway of one of the smaller huts; a smaller soldier, wearing headphones, was peering over his shoulder.

'What the — ?' Davies began. Then his face split into a smile. He pushed through the soldiers surrounding them, ignoring the menace of their guns, and strode up to the officer. 'Kikuji! What are you doing here, you old devil?'

'And no one said they send you.' Kikuji threw back his head and laughed. 'English *primeiro de todos!*' he bellowed, and pumped Davies' hand.

Davies grinned. He had served with the FNLA officer some years earlier in Angola, and the 'English number one!' slogan had become something of a catchphrase between them.

Tippett followed Davies over and greeted Kikuji with equal enthusiasm.

'Jesus, mate,' he said, 'I thought your crowd was going to finish us off half a minute ago.'

Kikuji apologized profusely. He explained — using a mixture of sign language, Portuguese, English, Spanish and French which all three men understood perfectly — that his men were not expecting the mercenaries until next week. The FNLA headquarters at Kinshasa should have radioed the news of their arrival last night, but there had been the usual blunder: the news had only reached the camp a few minutes earlier. The little radio operator nodded vigorously behind Kikuji's back in confirmation.

Davies nodded. The anxiety of the last few minutes had vanished with the discovery that his old friend was the *commandante* here. Liaison between mercs and African soldiers was often a problem; but with Kikuji there should be little difficulty. Not only was the African a superb fighting man, but he had earned Davies' respect both as an officer and as a comrade. They had saved one another's lives more than once in the bitter fighting around Maquela.

Kikuji soon rustled up the coffee Tippett so badly wanted and a rudimentary but filling meal. When everyone was fed and rested, the Africans and the mercenaries were paraded. There were about eighty black soldiers; their turn-out and discipline were better than Davies had anticipated after his Angolan experiences; and their weapons were spotless.

Before the inspection, Davies quietly discussed his plans with Kikuji and Tippett.

He jabbed a thumb towards the Africans. 'We shan't need all of them. It would make the force too unwieldy.'

Kikuji nodded intelligently. He sucked on his cigarette, a wrinkle appearing on his glossy ebony forehead as he frowned in concentration. 'We take only the best, my friend. Too many men *non bom*.'

Davies rubbed the stubble on his chin, weighing the odds. Their force had to be small enough to be fast and flexible, yet large enough to be effective.

'We've brought ten lads,' he said at last. 'Suppose we pick thirty of yours, and split them into ten groups of four, each with one white and three blacks. With us three that'll give us a unit strength of forty-three.'

'We could take on Fort Knox with that number,' said

81

Tippett drily. No one laughed. The job in front of them wasn't much easier.

The first day passed quickly. The three leaders picked out thirty of the FNLA troops and integrated them with the ten younger mercenaries in squads of four. There were three major advantages to this arrangement, Davies thought, particularly as he had insisted that each group of four should work, eat and sleep together. The white boys would gain from learning how the Africans coped with the problems of day-to-day living in this harsh and uncompromising environment. The blacks would gain from the superior military training of the whites. Furthermore, the more they were in each others' company, the less chance there would be of a foul-up in communications. This training period should last for a fortnight: that should be enough time to build up a co-ordinated team.

There was a mountain of arms in the Nissen hut which served as the armoury. Davies ordered each man to select a Kalashnikov and three magazines on the first evening.

Tippett and Davies stood together watching as the young black and white troops jostled and joked in the armoury. The hostility between the two nationalities had vanished entirely.

'This is how that bastard Callan should have done it,' Tippett said quietly.

Davies laughed without humour. The megalomaniac mercenary leader had terrorized and alienated the black FNLA troops — and, for that matter, many of the white mercenaries as well. The MPLA enemy had benefited accordingly.

'I'm playing this a different way, mate,' he told Tippett. 'For starters, I don't intend to end up in front of a firing squad in Luanda.'

Over the following days the whites rapidly acclimatized to the new conditions, with the help of liberal supplies of salt and anti-malaria tablets. Davies and Kikuji kept up an unrelenting pressure of work which had the double effect of accelerating their training and keeping bickering to a minimum. By the end of the first week, the forty-odd men had come together as a unit.

Holden Roberto contacted them by radio: he was able to give them a further four days' grace before the start of the operation. Davies decided to put the breathing-space to good use. During that second week the three senior men spent a couple of days out of the camp, leaving the troops in command of the rapidly-maturing Sanderson and of Manuel, Kikuji's second-in-command.

They drove down to the border crossing-point at Portugualia in an elderly Land Rover which was largely composed of parts cannibalized from other vehicles. Kikuji had abandoned it as beyond repair, but Davies spent several hours beneath the vehicle, relying successfully on his genius for improvisation in the total absence of spare parts.

On their trips to Portugualia, Kikuji acted as the eyes and ears of the Englishmen. They soon realized that the frontier was a formality which was more significant on paper than in fact. Kikuji was able to lead them on foot into Angola without any hindrance whatsoever.

They concealed themselves in the bush on the Angolan side and monitored the crossing-procedures for several hours. The entire unit could, of course, have walked into Angola as easily as its three leaders had done; but Davies had his own reasons for wanting to enter the country by road.

No one disturbed them as they lay sweating in the bush through the long afternoon, barring a constant stream of insects and one small boy. The boy stumbled on them by accident. Kikuji bought his loyalty and silence, apparently for life, with a cigarette and a handful of escudos.

It soon became apparent that the thoroughness of the customs check was related by an inverse ratio to the amount of money with which the guards were bribed. The only travellers who were rigorously checked were those who had little and could therefore give nothing. One truck-driver proved an exception to the rule as they watched that afternoon. When he heard the amount of the bribe which the guards demanded, he unwisely exploded with rage. In consequence, the customs officials laboriously dismantled the truck, strewed its parts all over the road and complacently pilfered its cargo.

Tippett spoke for them all when he said, 'If we can't get through that checkpoint it could only be really bad luck or sheer bloody incompetence.'

Kikuji nodded. 'But it will cost a lot,' he warned in fractured English. 'You sure we shouldn't cross on foot? *Et pas de risques.*'

'No way,' Davies said firmly. He wasn't going to spoil this ship for a ha'p'orth of tar. The risk when crossing the frontier by road was minimal, and the advantages would be well worth the cost. 'Listen, mate, we want to keep the team and the logistics together on the outward leg. And everyone's going to be carrying quite a load. There'll be less to carry on the return journey when we'll have used a lot of the munitions. But the most important thing is speed, both going in and coming out. Surprise is one of the main things we've got going for us.'

The *commandante* spread his arms, acknowledging the force of Davies' arguments. 'Okay. So we move *rapido.*'

Tippett looked shrewdly at Davies. 'How are you going to persuade Roberto to invest even more money in us?'

Davies shrugged. 'If he wants the diamonds he'll have to agree to do it our way. He's not going to go walking into Henrique de Carvalho himself, is he?'

12

'Travellers, like poets, are mostly an angry race.'
Sir Richard Burton

Davies had the opportunity to enlist Roberto's assistance
sooner than he had expected. When the three men returned
to the camp in the Land Rover that evening, they found a
message from the FNLA president. Roberto announced
that he intended to make a surprise visit the following day.

Roberto turned up in a Range Rover — air-conditioned,
like his Mercedes — accompanied by three young, muscular Africans in slacks and bright, printed shirts. The bulge
of shoulder holsters under their armpits left no doubt about
their role in life.

The president was immaculate in a dove-grey lounge
suit. As usual his dark glasses made his expression difficult
to read, but he was clearly delighted by the progress which
Davies had made in the ten days since his arrival.

The camp now looked more like a military barracks than
an African village. The morale, discipline and efficiency
of the strike force was amply demonstrated by the series
of manoeuvres they performed. Davies was all the more
pleased because Roberto had given him no time to stage a
dress rehearsal before his arrival. The president was seeing
them as they really were.

The group had been subdivided into three small platoons, each with its own loose rank structure, and each with
a special role to play in the coming attack. Davies had taken
every possible precaution against failure. Each platoon

could, at a pinch, fulfil the others' functions. He had even tried the experiment of removing key men from the platoons to check that they could still do their allocated tasks.

Afterwards, Davies drew Roberto aside and explained his plan for entering and travelling through Angola. 'Ideally we want trucks the guards are used to seeing — trucks which often pass through Portugualia on legitimate business. And it would be all the better if their normal route took them south towards Henrique de Carvalho.'

The president agreed at once with the idea. The extra money didn't appear to worry him, which came as no surprise to Davies. He knew Roberto was practically on his last legs: the politician had no choice but to gamble everything on this desperate throw.

Roberto wasted no time. Before he left, he arranged for Davies, Tippett and Kikuji to meet a couple of truck-drivers who plied between Zaire and Angola; the men had smuggled contraband — occasionally and for a consideration — for the FNLA. They were well-known to officials on both sides of the border, if only because they bribed regularly and generously. Usually they took wheat into Angola and returned with a load of coffee. Best of all, their customary route took them south of Portugualia, through Henrique de Carvalho to Villa Luso, some three hundred miles further south.

The only possible problem was that the truck-drivers had never smuggled men before — only supplies for the FNLA guerrillas in the Angolan bush.

The three soldiers met the truck-drivers the next evening in a house which the FNLA leader retained in Tshikapa, the nearest town to the camp. Both men were Angolan-born but of Portuguese extraction. They were dark, squat men, heavy drinkers and smokers. Davies had the forethought to take a bottle of scotch along with him. When the mercenary had finished explaining what he wanted, there was a moment's silence.

'We can get you *into* Angola, and down to Henrique de Carvalho. That's no problem — so long as the money's right.' Alessandro, the older of the two drivers, slapped a mosquito on his arm, scratched where it had bitten and continued: 'We'd want payment in US dollars or Swiss francs. And seventy-five per cent of it in advance — '

Tippett interrupted with a whistle of astonishment; Davies silenced him with a wave.

'— and we would each require twenty thousand US, or its equivalent. Furthermore, we can give you no guarantee that we can pick you up on the journey back to Zaire.'

Tippett could be restrained no longer. 'For that amount of money, how do you plan to get us there? Concorde? And why can't you bring us back?'

'We will if we can, *senhor*,' Alessandro said patiently. 'But it may be impossible.' His mournful brown eyes rested momentarily on the three Kalashnikovs leaning in one corner of the room. 'When there is . . . activity in Angola,' he explained delicately, 'the military are everywhere. All civilian trucks are herded into convoys and shepherded through the countryside by the army — usually right up to the border.'

His friend spoke for the first time: 'But there are collection points.'

Alessandro nodded. 'José is right. There are two just north of Henrique de Carvalho — one on the edge of town, the other twenty kilometres further on. If you, *senhors*, and your men can get there, we may be able to smuggle you on board.'

Davies suppressed a grin: the idea of leaving Angola under the protection of the army appealed to him. 'How long are the stopovers?' he asked.

Alessandro shrugged. 'It depends. Usually the second one lasts nearly until dusk. There is a secondary route into the interior, and the convoy always has to wait for a lot of stragglers.'

The mercenary abruptly changed the subject: 'Why do you ask for so much money?'

The truck-driver remained unruffled, though an unconscious look of arrogance flitted across his face. 'José and I are of Portuguese descent, *senhor*. We were born in Angola, but now there is no longer any place for us. Soon those black gangsters will steal our trucks and call it nationalization. Maybe they will kill us. Death finds many people in Angola since the communists took over. If this trip is successful, we can get ourselves and our families to Portugal — and have a little put by to start a new life.'

The three soldiers retired into another room to discuss the truck-drivers' terms. All three of them had been impressed, almost despite themselves, by the drivers' frankness. Alessandro and José could so easily have agreed that they would definitely transport the mercenaries on their return journey — and pocketed the payment in advance for that part of the trip without intending to do anything to earn it. It was one of those moments when you had to take a gamble on the integrity of others. Davies, Tippett and Kikuji were willing to do so.

Carrying a second bottle of scotch, Davies led the way back to the two Portuguese. 'Okay, *senhors*,' he said. 'You're on.'

Five days later, just after dawn, two large Mercedes truck rumbled up the slight incline to the gate of the camp with a great grinding of gears. Each towed a capacious thirty-foot trailer. The lorries and trailers were partially laden with sacks of wheat, stacked four sacks high and five wide.

All the troops helped with the unloading, working in relays. When the vehicles were empty, four heavy wooden cages — prefabricated over the last few days by the mercenaries — were manhandled aboard, one for each lorry and trailer. The cages were placed as far from the back as possible.

Davies gave the order to reload the sacks. The wheat was carefully packed around and on top of the cages and artistically arranged to make it seem that the trucks and trailers were fully laden with nothing but wheat. Davies personally checked the two vital requirements for each of the cages: there had to be adequate ventilation; and a narrow, concealed burrow had to lead through the sacks to the voids

88

created by the cages.

When he was completely satisfied, Davies gave his men the signal to board. For the purpose of the journey, he had divided the unit into four parties. He himself, Tippett and Kikuji were each in charge of one; with some misgivings, Davies had made the fourth one the responsibility of Sanderson, with Manuel as his back-up.

The mercenaries and their FNLA colleagues joked as they crawled laboriously into their darkened artificial caves. They took with them a formidable arsenal of weapons. In addition to their Kalashnikovs and spare magazines, each man carried a 66mm LAWS hand-held rocket, by its own sling. The pouches of their webbing harness held several grenades.

The unit as a whole was equipped with two mortars, each of fifty calibre. Six men carried Bergen rucksacks whose contents were Tippett's pride and joy. He had rustled up a variety of explosives. He had constructed several mines of the Claymore type; when these devices were exploded, they belched out both lethal ball-bearings and the concussive force of the blast itself in an arc of about thirty degrees over a range of some thirty metres. Tippett had also provided an assortment of plastic explosive, together with all the associated paraphernalia like fuses and detonators.

Davies was the last man aboard. He watched the drivers roping and sheeting their loads on the two trailers and one of the trucks. Finally he climbed in himself, and wriggled through the darkness. Ahead of him he could hear snorts of suppressed laughter: his young troops were riding high on a wave of nervous excitement.

The wave would subside, Davies knew, once they had time to appreciate the darkness, the danger and the discomfort. The sheer stench in there, he reflected, would soon make them all want to vomit. He wished that they had had time to give the men some indication of what confinement would be like.

They were fine after five minutes — but what the hell would they be like after thirty-six hours?

* * *

89

The mercenaries found themselves in the world of the blind. Their ears strained to catch every sound. Beneath them the trucks thundered into life. They pulled out of the compound and took the road to the border.

Each party had torches but, since replacement batteries had been unobtainable, Davies had ordered that their use be strictly rationed. Fortunately his watch had a luminous face. He had also — at considerable personal cost — forbidden the men to smoke for the duration of the journey: the ventilation in the cages just wasn't good enough.

He was able to keep a rough check on their progress by taking into account the passage of time and the halts they made. Their longest stop was at the checkpoint at Portugualia. The men sat in total silence, tensely cradling their Kalashnikovs. But there was no trouble: the guards didn't even bother to peer round the sheeting.

The problems began when the two-truck convoy hit the rough red shingle road inside Angola. The mercenaries were bounced on to one another by the irregularities of the road surface, like dice in a shaker. The road had been poorly-maintained. The heavy rainfall had eroded the hard pack shingle, and the surface was cut deeply with a lattice-work of ruts and pockmarked with holes.

The lurching of the trucks made the wheat sacks around them shift and resettle constantly, generating a fine mist of wheat dust which soon made breathing even more difficult. The wooden cages themselves began to shift to and fro as the constant motion chafed and loosened their bindings.

As the hours ticked slowly by, Davies became increasingly worried. The men with him grumbled constantly, and he had been forced to pistol-whip one African who had gone briefly berserk and attempted to fight his way out to the open air. Davies' controlled violence had the desired effect: his men sank into an apathetic torpor, partly conditioned by the intense, moist heat which enveloped them.

Davies had his own group under control; and he had no doubt that Tippett and Kikuji were maintaining discipline equally well. But the inexperienced Sanderson and Manuel were another proposition altogether.

He was right to be apprehensive. Sanderson had two whites and seven blacks in his trailer. One of the former was Jack O'Ryan, a hot-headed ex-SAS trooper of Irish origins. As conditions in the trailer worsened, O'Ryan took every opportunity to needle Sanderson. He demanded more room (at the expense of the others in the cage), he complained bitterly about the lack of air and several times threatened to crawl out to the top of the load. His attitude infected the others. After ten hours in this dark swaying hell, Sanderson and Manuel realized they were on the brink of mutiny.

Suddenly the breaking-point came. A match flared. In the light of the flame Sanderson saw that O'Ryan was lighting a cigarette.

'Put that thing out, Jack,' he ordered.

O'Ryan blew out the match. 'And who's going to stop me?' he sneered. 'You, Pete?'

Sanderson lacked experience but not courage. He flung himself across the intervening bodies towards the glow of the cigarette tip. He and O'Ryan grappled viciously, their pent-up aggression escaping in a series of jabs, slashes and punches.

Inevitably many of their blows went wide, hitting the soldiers around them. Manuel tried to come to Sanderson's aid, but his blind, clumsy movements only made matters worse.

One of the blacks screamed — the shockingly high, piercing sound of a man on the edge of hysteria.

The scream triggered a panic among the remaining blacks. They began to scramble out of the cage, desperate to escape from that confined airless space and the flailing limbs of the two struggling white men.

Sanderson, his mouth full of blood from a lucky punch of O'Ryan's, was dimly aware of what was happening. He shouted, 'Stop!' He was hideously aware that if any of the men got out, they would almost certainly jeopardize the entire attack. He tried to pull himself away from O'Ryan to deal with this new, more serious problem. Manuel was swearing monotonously in French.

The young ex-Para jabbed his elbow in O'Ryan's face and wrenched himself away. Despair washed over him: he had not only put the operation at risk but, on a personal level, he had failed Davies who had entrusted him with this command.

One of the escaping soldiers stumbled over Sanderson. A boot crashed with accidental brutality into the side of his head. A wave of unconsciousness surged up and swallowed him.

13

'Danger and delight grow on the same stalk.'
English proverb

'Bravo!' The stoop-shouldered patriarch beamed like a boy, his brilliantly white false teeth contrasting sharply with the deep tan of his face. He turned to the slim, pockmarked man by his side. 'They both ride well, hey?'

D'asser nodded in reply, without taking his eyes from the two riders. They had now reached the last corner of their informal race course in the huge, park-like garden, and were pulling into the final straight. D'asser's normally impassive face was less guarded and more animated than usual. Here, on the Rodriguez estate which he had known since childhood, he felt almost one of the family. Indeed, the Rodriguez were now the only family he had.

The old man ran a gnarled, mahogany-coloured hand through his shock of white hair, a characteristic gesture of delight. 'Jorge is still in front.'

His younger grandson was in the lead by half a length, crouched low over the neck of his red mare. The watchers could see him urging the horse to put on a final spurt to keep him ahead of his brother. Antonio's mount was larger — a jet-black gelding with a flowing mane which matched its rider's hair.

D'asser clenched his hands, the knuckles whitening. Secretly he wanted sixteen-year-old Jorge to win. It would give the boy so much pleasure; Antonio would surely be generous enough to give his brother the illusion of victory.

But as they watched, Antonio Rodriguez dug his heel into the gelding's flanks. The powerful horse responded immediately, his movements in perfect harmony with his master's commands. The gelding nosed inexorably past the red mare. He flashed past the crimson rhododendron bush which served as the finishing-post, the winner by at least a length.

There was a sigh of disappointment from the two spectators.

'Antonio could have let the boy win,' the patriarch muttered with the wheezing petulance of old age. 'Just this once.'

The two horsemen reined in their mounts and cantered over to their grandfather and D'asser. They jerked the reins, slewing the horse to an abrupt halt, and dismounted. Both of them had broad smiles on their faces.

'I was winning all the way,' Jorge boasted cheerfully. He bore no malice towards his elder brother.

'Except at the end!' Antonio joshed him. 'Come on, let's go round to the stables.'

Antonio led off his mount in the direction of the range of outbuildings which housed the stables. Jorge flashed a smile at his grandfather and D'asser and moved quickly to overtake his brother, still chattering excitedly.

Their grandfather stood watching them for a moment, leaning heavily on his sturdy ebony walking-stick; his disappointment was still evident in his face.

'When Jorge is a year or two older,' D'asser said abruptly, 'he'll beat Antonio every time. He's a better horseman even now.'

The old man snorted. He wasn't interested in what would happen in a year or two's time: he mightn't be alive by then. Still grumbling under his breath, he limped off towards the vast white house which had been in his family for well over a century.

D'asser stared down at his feet and, like the small boy he had once been, unconsciously scuffed the rich red African soil with one of his gleaming toe-caps. He wondered how long the communists — of whom, of course, he was technically one — would allow this efficiently-run but semi-aristocratic estate to remain in the hands of the Rodriguez. He shrugged and followed the old man into the house.

He crossed the deep veranda to the french windows and entered a large, white-washed sitting room. Its cool interior was a relief to him after the muggy, oppressive heat of the noonday sun outside. It was February — and that meant, in this part of the Dark Continent, that it was also the rainy season. Heavy tropical downpours were interspersed with strong hot sunshine. The combined heat and humidity made it almost impossible to live and work, even for those who had been born in the climate.

The well-trained staff had heard him coming in. A few seconds later a houseboy in a neatly-pressed white jacket materialized through the door at the other end of the room. He had correctly anticipated D'asser's needs: his tray held a long glass of freshly-pressed lime juice, clinking with ice.

The old man joined him, his stick tapping on the uncarpeted floor. Shortly afterwards Antonio and Jorge came in, the latter still flushed and laughing after the race. Their grandfather tactfully swallowed his disappointment, clapped them both on the back, and congratulated them on a well-run race. D'asser said nothing to Antonio, but gave Jorge a tip about the handling of his reins. Jorge wasn't going to lose next time if D'asser could help it.

Old Rodriguez took little part in the conversation of the younger men but sat dozing in his chair.

'I wish your leave was longer,' Jorge said to his brother and D'asser. 'There's only two days left.'

Antonio shrugged. 'We were lucky to get three weeks — I thought they'd give us seven days.'

On their return from Libya, Rodriguez and D'asser had been thoroughly debriefed by high-ranking party officials in Luanda and also passed on some of their newly-acquired military skills to ideologically-sound fellow officers. Someone must have been pleased with their achievements to give them so long a spell of home leave.

It was especially welcome because they had heard they were to be posted abroad on their return to duty. The three weeks had given them the opportunity to complete the amalgamation of D'asser's plantation with that of the Rodriguez family. Antonio had watched — with relief and some amusement — how Jorge's boyish charm had gradually affected the solitary and embittered D'asser. Anyone who knew only D'asser the dedicated and ruthless soldier would have been astounded to see him now — chatting happily with young Jorge. He had even been seen to smile once or twice when in the lad's company.

It was largely due, Antonio considered, to Jorge's personality. He was universally popular in the Quimbundo district, even with the estate workers. The boy lacked the arrogance usually associated with the families of big landowners; he had a ready and infectious smile; and was especially liked for his understanding and tolerance.

In return Jorge worshipped his brother and D'asser, his brother by adoption. The two men were legendary in the district as the two most feared soldiers in the Angolan army's northern command. In the few short years since the end of hostilities, the legend had been embellished until the local population had come to regard Antonio and D'asser as being practically superhuman. Jorge held the same opinion — and basked in the reflected glory of their company.

Antonio shouted for the houseboy to bring them fresh drinks. Thinking of Jorge reminded him of Rojer Eloi, the pleasant young Angolan on their course in Libya. He interrupted the others' conversation: 'Are we going to see Rojer Eloi tomorrow, D'asser?'

Before leaving Luanda, they had made a vague arrangement to meet Eloi in his hometown, Henrique de Carvalho, and take up his invitation to visit the local *canteena*.

D'asser reflected for a minute. It would give them a change of scene and a chance to get drunk without having to worry about the old man's ideas about propriety. There was also something to be said for getting away from the plantations — while they were here, there was always something to be done: the estate was a never-ending source of work.

'Okay,' he said in his dry precise voice. 'Henrique de Carvalho's only about a hundred miles.'

In the context of the vast distances of Africa, a hundred miles was nothing.

Jorge said nothing, but his face fell. He had hoped to have his two heroes to himself for the rest of their leave. But they wouldn't want him to tag along if they were going to see an old army comrade. He tried to mask his distress with a stream of jokes.

The houseboy shook Antonio Rodriguez awake an hour before dawn. The darkness outside was thick and impenetrable; but it was better to make an early start while the day was still relatively cool. He slipped out of bed and went next door to wake D'asser.

They dressed quickly and snatched a quick cup of coffee for breakfast. A few minutes later they slipped out of one of the house's side doors and walked briskly across the grounds. Both of them knew the area so well that they could have sprinted over it blindfold. They intended to walk down to the main highway, which skirted the Rodriguez estate for several kilometres before diving away into the interior of Angola. Once at the road they would easily be able to hitch a lift on one of the trucks carrying foodstuffs along this major east-west artery.

They had covered only a few hundred yards when D'asser laid his hand on Rodriguez' arm. 'There's someone behind us,' he whispered. His hearing was still trained up to combat readiness, even when on leave.

Rodriguez laughed at his friend's wariness. He could now hear running feet himself. A few seconds later, Jorge emerged panting from the murk.

'Antonio, D'asser,' he said breathlessly, 'please let me come too. I won't get in the way. After this leave, I won't see you again for *months*.'

Rodriguez glanced at his friend, one eyebrow raised in

enquiry. D'asser thought that the trip might make up for losing the race yesterday. He nodded.

'Okay, kid,' Antonio said. 'So long as you behave yourself.'

There was another reason to let Jorge come which all of them knew but none of them mentioned. D'asser and Antonio were soldiers who could be sent on active service at any moment. Jorge might have to wait longer than a few months for their next leave: he might have to wait for ever.

14

> 'When the elephants fight, sometimes the mousedeer
> between them is killed.'
>
> Malay proverb

The truck was a grey-and-white monster carrying a load of tinned pilchards. Its driver, a massively-built African who was almost as wide as he was tall, spread along the bench seat of the cab, leaving his three passengers little room. Jorge had to slot himself into the driver's bunk above the others' heads.

The driver was one of those convivial men who tell you their life history in the first five minutes you spend with them. Once that was out of the way, his conviviality switched to another direction.

'Here,' he said to Antonio, 'pass me that bottle in the glove compartment.'

The bottle was large, unlabelled and full of almost clear liquid. The driver cradled it affectionately with the arm which wasn't draped around the steering-wheel. It was home-brewed spirit, he explained; and he told them in exhaustive detail exactly how he had brewed it. He uncapped the bottle with his teeth and took a swig. His body jerked reflexively as the spirit coursed into him, and the engine revs wavered accordingly. He burped approvingly.

'*Calvados mucho calore*,' he said with pride. '*Mucho calore!*'

'Rubbish,' said Antonio Rodriguez with a cunning glint in his eye. 'Home-brew rots your guts and doesn't even get you drunk.'

99

The truck-driver indignantly passed them the bottle. For nearly an hour it moved between the four of them. Their swigs grew steadily longer as the liquor took hold and anaesthetized their throats. It was Jorge who started the singing — it was, in fact, the first time he had been properly drunk, away from the watchful eyes of his grandfather — and the others joined in with gusto. The driver was a man who prided himself on his sense of rhythm. Soon it affected his driving, and the truck weaved from side to side of the highway in time with their songs.

Everyone was surprised when Henrique de Carvalho appeared out of the heat haze: the hundred miles had seemed more like twenty. Swearing eternal friendship, the driver dumped them outside the *canteena* where they had arranged to meet Eloi.

As soon as Jorge's feet touched the pavement, his face turned an unhealthy shade of green. D'asser took one look at him and grabbed him by the arm. He led the boy into the alleyway alongside the one-storeyed, tin-roofed bar and propped him up against the wall.

'Come on, lad,' he said sardonically. 'What goes in must come out.'

Eloi arrived just as Jorge was being sick for the third and last time. The three men greeted each other with the usual expressive Latin hugs. The white-faced boy trailed after them into the bar. He privately resolved he would never touch alcohol again. Eloi, ignorant of this, bought him a beer; Jorge was pleasantly surprised to find that it went down very well.

He sat up and began to take notice of his surroundings. The bar interior was cool, and they had it to themselves apart from the pretty young girl who had served them. Eloi, Antonio and D'asser were deep in reminiscences of Libya. Jorge found his eyes returning again and again to the girl behind the bar. There was a flash of interest in her dark eyes.

Eloi ordered them a hot spicy meal, which gave Jorge the chance to start talking to the girl. After he had eaten the meal — and consumed another couple of beers — he felt even better than he had felt in the truck of the cab. He left the men, still absorbed in a conversation which was becoming steadily more technical, and wandered up to the bar. In short order he had bought the girl a drink and learned that her name was Maria and that she was some sort of second cousin of Eloi's. They rapidly progressed to that stage of courtship where the smitten participants neither speak nor listen to anything beyond themselves. Jorge and Maria were wholly taken up with gazing into one another's eyes.

Suddenly a perceptible tremor ran through the bar: the tables and chairs shook, and the glasses behind the bar vibrated noisily. The three soldiers sobered instantly. They heard — though the youngsters did not — the far-off roar of an explosion which belatedly followed the wave of vibration.

D'asser and Rodriguez looked enquiringly at Eloi. There could be many reasons for such an explosion — civil blasting at the nearby diamond mines, for instance; Eloi should be able to explain it.

But Eloi wordlessly shook his head. Simultaneously the three soldiers were on their feet, strapping on their Tokaref army-issue pistols and unbuckling the flaps of their holsters.

Eloi was the first outside. Shading his eyes with his hands, he searched the sky for signs of the explosion. A long thin finger of oily smoke pointed up from the aerodrome in the shimmering noon air. He pointed it out to Rodriguez and D'asser. As they watched, two more black plumes joined the first, each accompanied by vibrations and followed by the distant thunder of the explosions.

More explosions were succeeded by the far-off chatter of automatic gunfire.

'Guerrilla activity, I suppose.' There was a faint question in Eloi's voice. The FNLA guerrillas did not usually come so near the town with its heavily armed garrison of regulars.

Their attention was diverted from the explosions by closer sounds — the shouting of orders, the revving of engines and the slamming of doors. The three men turned to look in the other direction. At the far end of the long, dusty street was the high brick wall which enclosed the military barracks.

The additional noise even penetrated through to love's young dream. Jorge and Maria stumbled out on to the pavement and stood very close together watching the pillars of smoke above the aerodrome.

The heavy doors of the barracks swung inwards and a stream of vehicles poured into the street, swung past the bar and set off at speed in the direction of the aerodrome, with sirens wailing. Civilians emerged from offices, shops and bars and stood blinking in small knots on the pavement, staring at the convoy as it passed.

The soldiers on board the vehicles were in various stages of undress. Many were attempting to tie bootlaces, tuck in shirts or fasten their belts. The column accelerated fast until it vanished into its own cloud of thick red dust.

D'asser shrugged. 'Nothing we can do. Let's have another beer.'

Eloi nodded absently but did not follow his friends back into the *canteena*. His attention had been caught by a group of office girls who had come out of the mining offices directly opposite to watch the convoy. All of them seemed pretty: to him they looked as delectable as birds of paradise.

He called across the road, inviting them all to come and have a beer with him and insinuating that he had unimaginable delights waiting in store for them. They rejected his advances with hoots of laughter and giggles; but there were enough genuine smiles in his direction to make him feel that his luck might be better in the near future. He watched appreciatively as they returned to their offices.

As he was on the point of returning to the bar, a jeep came roaring out of the barracks, carrying an officer who knew Eloi slightly. The jeep slowed as it passed the *canteena*.

'Terrorists are attacking the airport,' the youthful captain shouted above the roar of the engine. 'You'd better get inside — they might lob a few mortars in the town.'

The captain tore off in hot pursuit of the column while the

gunner manning the heavy swivel-mounted machine-gun on the back struggled to keep his foothold.

Rodriguez had ordered them more food and beer. While he ate, Eloi had to endure a good deal of ribald chaffing about the reception the office girls had given him. There were more explosions, but they ignored them, though they did speculate about who was responsible and how they would counter the attack.

But the questions were academic: they were on leave.

Jorge soon left the men alone and sidled back to Maria at the bar. Eloi thought bitterly that, within his age-group, Jorge was having better luck than he was. He threw down his fork and leant back in the chair, lighting a short fat cigar. He contributed a few half-hearted remarks to the military conversation of his companions, but his mind was still on the bevy of girls from the office across the road. He stared wistfully through the open door of the *canteena* to the closed door of the mining offices. He almost forgot the excitement of the attack as his mind drifted into a fantasy land of petticoats, suspenders and hot, thrashing bodies.

Abruptly, he sat up and blinked, his reverie rudely shattered. A group of running men, both white and black and dressed in unfamiliar combat uniforms, ran across his field of vision and disappeared into the door of the mining offices. One soldier stayed in the alleyway nervously fingering what looked like a rocket launcher.

Eloi's initial reaction was total disbelief. But, in less time than it takes a man to blink, his war-schooled reflexes took over. He slid snake-like from his chair, one hand groping for his pistol, and crawled noiselessly across the floor to one of the open windows which flanked the door on either side.

D'asser and Rodriguez picked up on his cue immediately; they followed his lead and took up their position at the other window. They peered cautiously over the sill, concentrating on the drama being played out over the road.

Their concentration was so fierce that they forgot about the two youngsters who were still oblivious of everything outside themselves at the other end of the bar. The three soldiers automatically and stealthily cocked their hand-guns. A silence hovered over the *canteena* for a long moment, as pregnant as a rain cloud on the verge of bursting.

There were three muffled shots in the building across the road. Still no one moved in the bar. Besides the sentry at the door, there were more armed men just within the building. The Tokaref pistols which the three Angolans carried were of far too small a calibre to do anything against the grey-green, metre-long tubes of the missile launchers of the attacking force.

Their best hope of survival was to lie absolutely still — and watch.

But they had forgotten that Jorge was ignorant of the craft of war. Maria had heard the muffled shots as well, without realizing what they were. She looked up and saw the three men crouching by the window. She touched Jorge's arm and, with a smile in her pretty eyes, indicated what they were doing.

Jorge grinned broadly: the three grown men were playing at soldiers. Maria gave a tiny gurgle of laughter. The two youngsters were united in the eternal conspiracy of adolescents against adults. Jorge picked up his glass and swaggered down the room towards the front of the bar.

'Hey, Antonio,' he called cheerfully, 'I thought *I* was the one who couldn't hold my drink. You should see yourselves now!'

Rodriguez, D'asser and Eloi swung round.

Simultaneously the soldier across the street saw the movement — and perhaps the glint of Jorge's glass — in the *canteena*'s shaded interior. He threw the 66mm rocket launcher to his shoulder. He paused for only a fraction of a second to sight it, and squeezed the black rubber-covered activator tit on top of the tube.

There was a flash at the muzzle of the disposable glass fibre tube. The rocket flew with unerring accuracy across the still, dusty road and through the open doors of the bar.

A millisecond later, it exploded.

15

'A whiff of grapeshot.'
Thomas Carlyle

The African dusk slipped swiftly into night. José, at the
wheel of the second truck, rubbed his eyes and stared ahead
along the powerful beam of his headlights. As they manoeuvred round a sharp bend he caught a sideways glimpse of the
trailer behind Alessandro's truck in front of him. Surely the
load of sacks was sagging in the middle? His dreams of a
happy, secure future in Portugal were abruptly uprooted
and replaced with pure nightmare. The ties had loosened;
the sacks would slip off; the wooden cage would be revealed
with its human captives in the remorseless glare of a spot-
light mounted on one of the military patrol vehicles.

He flashed his lights hysterically, and went on flashing
them until Alessandro found a suitably secluded spot to turn
off the road.

The bush shrouded the two parked trucks from prying
eyes. Both drivers leapt out of their cabs to confer. At once
they became aware of shouting and the sound of struggling
in Alessandro's trailer. They ran to release Davies.

After half an hour, the mercenary leader ruefully conceded that the damage could have been a lot worse. He had
found Sanderson out for the count, but the boy had now
come round and had nothing worse than a splitting head-
ache. He had dug out O'Ryan and Manuel from beneath a
pile of sacks which had collapsed on top of them, effectively blocking the escape burrow from their cage. They were

locked in a ferocious embrace. Davies had pulled them apart, discovered what had happened and given O'Ryan a belt round the mouth. It was an impromptu but effective field punishment which had restored order and would prevent the Irishman from eating anything solid for a day or two. The fresh air calmed down the others who had been trapped inside the cage.

Davies opened up all the loads and gave everyone a breather. All the troops were in poor condition. If this went on much longer, Davies reflected, they would be in no condition to fight a major engagement at the other end. In consequence he decided to alter his plan.

It took four precious hours to reshuffle the loads. They dared not use too much light for fear of betraying their position. The wooden cages were discarded; and the sacks were piled up in such a way that there was a hollow on the top of each load. The men sat in these, hidden from overhead by the heavy tarpaulins which secured the wheat.

It was a risk worth taking, Davies calculated. Now they had passed the border, a thorough inspection was unlikely.

The lorries rolled on through the night. They made better time than expected but were still behind schedule, owing to the unanticipated delay.

At dawn next morning Alessandro and José pulled off into a clearing out of sight of the road. The men extracted themselves from their mobile prisons and helped to rearrange the sacks of wheat. They brushed the grit and dirt from themselves and, more meticulously, from their weapons.

While this was going on, Alessandro and Davies walked a few hundred metres up the deserted road. The truck-driver pointed out a broad rutted lay-by which extended from the side of the road into the bush.

'This is the staging-point for the civilian convoy when the military escort us. If we can, we will be here within forty-eight hours. We'll try the clearing first — if you aren't there yet, we will have to come on here.'

'Failing that we'll try and contact you at the collection

106

point you mentioned further north.' Davies ground his cigarette butt beneath his boot heel. 'We appreciate this,' he said. 'There may be a bonus for you.'

'Thank you, *senhor*.' Alessandro's face darkened. 'And we are glad that you come to make havoc among these black gangsters who rule our country.' He spat to emphasize his point.

Davies and Alessandro walked back to the clearing. The truck-drivers were anxious to get going. Their personal danger increased every moment they remained in the mercenaries' company.

Once the Angolans had left, the three leaders of the expedition held a quick conference. They had decided their basic strategy long ago in the Zairois camp. Their delayed arrival made it necessary to alter a few minor details, but essentially the plan held good.

Afterwards there was little need of conversation. All the men knew the broad details of the battle-plan and had been drilled in advance. When Davies gave the word, they set off across country in a loose but highly co-ordinated formation. In less than an hour they reached the road which linked Henrique de Carvalho with its airport. Here the force split into two parties.

Davies took ten men, including Kikuji who knew the layout of the town well. Keeping well under cover, they moved towards the fringes of the settlement. Tippett took command of the remainder — with himself he had thirty-two men. Although the lanky explosives expert lacked some of Davies' military experience, his special skills were vital to this aspect of the operation. Both Sanderson and Manuel accompanied him.

Tippett advanced towards the airport, keeping within sight of the road. When they had gone a couple of kilometres, they reached a saucer-shaped depression, bisected by the muddy red ribbon of the road.

As the maps had suggested, it was perfect for his purpose. Tippett subdivided his force. Twenty men, led by himself, would remain in this shallow valley, while the rest, under

Sanderson's command, moved up to the airport and took their positions there.

Tippett worked fast, blessing the foresight which had made him train several of his men to handle explosives. He had approximately three hours to lay his trap.

At the bottom of the dish-like valley he laid out all but two of the Claymore mines at his disposal. He positioned them so their field of fire would saturate a three hundred yard stretch of the road with millions of hardened steel ball-bearings, each with the velocity of a bullet from a high-powered hunting rifle. He deployed his men well back from the mines in heavily-camouflaged positions. Their LAWS rockets would provide a vital — and more accurate — back-up to the mines.

The preparations were completed just after eleven a.m. The next forty minutes were the worst that Tippett had so far experienced on this contract. He hated the waiting — when you were all screwed up to go but waiting indefinitely for the starter's pistol.

At last the walkie-talkie set beside him crackled into life. 'Ready and waiting.' The tension brought out the Somerset burr. 'Sanderson — out.'

Tippett gave Manuel a thumbs-up sign and pressed the button on the handset to transmit. The sets had short ranges, and Tippett was the vital link between Sanderson and Davies.

Davies was on the air a few seconds later. 'In position,' he said laconically.

Tippett called up Sanderson. There was only one word to say: '*Go!*'

Sanderson sighed with relief as the monosyllable emerged over the static. He was desperately anxious to prove himself to Davies and Tippett — to show that his failure to maintain discipline the previous night was not a typical performance. He had half-feared that he would be relieved of his independent command.

He swiftly ran through the list of priorities which Davies

had given him. He mentally checked the dispositions of his companions whom he had stationed at fifty yards intervals along the perimeter of the airfield.

It was 11.43.

Sanderson raised the LAWS missile-launcher to his shoulder and sighted carefully on two small helicopters a hundred and fifty yards away. They exploded on the tarmac runway into twin balls of flame.

Seconds afterwards, the mortar team on his left scored a direct hit on the low barracks building which ran to the right of the control tower. Men scurried out of it into the open, attracting a crackle of small arms fire.

Sanderson grinned with satisfaction and wiped the beads of sweat from his forehead. More hits followed, swiftly reducing the barracks to rubble and flame. He picked up his second LAWS, which he had taken from a man in the mortar team, and shifted his position so the tube was in line with his next target. He squeezed the rubber tit as tenderly as if it had belonged to a lover.

There was a dull *crump*, immediately followed by a great gout of flame and a series of subsidiary explosions. Sanderson's second rocket had sunk deep into the huge stockpile of forty-gallon drums which were neatly stacked within their own wire-fenced compound.

The force of the explosion was so immense that it knocked flat the two steel hangars adjacent to the compound with the ease and speed of a finger destroying a house of cards. But the most spectacular effect of the destruction of the fuel dump was the enormous crimson ball which rose over the site like a gross hot-air balloon.

Over on the far side of the aerodrome, Sanderson could hear the sound of automatic gunfire. For a moment it disturbed him, but then he realized what it was: the frightened sentries were blazing away at random into an area of bush where none of the mercenaries was concealed.

'Sanderson!' Tippett's voice came eerily from the radio set strapped to Sanderson's wrist. 'Relief column's on its way. Take out final target and withdraw.'

Sanderson sighted his third LAWS on the upper storey of the control tower. His main purpose was to destroy the huge radio antennae above it, crippling the defenders' attempts to call for help from further afield than Henrique de Carvalho. Manuel pumped another rocket into the base of the tower for good measure. The entire erection crumpled to the ground.

This was the signal for the attackers to withdraw. The two mortar teams let fly their final rounds. Each of the mortars was then booby-trapped by placing grenades with their pins withdrawn beneath the base plates. If the Angolans tried to move them later, there wouldn't be much left — of the mortars or of the Angolans.

The men regrouped around Sanderson and set off for their rendezvous with Tippett. They had much less to carry now, and their pace was correspondingly faster. They had not gone much further than a kilometre when Manuel put his hand on Sanderson's sleeve.

'You hear?' he said cheerfully. '*Bom, bom!*'

Despite his fatigue Sanderson's grimy face split into a smile. They had both heard a dull, thud-like explosion: the Claymore mines had been sprung.

For Tippett the wait had become intolerable. His mind ran wild with pessimistic speculations. Suppose their calculations had been wrong? Suppose there was another significant Angolan force in the area, nearer to the airfield than the one in Henrique de Carvalho? Suppose . . .

His gloom lightened when Sanderson's attack on the airfield opened. There were a good three kilometres between them, but Tippett could just distinguish the explosions which signalled the destruction of the helicopters. But he was totally unprepared for both the noise and the visual spectacle when the fuel dump went up. The size and splendour of the fireball amazed him; he and his companions ducked as the thunder of the massive explosion rolled over them, instinctively feeling they were under attack.

Tippett was a connoisseur of explosions — in civilian life

he had been a cracksman at the top of his profession — and for an instant he felt distinctly envious of Sanderson.

When Davies radioed the message that the relief convoy was on its way from the town, the tension deepened. Their enforced idleness made it worse. Tippett's group pressed themselves further into the ground, their fingers curling round triggers. They were down to minutes now.

Curiously enough, Tippett was so intent in watching the colourful sideshow in the sky above the airfield that he nearly missed the arrival of the column. The rim of the saucer masked the rumble of its engines.

Suddenly a jeep cleared the rim and accelerated down into the depression. There was a young officer sitting beside the driver, his pistol already drawn. Tippett wondered if he knew how futile his weapon was. The mercenary watched with baited breath as the line of vehicles poured after the jeep over the crest of the hill. The Angolans were putting speed above caution, and their vehicles were tightly bunched together.

Down to seconds . . . Tippett thought, his eyes riveted on the dead branch he had placed by the side of the road, shortly before it began to climb up the far slope of the depression. The lead jeep hurtled past the branch, its driver gearing down to manage the incline ahead.

Tippett jammed down the tee-shaped bar on the hand generator. A surge of high voltage current ripped along the multi-coloured flex towards the detonators. Tippett threw himself flat, covering his ears with his hands.

The enormous explosion was cupped by the circular valley and temporarily deafened the attacking party — even Tippett, despite his precautions. The detonation immediately threw tons of dust and earth into the air, masking the column at a stroke. Tippett jumped to his feet, searching through the fine, rust-red mist for a glimpse of the vehicles below.

The billowing clouds thinned suddenly on the side closest to the air-field. The lead jeep dramatically materialized before Tippett's eyes. Its engine was revving high. To his horror it seemed unscathed. A thin blade of panic twisted its way into the mercenary: he must have set the Claymores incorrectly and missed their target. He threw his Kalashnikov up to his shoulder.

The jeep swerved abruptly to one side, tossing out its driver and passenger. They lay motionless, their limbs grotesquely splayed and sticky with blood. The machine-gunner, who had been struggling to maintain his foothold on the back ever since the column left the barracks, had long since vanished.

Tippett slowly lowered his rifle. Maybe the Claymores hadn't missed. He peered through the swirling fog which still blanketed the rest of the column. His main concern was the two armoured cars which had been close on the heels of the lead jeep. His stomach turned to water at the thought that they might be as undamaged as the jeep, lurking behind the mist until their attackers showed themselves.

'Launch the LAWS!' Tippett shouted. To his deafened ears the words sounded distorted, as if spoken through a long metallic tube. But his men were equally deafened: only the soldier nearest to the commander actually heard the order and fired his rocket.

The projectile sunk deep into the red cloud, causing great mushrooms of dust to billow out of it. The rest of the men followed their companion's example. The rockets punched into the fog like hailstones on water. There were *cracks* and *snaps* as ammunition exploded; thick, sooty smoke mingled with the red dust as diesel and rubber burned.

Then there was silence, broken only by the crackle of the flames and the explosion of the occasional round. Tippett stood up and waved his men to advance. His mind raced as he calculated the angles: if they were alive, the enemy would have tried to break out from that living hell down there; or they would have opened fire at random; surely they must be dead?

But fear still gnawed at him as he thought of those solid armoured fighting vehicles. If they had missed the main force of the blasts, anything might happen.

112

When the line of attackers reached the eddying boundary of the pall of fog, each man came to a halt without waiting for orders. Tippett loosed off an entire clip of ammunition from his Kalashnikov, firing blindly into the red fog. Everyone else did the same. They retreated back to their positions of concealment and waited to see the effects of their handiwork.

The mist gradually thinned. Bizarre outlines slowly emerged on the floor of the little valley. Every shape was covered with a mantle of red dust which somehow masked the ugly realities beneath. Here and there they could see a twitching limb or a figure on hands and knees, crawling blindly.

The colour returned to Tippett's face when he saw the armoured cars. Their drivers and commanders had been watching the road ahead, with their hatch covers wide open. All four men had been instantly decapitated. The lead vehicle had gone over on its side. The second armoured car had ploughed straight into the underbelly of the first before it too flipped over on its side.

The rest of the convoy had consisted of five trucks and two more jeeps. Now there was little to see besides a scrambled mass of wheels, some still turning, the blackened and distorted shells of the vehicles and a litter of smaller fragments around them.

A force of nearly two hundred men had been utterly destroyed in a few seconds.

The mercenaries prowled cautiously through the wreckage, despatching the wounded with terminal cracks of their Kalashnikovs. In places fires were still raging, and the choking black smoke made them cough. Tippett was almost grateful for the dust and his deafness: the dust soaked up the blood like blotting paper and gave a welcome unreality to the burned bodies and tangled limbs, while the deafness made it harder to hear the cries of the mortally wounded.

It also emphasized the silence which followed the ambush, making it more oppressive. Tippett, aware that the adrenalin-filled minutes of combat could be succeeded by an emotional slump, bullied his men away with a mixture of shouts and gestures.

The twenty men wearily pulled themselves together while Tippett called up Sanderson on the walkie-talkie.

Sanderson sounded cheerful. 'No problems this end. See you at the rendezvous. Our ETA is about half an hour.'

No bloody problems, Tippett thought sourly. *Yet*.

For two hours after the mercenaries had gone, there was no sign of human life at the scene of the ambush. The wreckage smouldered. Insect scavengers arrived to survey the feast which was waiting for them.

Suddenly the birds of prey which had been wheeling overhead made off in alarm. A bedraggled but recognizably human figure emerged from the bush near the lead jeep.

It was the young officer. His combat uniform was in tatters, and smeared with dust and coagulating blood. He staggered unsteadily on to the road and collapsed against the remains of his jeep.

'Miguel!' he called; his voice came out as a hoarse whisper. 'Help me. I cannot see. Give me water, for the love of God.'

His hand shook as he raised it to touch the bloody mess which had once been a smoothly-handsome olive-skinned face.

'Miguel,' he moaned. 'For the love of God.' He took a pace forward and stumbled over something which felt soft, slippery and yielding.

He had found his driver Miguel.

16

'If you dip your arm into the pickle pot, let it be up to
   the elbow.'

Malay proverb

Davies had one inestimable advantage before he started his
end of the operation: he felt he knew the sprawling shanty
town of Henrique de Carvalho backwards before he had
ever set eyes on it. There were two reasons for this: Dorian's
research department had got hold of the latest plan of the
town, together with detailed information about it; and
Kikuji had grown up there — and still made secret visits to
it occasionally.

Kikuji led Davies and the other nine men of the detail by
devious routes through the outskirts of the town. Their task
was made easier by the fact that the bush was relatively thick
even close to the single main street.

They reached their immediate destination in safety. It
was an unoccupied and near derelict hut which had once
belonged to Kikuji's mother. It faced a strip of parched
wasteland, twenty yards broad; a few scraggy chickens
pecked forlornly at the dirt. On the other side of the wasteland was the large, foursquare building which housed the
mining offices.

The offices were built of brick, a rare sight in Henrique de
Carvalho. Only the bank and the barracks further along the
main street shared this distinction. There were heavy steel
bars at all the windows. Davies could see no sign of an
entrance at the rear. He questioned Kikuji about it.

115

The big negro shook his head, though the smile never left his face. '*Uno* door.' He waved a finger for emphasis. '*Uno*. We go in front way.'

Davies brooded for a while over the problem. They could easily smash their way through the back with the LAWS rockets but that would bring the remainder of the garrison and the townsfolk round about their heads. It was vital to the success of the operation that no attention was drawn to his small party until they had left.

The *commandante* nudged him, still grinning. 'We go in, out,' he said with relish. 'Bang, bang!'

'Sure, Kikuji.' Davies' tone was dry. He turned away and investigated the shack they were in. He found a small, glassless window at one end. 'O'Ryan,' he called, 'come here.'

The burly Irishman lumbered over. The bruises which Sanderson had given him glowed lividly on his face.

'I want you to stand here,' Davies said curtly. 'Keep your eyes on the gap between the mining offices and the shop next to it. I want to know the moment there's any military traffic going down that road.'

The radio around his waist crackled into life: Tippett and Sanderson were ready.

The minutes ticked slowly by. At last Davies' ears caught the sounds they had been straining to catch: the thump of distant explosions at the airfield. Immediately the small group extinguished its cigarettes and stopped its whispered conversations.

'The relief column's on the road.' O'Ryan's voice was hoarse with tension. Davies was instantly beside him at the window, just in time to see the last lorry-load of troops and the officer's jeep screeching along the dusty street.

'Okay. Let's go.' Davies led his men out of the hut. They sprinted across the wasteland, sending the chickens scattering in all directions. Following their instructions, six men peeled off from the rest of the party. Three ran to the right, and three to the left. They took up positions at the two corners of the mining offices' frontage, covering the road.

116

Davies, Kikuji, O'Ryan and two blacks ran on to the front door. The mercenary leader noted with relief that no one had seen them — the explosions at the airport had diverted the attention of civilians, as well as that of the military. He glanced across the road at the only building which looked directly on to the office door. It was some sort of bar, he reckoned. It looked empty — probably the occupants had gone to see the fun.

He rapped on the steel-ribbed wooden door. Seconds later it was opened by a pretty black girl. Her welcoming smile congealed on her face as she saw the five armed men in combat gear. Before she had time to scream, the party was in the building.

O'Ryan, obeying previous orders, stayed in the alleyway. He shifted his LAWS; his eyes roamed nervously around the deserted street.

The rest of the mercenaries pushed into the large sorting-hall immediately beyond. In front of them was a series of baize-topped tables, on which lay small piles of uncut diamonds. The sorters and graders who sat behind the tables were all women, most of them as young as the one who had opened the door.

Davies and Kikuji gave them no time to think, let alone resist. The two men herded the sorters into a small back-room, whose barred window looked out over the wasteland they had crossed a few seconds earlier. Meanwhile the other two soldiers ran for the stairs. The administrative offices were all on the first floor.

Kikuji pointed out a square slab of steel set in the wall of the backroom. His smile was even broader. Davies nodded: it must be the vault door.

The two black soldiers clattered downstairs, holding four middle-aged black men at gun-point. All wore dark suits; their hands were clamped on top of their heads and the whites of their eyes were showing.

The oldest and fattest of the four stumbled forward. He fell to his knees, imploring Davies for mercy in a gabble of Portuguese. Davies was carrying a Browning High Power

117

9mm in his hand; he thrust the muzzle into the office manager's mouth and gestured eloquently towards the door of the vault.

The manager nodded violently, jarring his teeth against the pistol. He stood over the combination-lock in the centre of the vault door, peering short-sightedly through his glasses and manipulating the lock with trembling hands.

The heavy door swung inwards, revealing a steel-lined cell beyond. The manager, without waiting to be asked, stumbled into the vault and unlocked the three safes it contained.

Davies resisted the temptation to laugh. *Jesus!* he thought, *this man wants to live!*

Two of the safes contained hundreds, if not thousands, of small white envelopes, each containing a parcel of sorted and graded stones. When Davies saw the contents of the third he gave a silent whistle. They had been given an immense bonus.

The safe held more currency than he had ever seen in his life. He riffled through several bundles, his eyes widening. They were all large denomination notes — green hundred dollar bills, blue Deutschmarks, brown French francs, fifty pound notes and several others.

The four soldiers took it in turns to guard the staff in the backroom while the others stuffed diamonds and currency into their Bergen rucksacks and pockets.

Davies was just coming out of the vault when the youngest of the four administrators leapt at the smaller of the two FNLA troopers.

The trooper staggered back, with the administrator trying to wrest the Kalashnikov from his grasp. The soldier counter-lunged and pressed the trigger. The bullet caught the administrator in the groin, flipping him backwards among the screaming girls. The soldier pumped another round into his head. The administrator slumped to the floor.

A couple of minutes later, it was time to go. The four marauders shepherded the petrified office workers past the corpse of their companion. Davies slammed the door behind them. He was in the process of hefting his bulging Bergen on to his back when there was a shattering explosion from the front of the building.

Davies led the run to the front door. The scene outside told its own tale: the charred ruins of the bar, the discarded LAWS tube on the ground and the pleased look on O'Ryan's face.

'I hope that was fucking necessary,' he snarled as he ran past the Irishman. All five of them dashed from the building. The other six men joined them and the whole party left town at a trot.

They attracted no fire. They passed only one bemused pedestrian who was too surprised to be afraid.

They paused for breath when they were three hundred yards into the bush, completely sheltered by the dense vegetation. Davies and Kikuji shrugged off their rucksacks and gave them to two unencumbered soldiers. After a swift survey of the terrain, they set two simple grenade traps which would be sprung when someone stumbled against their tripwires. The traps might not be up to Tippett's exacting standards, but Davies was nevertheless pleased. There would soon be pursuers in plenty, and there was no sense in making their job too easy for them.

Kikuji took the lead when they moved off again, heading for their rendezvous with Tippett and the rest of the party.

Davies fell in beside O'Ryan. 'What the hell was that rocket all about? You realize it must have alerted the garrison and speeded up their pursuit, maybe by hours?'

The smug expression faded from O'Ryan's face. 'There was someone walking down that bar towards the door, and I think he had a weapon.' The Irishman's brogue became more pronounced as he strove to justify himself. 'And there was at least a couple of others kneeling at the windows and watching us.'

Davies moved away from O'Ryan. 'I just hope you haven't buggered up the whole operation,' he said over his shoulder. 'For your sake.'

17

"'Will you walk a little faster?' said a whiting to a
snail. "There's a porpoise close behind us, and
he's treading on my tail . . .'"

Lewis Carroll

Kikuji's bush-trained ears caught the sounds before anyone
else's. He stopped abruptly and slid sideways behind a
gnarled thorn tree. The rest of the party picked up on his
lead with the speed of well-trained men. They slipped
immediately behind cover, using the stunted bushes, trees
and boulders which littered the terrain they were passing
through.

Davies was in the centre of the line. He chose a low bush
with grey-brown spikes. One of them ran into the back of his
hand as he crouched down. He cursed silently and sucked
the scratch automatically. His full attention was trained on
the silence around them.

A stick snapped, perhaps fifty yards ahead. Davies eased
the safety catch of his rifle on to the fire position. A constant
background of rustling developed, rapidly growing louder.
A body of men was moving quickly through the bush, aim-
ing to strike the very path which they had just left.

Another stick snapped. *Someone's being careless.* But Davies
didn't think it was the pursuit — the Angolans would have
almost certainly been noisier.

'It's Tippett, I think,' he whispered to the man closest to
him. 'Don't fire unless I do — pass it on.'

Nevertheless, the mercenary didn't move: he lay waiting

with the Kalashnikov ready for instant use. It was unwise to rely on almost-certainties in the bush. If you did, there was a nasty tendency for you to end up dead.

Tippett's lean figure came into view on the path. The tension seeped away from Davies. He scrambled to his feet. Suddenly he realized that his friend's face and combat jacket were saturated with blood. The men behind him were the same. Christ, that was the last thing they needed — it looked as if the larger part of his force had been badly mauled in a fire-fight. Quite apart from the loss of those killed, they would have to cope with the wounded.

But as he got closer, he saw there was a broad grin on Tippett's face.

'It's the fucking dust, mate.' Tippett laughed. 'It's in *everything*.'

Now Davies was closer, he could see that the long crimson stains were not blood but that omnipresent red dust, mingled with sweat. 'For one horrible moment I thought you'd all copped a packet.' As he spoke, Davies scanned the line of men coming up. There seemed to be no one missing.

'It's the other bastards who copped a packet.' Tippett pulled a half-crushed packet of cigarettes from his breast pocket and offered one to Davies. 'I don't think we'll be seeing too much of them in a hurry.' Davies passed him a canteen. Tippett drank thirstily before continuing. 'Sanderson reckons he had a ball at the airport — got the antennae and the choppers, he says —'

'Thank God he did,' Davies interrupted. 'We'd have had no chance with a couple of fucking gunships up our arses.'

'Did you see the fuel dump go up?' Tippett asked. 'Jesus Christ! They must have heard it in Luanda.'

Tippett flopped on to the ground. Davies took control of the whole force, issuing a stream of orders. He set a guard back on the path, and told two of Tippett's trainees to manufacture a booby-trap for any pursuers who were coming too quickly for their own good. He found time to congratulate Sanderson. The young ex-Para flushed with pleasure, confident that the unfortunate episode with O'Ryan had been forgiven if not forgotten.

The rest of the men settled down for a breather. Tippett's party took the opportunity to clean their dust-covered weapons. Davies noticed with satisfaction that no one had to tell them to do it.

Tippett looked up as Davies returned to where he sprawled on the ground. 'How did *you* get on?' A sardonic grin flashed briefly across his filthy face. 'Are we stone-rich or have we just had a good time?'

Davies face remained impassive but he gave a small nod in the direction of the four well-stuffed Bergen rucksacks. Tippett crawled over to the nearest and unfastened its straps. He gave a low, appreciative whistle as he saw the wads of currency crammed on top. He dug his hand through the top layer and came out with half a dozen enormous uncut stones in his hand.

'They feel really cold,' he said as if to himself . He looked up at Davies. 'Almost like ice, aren't they? But very nice ice.'

He chuckled quietly as he refastened the top of the khaki bag.

Davies lit another cigarette and squinted through the smoke. 'It's as useless as real ice,' he said, 'unless we can keep it — and stay alive long enough to spend it.' His voice hardened as he switched to practicalities. 'You got any explosive gear left, mate?'

Tippett's smile faded, leaving his face sombre. 'Two more Claymores and some grenades. A few odds and sods — tripwires, dets and that sort of stuff.'

'We'll be needing them a little later on, in case they find this trap.' Davies glanced at his watch. 'Another ten minutes and then we gap it, mate.'

Tippett nodded and began to clean his rifle.

Kikuji and Davies took point when the party set off on the next stage of its journey. Each of the forty-odd men knew that his survival depended on his own legs and his individual ability to keep going. There was no room for passengers in this force. Davies had made it clear to everyone that those who couldn't keep up with the main force — for whatever reason — would have to be left behind.

The trail they blazed was due east, the direction which led straight to the nearest border with Zaire. Davies intended to leave behind the impression that the mercenaries were fleeing to the sanctuary of the neighbouring country by the shortest possible route.

They marched quickly through a tough, inhospitable terrain. In every direction stretched a seemingly-endless sea of ten-foot-high elephant grass. This undulating expanse was scattered with thorny thickets of low, dense bushes. Shallow gulleys meandered across the ground; since it was the rainy season these had filled with water.

The red soil was as heavy and clay-like as the soil of the East Anglian Fens. The earth stuck to the men's boots, building up layer by layer until walking became impossible. At some point everyone had to pull out of line to scrape off the clay.

They pushed through the high, sharp grass for three gruelling hours. The relentless heat of the mid-afternoon sun gradually took its effect: the pace of the march flagged and grumbling increased. Davies called a ten minute break. When they resumed, Tippett and Sanderson relieved Davies and Kikuji a point.

Nearly an hour later Tippett sent back word to Davies that he had found a suitable site for the Claymore mines. Davies and the rest of the party pressed on, leaving the lanky explosives expert to do his job.

The place, Tippett considered, was as near ideal as he was likely to find. On the left hand side of the path they had blazed was a spur of rocky ground. Tippett scrambled on to it, taking care that he left no footprints on the muddy path which could betray the manoeuvre.

He walked backwards, in the direction they had come from, keeping to a course which was parallel to the path. The rocky spine lay beneath him like the half-buried skeleton of a gigantic prehistoric beast. The hard ground retained no trace of his passage.

After a hundred metres the rocks began to peter out. Tippett cautiously worked his way down to the trail. He laid the Claymore mines in a way that maximized their arc of fire. The path was narrow, so penetration in depth would not be so important. He concealed the tripwire to trigger the detonator with a fallen branch which the mercenaries had torn down as they blazed their way through the bush.

Previous experience enabled him to assess the likely sequence of events with a fair chance of accuracy. In all probability, the pursuit column would be led by one or two expert trackers. Such men were cautious by their very nature: they would step over small obstacles with care. The main body behind them, on the other hand, would feel that the path must be safe since the trackers had already passed along it; consequently the bulk of the column would exercise less care than the trackers in advance of them.

Furthermore, the spot which Tippett had chosen was calculated to make the pursuers overconfident. At this point the trail cut through the tall grass in a straight line — several hundred yards of it were visible in both directions. The ground on either side was too exposed for an ambush to be hidden. If he were the commander of the Angolan column, Tippett reckoned, he would push ahead as fast as possible along this section of the path, without worrying over much about the risk of a counter-attack.

Tippett carefully retraced his steps along the spine of rock and rejoined the path where he had originally left it. He set out at a jog-trot after the rest of the mercenaries, keeping a wary eye out for any sign of pursuit, either behind him or in the air.

Nightmarish possibilities seethed in the back of his mind. He tried not to think what would happen if he slipped and broke his ankle, or if the Angolans got hold of a helicopter, or if the rest of his own force were making better speed than he was.

It was with immense relief that Tippett came up with the two white mercenaries who formed the rearguard, some fifty minutes later.

Half an hour before sunset the file of men came up against their first major obstacle, the river Chiumbe. It was cooler now, and Davies was anxious to cover as much ground as possible before the light went. But when he saw the muddy, fast-flowing waters of the river he stopped in his tracks. For once he was speechless.

The Chiumbe was one of the tributaries of the mighty Congo river. Roberto, who had passed through this part of Angola several times, had described the river as a minor one; his exact words had been, 'You'll find it easily fordable.' The maps supplied by Dorian seemed to support this contention.

But the planners had overlooked one vital point: they were now in the middle of the rainy season. The Chiumbe was no longer a placid, overgrown stream: it had been transformed into a torrent of water eighty yards wide. Its waters were reddish-brown and boiled turbulently with the force of the current which drove them relentlessly down to the Congo. Full-grown trees had been torn from the banks by the angry, swollen waters which tossed and turned them like shirts in a washing-machine.

Tippett, a frown creasing his lean face, came up to join Davies. They stood silently on the bank for a moment, staring at the broad and treacherous river. It seemed to Davies that nature was ganging up against them, never mind the Angolans. Soon it would be dark — and the night would trap them on the wrong side of the river, leaving them to the tender mercies of the pursuit column at first light. To cap it all, Davies could hear an angry murmur swelling among the rank-and-file of the white mercenaries and their FNLA comrades.

'Bloody hell,' Davies snarled to Tippett. '"Easily fordable", Roberto said. And Dorian said it would be as easy to cross as the Serpentine. The bastards didn't mention we'd need an inflatable boat.'

18

'The best laid schemes of mice and men . . .'
Robbie Burns

'Snap out of it. This ain't a bloody picnic party.' Davies'
voice cut sharply into the whispers of dissension among the
men. Kikuji, Davies and Tippett stood shoulder to shoulder
on the river bank; Sanderson and Manuel drifted over to
join them, both looking rather foolish.

The mini-mutiny had been quelled before it had started.
Davies' eyes roved among his men, quickly identifying
potential ringleaders. 'O'Ryan,' he snapped, 'drop back on
to the trail as a rearguard. Agostinho, get upstream, and I
want Smith downstream to watch our flanks. *Move!*'

Once the barrackroom-lawyers had been isolated from
the rest of the force, Davies told the remainder to rest. The
three leaders held a conference by the river.

'The original plan,' Davies said quietly, 'was to get across
the Chiumbe so the Angolans thought we were heading due
east for the border. As you know, once over the river we
were going to slip north in a long arc back to the main road
where the lorries are waiting — and leave the pursuit to
chase their own shadows up to the eastern border. That's
what we arranged with Roberto and Dorian.'

'Well, there's no way we can do that now, mate,' said
Tippett angrily. 'Those two have buggered us up properly.'

Davies interrupted: 'Which they planned to do later in
any case.'

As he spoke, he watched Kikuji. The big Nubian could

understand English far better than he could speak it. His habitual smile faded. 'Please, *commandantes*,' he said to the two white men. 'What is this?'

Davies had already told Tippett about the fragments of conversation he had overheard in the house at Hampstead after stealing the courier's diamonds for Dorian and Roberto. He now took a gamble and decided to tell Kikuji as well. The mercenary was banking on two things: he liked and trusted the Nubian and felt confident that the feeling was reciprocated; and he had a shrewd suspicion that Kikuji's motive for joining the FNLA had more to do with a hatred of the communists and a love of fighting than with any respect for Holden Roberto, either as a man or as a politician.

'Once we get back to Zaire,' the mercenary explained, 'your boss and Dorian are going to have us all liquidated — so they get a bigger cut of the proceeds, and so there aren't any inconvenient witnesses.'

It took a while for the African to grasp what the mercenary was saying. His face was furrowed with worry and anger.

'*Commandantes*,' he said at last, 'ees *importante* you understand me and my *soldados* . . . together with English *soldados* — *camarades*.' He clasped his hands together to emphasize his point. 'I think . . . you are all good men. But Roberto — he is *non bom*.' He unclasped his hands and chopped with his right at the open palm of his left. Both the white men had the vivid impression that Kikuji was mentally breaking Roberto's neck.

Davies and Tippett glanced at each other, not bothering to conceal their relief. With Kikuji and the rest of the black contingent behind them, they could at least act as a united force — both now, in their present predicament, and later, when — and if — they got back to Zaire.

'Tippett and me were going to turn the feint escape into the real thing,' Davies told Kikuji. 'After this river we were going to continue east and go hell for leather for the Zairois border. We'd have to cross one more river, the Luembe,

127

but after that we wouldn't have much more than twenty kilometres to go.'

'But the communists — ' Kikuji began.

Tippett gestured towards his remaining store of explosives. 'A few booby-traps along the way would have delayed the pursuit column — maybe even stopped it. That's why it was so important to get the copters — they could have leap-frogged ahead of us to the border.'

Davies answered another of Kukuji's unspoken questions: 'If we could reach southern Zaire, we'd be laughing. We'd sidestep any reception Roberto and Dorian have arranged in Tshikapa. And there are plenty of airfields in the south. With the amount of loose cash we've got, there'd be no problem in getting a flight elsewhere. Whatever happened we'd be in a very strong bargaining position.'

'We would have been,' said Tippett bitterly. 'Talk about being between the devil and the deep blue sea.'

'Maybe we have *uno* chance,' Kikuji said hesitantly. 'There is a village about ten kilometres north . . .' He explained in a halting blend of English and Portuguese that his aunt's cousin lived there. The river was narrower and deeper at that point. When Kikuji was last there, he had heard talk of plans to build a bridge.

Davies shrugged. 'What it boils down to is that we can't go on, we can't stay here and we can't go back. So we have to go north or south. And if we go north, there's a chance we might find a bridge still standing.'

'Always supposing they built the bloody thing in the first place,' Tippett added drily.

The three leaders got their weary men together and bullied them into motion. The chain of soldiers kept close to the line of the river. Thick vegetation and the gathering dusk made their going difficult; sometimes Davies wondered if it was only the fear of pursuit which kept them going. He himself would have willingly traded a rucksackful of diamonds to be back in his living-room at Camberley. Or even two or three rucksackfuls. Wealth lost its significance when you couldn't use it.

Everyone was relieved when they ran into a muddy but well-used path along the riverbank. It made the going easier — and it suggested that they couldn't be too far away from the village and the bridge.

The column stopped to rest while Kikuji and Manuel went ahead as scouts. They returned with good news: a small bridge had been built; it was unguarded and still standing; and it was out of sight of the village itself.

The whole party pushed forward up the path. By now it was practically dark. Each man could hardly distinguish the shape of the man ahead of him.

But Davies' sudden optimism vanished equally suddenly when he actually saw the bridge. At the best of times it must have been a flimsy structure. He examined it as well as he could in the darkness.

The bridge crossed the river on the precarious support of piers made of trees. The narrow walkway consisted of planks which had been lashed together. A rudimentary ropeguard stretched above the planking. Davies suspected that the support it would give must be more psychological than real.

But the most disturbing feature was the river itself. It seemed far faster and more turbulent than it had upstream, perhaps because the channel here was narrower. The level had risen so high that the piers were now submerged, except when some particularly violent eddy revealed a brief glimpse. In places the water was crashing over the walkway itself, slapping and sucking mercilessly at the wooden structure.

'We'd better hurry,' said Tippett. 'It doesn't look as if it's going to be standing for much longer.'

'Too right, mate,' Davies came quickly to a decision: 'I want you and the Bergens to go over first. Kikuji and me had better stay on this bank in case of trouble.'

With Tippett in the lead, the line of men began to snake across the bridge. The going was slow. It was too dark to see much, and one false step could send any of them slithering into the boiling waters below.

The middle section was the biggest problem. It was slung lower than the rest of the bridge, and the water was already crashing and frothing over it. Davies ordered them to negotiate it one man at a time. Tippett and the lads carrying the other three Bergens went first.

One by one the men filed over. The gathering darkness and the roar of the river intensified the suspense. The men awaiting their turn became particularly jumpy, convinced they could hear the sounds of pursuit behind them. Davies had to restrain O'Ryan from emptying his magazine into the bush at random. Beads of sweat gleamed eerily on the Irishman's face.

Davies counted the men who were left: only nine now, plus himself and Kikuji. They were going to make it. His mind ran ahead: they couldn't afford to rest now — they must press on, destroying the bridge behind them.

Night had completely fallen by now. Davies and Tippett were maintaining contact by radio. Knowing the effort was useless, Davies strained his eyes to follow the progress of the men now on the bridge.

No one saw the huge tree that came down the river out of the night. No one could have done anything, even if they had.

The malevolent force of the current smashed it against the groaning timbers of the bridge. There was a rolling crash which temporarily drowned the roar of the waters.

It hit the bridge right in the centre of the vulnerable middle section. The current flicked it effortlessly on to the half-submerged walkway itself. The tree's immense weight descended like a sledgehammer on the fragile planks, splintering through the wood and tearing apart the rope thongs.

The indefatigable current pushed it onwards, seemingly gaining in strength and fury from the obstacle. The tree plunged away from the bridge, taking with it the two sets of piers closest to the collision and most of the middle section of the walkway which they had supported.

The whole process happened so fast that Davies only

130

reconstructed the probable sequence of events much later. At the time, it all seemed to happen simultaneously.

Then and later, what he remembered most clearly was the screams.

There were two of them — high, despairing and ruthlessly truncated by the swirling waters of the muddy river Chiumbe.

19

'When they concentrate in the bush, they make easier their own annihilation.'

Candido Mondlane (Fremlino).

I've been nailed in my coffin and buried alive!

It was the first lucid thought which seared through D'asser's mind as he returned to consciousness. He was trapped in total darkness. There was something gritty in his mouth. An immense weight lay across his chest; another pinioned him across the thighs. A variety of pains — from dull aches to acute stabs — inhabited all areas of his body.

He moved his right arm tentatively, flexing each of his fingers in turn in an automatic attempt to assess the damage. The prickle of a cough rose inexorably in his throat. He tried desperately to contain it, sensing that noise could betray him. But his dust-filled lungs erupted in a series of dry, spasmodic retchings.

D'asser tried to channellize the swirls of confusion which eddied around in his head. His mind, he recognized dimly, was enveloped in the silky folds of shock: he had to force his way out and find some reference point.

Snippets of memory returned, as disjointed as a surrealist film. A million years ago, he remembered, he had knelt at a glassless window, in a cool place. There had been friends with him, but he could not focus on their faces. They must have been watching something outside — but what?

Another fragment of the past presented itself for inspection. He recalled a flash across the street and the *whoosh* as a rocket flew past him only inches away. The acrid stench of the missile's propellent was still in his nostrils.

But the rest was a blank, screened from D'asser's consciousness by the safety curtain of shock. Indeed, the pock-marked man would never remember the blinding flash of the explosion or the tearing crash as the rocket impacted against the long wooden bar. The blast also blew out the closed windows in the bar, stripped the plaster from the ceiling of the long room, and brought down the beams above. Two of those massive timbers now lay across D'asser's supine body. If their fall had not been broken by a nearby table, they would have pulped the life out of him in an instant.

He had been unconscious for over twenty minutes. It was fortunate that he failed to suppress the cough: its racking sound was heard by the score of soldiers who were combing the wreckage for survivors.

They found him at last, buried beneath a mass of wood and plaster. They carried him out into the strong midday sunshine. One of the soldiers held a canteen of water to the lips of the injured man. D'asser drank greedily.

The white-coated doctor from the barracks turned away from a huddle of wailing women and came over to D'asser. It was a quick, professional check: the small man was badly shaken; he had a lot of minor cuts and bruises — but he had miraculously missed any major injury.

D'asser's faculties came flooding back in the warm sunshine, helped by the familiar uniforms around him and the recognizable vehicles in the road. He was back in a world he recognized. He pushed aside the doctor and unsteadily got to his feet, using the wall beside him as a prop. He swilled the water around his mouth and throat and spat out an amalgam of dust and plaster.

He began to make sense of the scene around him. There was a throng of people, both military and civilians, around the ruins of the devastated *canteena*. Relief washed over him as he caught sight of Eloi. The young man was dusty and tousled, but he looked unhurt. D'asser staggered towards

133

his friend, refusing an offer of help from one of the medical orderlies. His doggedness was rewarded: the further he walked, the more his strength returned.

Eloi looked up as D'asser approached. The youth and gaiety had been drained from the younger man's face. 'Thank God you're safe,' he croaked.

But D'asser didn't hear him. His attention was riveted on his friend Rodriguez who sat slumped against the wall clutching what appeared to be a filthy bundle of rags. D'asser stared stupidly at him for a moment. Rodriguez, his face contorted beneath its mask of grime, didn't look up and made no sound.

'What's he doing?' D'asser asked Eloi; his state of shock prevented him from providing the answer himself.

Eloi put an arm around the older man's shoulders, a protective gesture which oddly reversed their usual roles. 'Hush,' he said softly, his eyes still on the stricken figure of Rodriguez.

D'asser looked blankly at the pile of rags. Blood was seeping through the dust, he realized with a sudden shock. And the small round object which glistened in the folds of the rags was surely an eye detached from its socket.

The truth hit him abruptly. D'asser, still groggy, fell forwards on to his knees, with tears starting involuntarily from his eyes.

The rags which Rodriguez held contained all that was left of young Jorge.

A few minutes later the rescue squad emerged from the bar with Maria's body. They laid her on the hard ground near the three grieving men. Her dress and half her face had been ripped away by the blast, leaving her battered body obscenely on display to prying eyes.

Eloi shuddered. He removed his shirt, tearing off the buttons in his haste, and covered the still, broken body as best he could. The explosion had shattered one of his young cousin's legs, bending it upwards. This remained in view — a cruelly vivid illustration of the effects of war, the single horseman of the Apocalypse.

It was another half an hour before Eloi managed to get his comrades away from the corpses. The young man was friendly with the officer in charge of transport at the barracks, and succeeded in borrowing a jeep. They deposited the mortal remains of Jorge in a makeshift coffin. Shortly afterwards Rodriguez set off for Mona Quimbundo with his brother lashed to the back of the vehicle.

Eloi and D'asser watched the jeep until it was out of sight. D'asser, his face and clothes still smeared with blood and dust, looked half-dead on his feet. But his mind was alive with a terrible emotion which gave him a seemingly-inexhaustible supply of energy.

For him, Jorge's death meant only one thing: D'asser was reliving what he had felt when he had found the corpses of his family during the civil war. One emotion predominated above all others: he hated the men who had destroyed what he had loved. So intense was his hatred that it pushed his shock and his injuries to the back of his mind. Hatred fuelled him with pure adrenalin.

'You know where to find the *commandante* of the town?' he asked Eloi. 'Take me to him.'

The two men made their way to the barracks which were a hive of activity. The guards were unwilling to let them in during such a crisis; but the combination of D'asser's set white face and his awesome military reputation finally won them an interview with the *coronel*.

'I want a fresh uniform and all the men you've got,' D'asser snapped, unmindful of the difference in rank between himself and the colonel, 'Plus all available logistic support. The pursuit column's got to start *now* if we want to get those bastards.'

The colonel — a portly man of Portuguese extraction, whose pot-belly was to some extent set off by the formidable row of medal ribbons on his tunic — sighed. 'I am sorry,' he said firmly. 'The defence of the town must be my priority. I can do nothing until I hear from the relief column we sent to the airfield.'

D'asser argued, even pleaded. Only his reputation

135

prevented the colonel from throwing him out of his office. Instead, the senior officer patiently and plausibly argued that he had only enough manpower left in the town to defend its perimeters; he could spare no one until the relief column returned. He even produced the nominal roll of his garrison to prove to D'asser that he simply hadn't got the troops available.

The *coronel* lit his tenth cigar of the day. 'And we may have further problems,' he said grimly. 'There have been more explosions, some nearer to the town than the airfield, and there was a cloud of dust in the sky.' He shook his head. 'No, I can take no risks at this juncture.'

D'asser tried to argue, but the old man remained obdurate. The *coronel* was becoming visibly irritated when suddenly their conversation was interrupted by more explosions. There were two of them — and they sounded much closer to the town than their predecessors.

The colonel was immediately galvanized into action. He ignored D'asser, called together his remaining officers and soon had his men deployed in a tighter defensive perimeter around the town. He believed — and even D'asser agreed it was a reasonable supposition — that the explosions signalled the beginning of a mortar attack on the town itself.

Two tense hours followed, with the Angolan regulars desperately hoping to hear from the relief column which had gone to the airfield. D'asser and Eloi spent some of the time finding fresh uniforms and arms, and commandeering a jeep. At the end of the time, D'asser won permission from the colonel to investigate the latest explosions.

He and Eloi soon returned, with the bleak expressions of men who have yet again viewed the totally unacceptable face of war.

D'asser made their report, his dry, almost academic voice giving no hint of the emotions which boiled beneath.

'The enemy left a couple of booby-traps in the bush, just outside town, sir — presumably to delay any reaction sticks of commandos we could send after them. But civilians — a mother and two young boys — sprung them. Maybe three

136

kids — it was hard to tell because such a mess had been made of them.' His voice momentarily faltered. 'They must have been making for the town in order to avoid the fighting.'

There was silence on the small, smoke-filled office. A bloated fly landed on the colonel's sleeve. He made an ineffectual attempt to crush it. His face was grey beneath his heavy tan.

'In your absence there has been no news from the relief column or the airfield. Just total radio silence.'

'May I make a suggestion, sir?' D'asser did not wait for permission to continue. 'If we could take a jeep and a couple of men, Lieutenant Eloi and I could investigate the road to the airfield. We can do nothing until we have some hard information.'

The old colonel slowly nodded. At least such a patrol would not seriously diminish his remaining garrison. The years of comparative peace had slowed his reflexes. He was almost glad that D'asser was around to make the decisions.

Minutes later, the Soviet-type jeep swung out of the barracks with a screech of protesting rubber. D'asser and Eloi were in front; there were two privates behind, one manning the heavy machine-gun on the rear of the vehicle.

Once they had left behind the security of the town, D'asser slowed their speed. His caution had been bred into him by many such patrols. Despite his sense of urgency he had no desire to rush into a trap. Dying itself didn't worry him; what did was the fact that dead men could take no revenge.

It took them thirty minutes to reach the saucer-like defile on the way to the airfield. It was still filled with dust. D'asser braked sharply as he came over the rim of the little valley. The dreadful scene of carnage confronted them like a scene from hell. The machine gunner promptly leant over the side of the jeep and vomited.

D'asser thrust the jeep into first gear and moved slowly along the side of the road, in parallel with the shattered column. Right along the line, there was nothing but dead men and broken vehicles, covered in a phantasmagorical veil of red dust.

'Look,' said Eloi, his voice straining with disbelief. 'There's someone moving up there.'

D'asser accelerated to the head of the column and pulled to a halt beside a bedraggled figure who was staggering uncertainly around the remains of the lead jeep. Beneath the blood and dirt could be distinguished the outlines of an army uniform. The left-hand side of the face was an unrecognizable mass of raw flesh, like something from a butcher's slab. The man turned. Eloi gasped as the other side of the survivor's face came into view. It was the young officer who had warned him to keep off the streets in Henrique de Carvalho.

'Miguel? Miguel?' The officer tottered, his hands outstretched as he tried to touch the newly-arrived jeep. His voice was high and cracked; he had crossed far beyond the boundaries of sanity. 'Miguel,' he wailed, 'I am blind. Give me water, for the love of God.'

They took the captain on with them to the airfield. He was the sole survivor of some two hundred men, as a quick check along the line of the convoy had established. Eloi wondered if survivor was the right word: in the captain's position, he would have welcomed death itself with open arms.

The airfield itself was a desolation of smoking ruins. The jeep came under intense but completely inaccurate small-arms fire from the thoroughly demoralized defenders. D'asser and Eloi held a five minute shouting-match with the soldiers within, before the latter were convinced that the newcomers did not intend to destroy them.

The jeep returned to Henrique de Carvalho through the gathering dusk, with the blinded captain gibbering in the back. The *coronel* received their appalling news with an impassive face: he was too experienced not to have feared that a disaster like this might have happened.

D'asser asked him what he planned to do now. The senior officer shrugged his heavy shoulders.

'We shall have to wait for first light. We have no option. Thank God the radio here is powerful enough to reach Luanda — otherwise we would have been totally cut off from reinforcements. The enemy were damnably efficient. We don't even know who they were.'

'Those FNLA bastards are up to their old tricks — they were led and trained by white mercenaries.' D'asser's lips tightened. 'I'll crucify the lot of them when I catch them.'

The colonel sent an orderly to despatch trucks to bring in the dead and the wounded. When they were alone again he turned to D'asser.

'You realize the attack on the airfield and the ambush were just feints designed to leave the town defenceless? The enemy's real target was the mining offices. And they were clever about it: they lifted a fortune in diamonds and currency and locked the staff in the empty vault. I had to get the under-manager out of hospital to unlock the door. I'll say one thing for them, they only killed one man.'

'You forget the bar,' D'asser said in a voice like a hacksaw. 'They also killed a teenage boy and a girl.'

All through the night the staff at the mining offices worked on the stock figures, trying to assess the value of what had been stolen. Via the barracks they were in constant contact with the authorities in Luanda. Their estimates rose steadily in value as the long night crawled slowly towards dawn. De Bloom's in South Africa were also informed, since the loss would affect them as much as Angola itself.

A flurry of radio messages, some hysterical in tone, returned from Luanda. The colonel laboured under a double shock — the loss of most of his men and the loss of the assets entrusted, in effect, to his care. Age and fatigue also took their toll.

Shortly before first light the colonel sent for D'asser. When the small man reached the operation room, he was shocked by the change he found in the colonel: the man seemed to have aged twenty years and lost two stones in a matter of hours. But D'asser wasted no sympathy on him — he needed all his emotional capital to feed his hatred.

The colonel looked for a long moment at the slim man before him, his lids drooping over his bloodshot eyes.

'You get your chance, young man,' he said at last. He tapped the transcript of a radio message which lay before him on the desk. 'I've been ordered to despatch a hot-pursuit commando, with you in command; you can take Lieutenant Eloi as well. Reinforcements are already on their way, both by road and by air. A couple of Hind gunships are being sent from Benguela — they should arrive by mid-afternoon.'

The colonel's clipped military voice faltered. In an undertone he added: 'I hope you make those bastards wish they had never been born.'

Two patrols left the township just as fingers of light were beginning to poke into the east of the night sky. D'asser had decided to divide his force into two, at least for the time being, maintaining radio contact between them.

Eloi led one patrol along the road to the airport, hoping to pick up the spoor of the men who had attacked it and of those who had set up the ambush.

D'asser's patrol had less far to go: they concentrated on finding traces of the enemy around the clearing in the bush where the mother and children had been blown up yesterday.

Neither of them was in town when a small two-man helicoptor landed at the barracks a couple of hours later. Rodriguez was the passenger; the pilot was a friend of his from Mona Quimbundo. While the pilot refuelled the helicopter, Rodriguez persuaded the colonel to allow him to join his comrades in the pursuit.

Antonio Rodriguez was gaunt and unshaven. He had had no sleep. Two images lived in his mind and kept him awake: his brother's body, cradled in his own arms; and the expression on their grandfather's face when the old man had seen the remains of his younger grandson.

The slim Latin was given a Kalashnikov from the

armoury. He returned to the helicopter and strapped himself into the diminutive perspex bubble of its cockpit. He elected to join up with D'asser rather than Eloi, since the former was nearer.

It wasn't difficult to pick up the starting-point of the trail which D'asser was following. In the middle of the bush there was a jagged black smear, vivid against the green undergrowth, where the tripwires and grenades had done their deadly work.

But in the interim there had been a rain shower, which made the following of D'asser's route a harder business than Rodriguez had anticipated. He picked it up in the end and soared along their line of march in the air, a few metres above the level of the bush. They passed over a small hill where a second trail joined the first. Rodriguez correctly guessed that Eloi's party had joined D'asser's.

Shortly afterwards, Rodriguez overflew an area of grass which had been methodically trampled. He recognized the pattern of the bootprints: D'asser was using the techniques they had developed in the civil war to check an area for booby-traps. It made sense, Rodriguez conceded: the enemy had already shown that they had a talent for that kind of trick; their explosives expert must be first class.

The chopper flew on for another kilometre. The trail was progressively easier to follow. The pilot gave a thumbs-up sign as he spotted the tailend of the fast-moving patrol snaking through the bush ahead.

The men on the ground halted as the helicopter flew over them, staring up at the machine. Some of them waved. The pilot took them over the whole column, looking for a level site where he could safely land. He noticed a strip of rock poking up through the soil a few hundred metres ahead. It ran parallel with the trail and was bare of vegetation. In the centre of the rocks was a small flat area, an almost-perfect oval in shape, where a couple of helicopters could have landed in safety.

The pilot eased down the blue and silver machine. Rodriguez jumped out as soon as the chopper touched the ground. He ran half-crouching down to the trail, with the wash of the still-turning rotors churning up the air around him.

Eloi and D'asser were soon conferring with their old comrade. They waved on the rest of the patrol and quickly exchanged their news.

'Has the colonel got a revised ETA for the two gunships?' D'asser demanded. 'It's vital that we get them as soon as possible.'

Rodriguez shook his head. 'No, they're still due at — '

Tippett's Claymores exploded.

The concussive blast of the huge explosion flipped the three officers on to the ground. Behind them, the helicopter's blades were still spinning rapidly — and acting like an aerofoil. The blast lobbed the chopper twenty metres into the air.

The pilot's reflexes fought to regain control of the machine. He twisted the throttle wide open in an effort to keep it airborne. But it was too late: he ran out of time in an instant. The rotors gathered speed too slowly.

The helicopter plummeted tail-first to the ground. The elegant blue and silver machine crumpled immediately into a mass of distorted aluminium and shattered perspex. Blossoms of flame seared from the wreckage. The flames took only seconds to reach the fuel tanks.

Weaving like drunks, Rodriguez and Eloi got to their feet. D'asser lay where the back-blast had thrown him, totally unconscious for the second time in less than twenty-four hours.

The two officers stared down the trail, the direction from which the blast had come, where the main body of their pursuit column was. Their eyes widened in shock.

Not *was*, but *had been*.

There were no soldiers now — just the screaming, the dying and the dead.

20

'Unhappy the general who comes on the field of battle with a system.'

Napoleon

'Forty-five kilos of diamonds!' Old De Bloom's voice was trembling with rage. 'And they were led by damned *rooineks*.'

'British soldiers? In Angola?' Reitz' surprise made him speak more loudly and with less respect than he usually did to his employer. After all, the old Boer with the withered red face was the chairman of one of the largest multi-national corporations in the world.

'Mercenaries, you fool.' De Bloom leant forward in the rear seat of the huge silver Mercedes. 'I'm sending eight men with you from our own security force. *You will get those diamonds back.*'

Questions bubbled into Reitz' mind. 'But — '

De Bloom waved him angrily into silence. 'Van der Gucht and Schmidt will accompany you. You will be fully briefed on the flight. Now *go.*'

Reitz emerged from the Mercedes and stood blinking in the hard clear sunlight outside the chrome and concrete of Johannesburg airport. He was a tall, lean man, with a crew-cut and a face which looked as if it had been badly sculpted in stone. His job as head of De Bloom's security had accustomed him to sudden crises; but he had never seen the old man in such a state.

He walked briskly into the terminal building and turned

right to the doorway which led to private flight departures. He knew little beyond the bare fact that the diamonds had been stolen from Henrique de Carvalho around midday yesterday. The importance of the mission was obvious — and made even clearer by the presence of Van der Gucht and Schmidt, two of the corporation's senior executive vice presidents.

The two Type-36 Lear jets were waiting on the tarmac, the sun glinting on their silvered sides. They had already been cleared for take-off — when De Blooms was in a hurry, the South African authorities were always unfailingly cooperative.

Reitz was the last to board. The jets took off immediately afterwards, climbing rapidly and setting their course for neighbouring Botswana. They had a fifteen hundred mile journey ahead of them.

Most of the passengers were in the same mould as Reitz — tall tough South Africans with neat haircuts, men who were quiet in both voice and action — until their special skills were called on. The vice-presidents were the exceptions: they wore sombre business suits; they were older, sleeker and slightly overweight. Their main responsibilities, Reitz guessed, would concern the international political ramifications of the raid.

Reitz unbuckled his seatbelt, crossed the cabin and slid into the seat beside Van der Gucht. A faint smile twisted his thin lips: their mission was in some ways ironic. Their flight was bound for Luanda — the capital of a Marxist country with which South Africa was at war. At this very moment, the South African army and airforce were laying siege to a large chunk of southern Angola — and, if the rumours were to be believed, were subjecting the civilian population there to all manner of atrocities.

But money was power — money would even make governments forget the wars they were fighting. De Blooms needed the diamonds from Angolan mines; the Angolans needed South African expertise and the foreign currency which the diamonds earned them. War or no war, the business arrangement had the blessing of both of the governments concerned.

Van der Gucht passed Reitz a thick manilla folder; he had an identical one on his lap.

'It's all there,' he said. 'You'll have to study it in depth, but perhaps I'd better outline the main points now. What you have to understand is that it's not so much the direct consequences of the loss of the diamonds which worry De Blooms — it's the indirect ones. And God knows they could be serious enough: the corporation itself is at risk — and our jobs with it.'

Reitz shrugged. 'The Angolans should have the situation under control by now. It's hard to believe that they can't lay their hands on a handful of marauders in the heart of their own country. They aren't *that* inefficient.'

'We can't take the risk.' Van der Gucht moved closer and spoke in a lower voice. 'If those stones reach the Western market-place, the whole balloon goes up. The diamond business is riding the same economic trend as everything else in the West: downwards. If a large quantity of cheap, good stones suddenly appear on the market, it will have the immediate effect of devaluing our own stocks. We'd stand to lose billions — it's that serious.'

'But the planned diversification should help offset that,' Reitz objected. 'The emerald mines —'

'Will go down the drain as well,' Van der Gucht snapped. 'If our stocks are dramatically devalued, our supply of credit will dry up — overnight. We acquired the emerald-mining rights in Zimbabwe under certain conditions — one of which is that we must make the mines productive within a year. If we can't borrow money to do that, Mugabe will simply hand over the concessions to someone else. He'd be acting perfectly legally. You can see his point — he needs the revenue. The main reason why he accepted our tender over the other competitors' was that our timetable was shorter than theirs.'

Reitz nodded. His mind moved on to another aspect of the subject. 'What's the Angolan angle?'

'They'll back us to the hilt, thank God.' Van der Gucht pointed at the manilla folder with a stubby forefinger. 'There's a detailed section on the country in there. Basically, the country's been on the verge of bankruptcy since the civil war. The war also ruined their agriculture, with the result that they're having to import most of their basic foodstuffs. And because of the Angolan political and economic situation, everyone who deals with them insists on being paid cash.'

Reitz' pale grey eyes narrowed. 'So they are totally dependent on their exports to earn the necessary foreign currency?'

'Right. The main money-spinner is the oil they get offshore Cabinda, that little enclave state in northern Angola. But the diamonds from Henrique de Carvalho are next on the list. If they lose forty-five kilos of diamonds, a lot of Angolans are going to go hungry.'

Reitz said one word: 'Famine . . .'

Van der Gucht lowered his voice still further: 'You know what that means: unrest leading to civil war . . . possible foreign intervention . . . a blockage in the flow of diamonds to De Blooms, possibly permanently . . . Christ, man, it could change the entire balance of power in southern Africa.'

Reitz felt for a cigarette. 'It adds up to a plus right now,' he said thoughtfully. 'It means the Angolans will pull out every stop to cooperate with us.'

Van der Gucht grasped eagerly at this straw of hope. 'Maybe the old man is over-reacting. By the time we reach Luanda, we may find the situation has been normalized for hours.'

Reitz made no reply. Angolan cooperation was not the same as Angolan efficiency. He himself was always a pessimist.

It didn't pay to be an optimist in his line of business.

Wingtip to wingtip, the two Lear jets flew on, their vapour trails leaving parallel white lines across the blue African sky. Reitz ploughed through the contents of the folder on his lap.

In the seat beside him, Van der Gucht was sweating. *They're all the same, these deskmen*, Reitz thought contemptuously. *They go to pieces in the field.*

There was a tap on his shoulder. The co-pilot respectfully touched his cap and handed over a radio message which had just come in. It was addressed to Reitz and Van der Gucht.

LOCAL FORCES MAULED BADLY BY ATTACKERS STOP PURSUIT OF ATTACKERS HAS CEASED REPEAT CEASED STOP TERRORISTS BELIEVED TO BE A MIXTURE OF BRITS AND BLACKS STOP THIS IDENTIFICATION NOW CONFIRMED STOP TERRORISTS MAKING FOR ZED REPEAT ZED STOP HAVE SENT MORE PERSONNEL TO KOL AND LUB STOP MOST URGENT THAT ANGOLANS ARE PERSUADED TO CONTINUE PURSUIT STOP REITZ TO GO DIRECTLY TO K REPEAT REITZ DIRECTLY TO K STOP

Reitz read the message twice and passed it to Van der Gucht. So those bloody kaffirs in Angola had cocked it up, had they? If the terrs were making for Zaire, that confirmed the idea that the black members of the contingent were FNLA-backed.

Kolwezi and Lubumbashi were sizeable towns in Southern Zaire, close to the Angolan border. They both had airfields and the associated civil airfreight traffic, so they were logical bolt-holes for the mercenaries to make for — and for De Blooms to block.

But why did the old man want him to go north to Kinshasa, the Zairois capital? He could think of only one possible explanation: the mercenaries must have shown themselves too clever to do the obvious.

Reitz chuckled — a thin sound like the rustling of paper, which sent a shiver down the back of the perspiring businessman in the seat beside him.

Too clever for Jan Reitz? He doubted it.

21

Two men were dead.

Davies felt a gut-anger at the thought. So far he had lost none of his men in this operation, and he had hoped to reach Zaire with no casualties. The fact that the killer was the river Chiumbe rather than an MPLA bullet didn't make it any better.

Radio contact between Tippett and Davies soon established the identities of the men who had died. Both were black. It was unfortunate that one of them had been carrying most of Tippett's remaining explosives.

Their new plan was forced on them by necessity. Time was beginning to run against them; and there was no way to get across the river now the bridge was gone.

Tippett, they decided, was to take his force and the booty and go hell-for-leather for the border. Once in Zaire, they were to wait under cover in the bush around the town of Sandoa. If Davies, Kikuji and the rest of the smaller party trapped on the western bank of the Chiumbe hadn't shown up in eight days, Tippett was to head south and take himself and the white lads out through one of the airfields there.

Meanwhile Davies and his party had no option but to follow the original plan — to make for the rendezvous with the trucks. Roberto and Dorian would be waiting for them at Tshikapa; but at least Davies now had one lever to use against any possible skulduggery. He no longer had the diamonds with him — but he did know where they were.

The two groups broke radio contact. Davies led his group on to the remnants of the footbridge and climbed down into the swirling shallows of the river itself, just beside the bank. He and his men waded north for twenty metres before climbing back on to dry land. Davies hoped that the manoeuvre would persuade the pursuit team that the whole body of men had crossed the river, destroying the bridge behind them.

The march which followed was a nightmare. Their course was a long arc, designed to take them back to the road. The dense grass and the heavy clinging soil made it hard going at the best of times; in the darkness it was ten times worse.

Davies and Kikuji goaded the flagging men along. They marched all through the night, stopping only for three twenty minute rests. At dawn Davies got his party under cover and allowed them the luxury of an hour's sleep.

The next day followed the same arduous pattern. Davies and Kikuji watched themselves and their men turn into zombies. They kept going only because their wills were subconsciously fuelled by the need to survive, and because marching had now become an automatic grind which required no thought at all. They continued well into the following night.

Just before dawn the three desperately tired men who held the unenviable position of point passed word back to the file of stumbling men behind them that they were on the outskirts of a hamlet of mud-and-wattle huts.

It caught Davies unawares: fatigue had dulled his senses and blunted his usual caution; he concentrated more on his aching legs than the world around him. It took him a few precious seconds to react.

With a low hissing noise he galvanized the men around him into action, breaking through their exhaustion by sheer force of personality. The plodding zombies were trans-formed, as if by magic, into wills-o'-the-wisp who melted into the lush elephant grass on either side of the narrow path.

Only the three men on point remained. They had spread out and stopped. Each man sought to blend in with his background. Their rifles were rock-steady; the safety-catches had been eased forward; index fingers were crooked around the hook-shaped triggers. Once again the miracle had happened — adrenalin surged through their jaded nerve centres and weary limbs, increasing tension and heightening perceptions to a level of total awareness.

Kikuji had the centre position at point. Fresh droplets of sweat studded his forehead; gradually they moved, forming rivulets which coursed down his face to the already saturated sweat-rag around his neck.

He advanced with agonizing slowness, his hooded eyes flashing back and forth across the whole of his field of vision.

It was still very dark, though the night had lost that sooty, impenetrable quality. The big Nubian could see he was very close to the cluster of huts now. But with every cautious step he took, his confidence grew. If the village were still inhabited, he should be able to hear the domestic animals stirring, ready for dawn; his flared nostrils, acutely sensing every smell, were downwind to the village — he should be smelling the lingering odour of charcoal, the decaying garbage and even the sweat of the villagers.

Tiny sounds behind Kikuji told him that the rest of the group were fanning out, covering the three men at point. He moved stealthily from hut to hut. All of them were deserted, their former inhabitants driven out by hunger, the guerrilla war or both.

The rest of the men relaxed as the village proved to be a false alarm. But Davies was aware that there was a price to be paid for this temporary alertness: the sudden anticlimax had left them more tired than ever. As it was, if this village had been one of the inhabited ones with its own militia, they could all have been dead by now.

He called a halt for a few hours. He set a guard and gathered the rest of the men into two of the huts.

With the suddeness of a burst water-pipe, the heavens opened: torrential rain bucketed down. Within seconds the air temperature had dropped by several degrees. The huts were not waterproof, so the tired soldiers burrowed in their packs for the thin green poncho-cum-groundsheets which all of them carried.

Davies repressed a yawn. 'This can't be bad — the rain will wash out our tracks, both through the grass and on the path. If we can get a small fire going, there's no reason why we shouldn't have a brew.'

He spoke to no one in particular, but a small African soldier gave him a tired grin and immediately began to gather twigs and small sticks. There was no need for him to go outside — the huts' builders had used plenty of wood on the interiors of the stuctures, packing it into the mud to increase their strength.

Davies' homely Cockney accent, the very idea of a brew after days without anything hot, and the sight of someone actually putting the idea into practice — all these combined to raise morale. Within seconds the other men had visibly relaxed and were helping to gather firewood.

The fuel was completely dry, so there was soon a small, lively fire in the centre of each of the occupied huts. The men sat with their backs to the walls, their feet stretched out to the dancing flames.

Davies stared round the ring of faces in his hut. The black ones were tinged with the grey of fatigue. The white faces showed similar signs — dark rings had appeared around their eyes and pallor had replaced the healthy pinkness of their skins. The dark shadow of stubble accentuated the sallowness of the faces.

The African who had initiated the fire appeared in the doorway with an aluminium pot in which he had collected rainwater. He placed the pot in the middle of the fire and pushed his way into the circle of men around it. Davies made way for him with a smile. The little African was often surly and miserable with both blacks, and whites, but he had one saving grace which had led Kikuji to recommend him for the operation. The man could produce a pot of food or coffee out of seemingly no ingredients and in next to no time, whatever the situation. For this reason he was tolerated and even grudgingly liked by his mates.

While he waited for the coffee to cool, Davies lethargically unbuttoned his shirt and rubbed his raw shoulders with a handful of soothing lotion. He winced as the liquid bit into the raw, chafed flesh.

Most men settled down to sleep at once after finishing their coffee. Davies, though exhausted, stared for a while at the hypnotic flickerings of the flames. Despite physical tiredness, his mind was still alert. One thought kept him awake, though he found it hard to comprehend its awesome implications:

He, Tom Davies, had led an operation which had achieved what was arguably the greatest robbery ever seen in the Dark Continent — or even anywhere.

Robbery, he mused tiredly, wasn't the right word, of course. As far as he was concerned, taking loot from communist forces was fair game . . .

The flames were burning lower. Davies flung another bundle of twigs on the fire. As they flared up, his mind ran ahead to the future. Roberto and Dorian should be together in Kinshasa by now: he must work out a strategy.

He noticed with detached curiosity that his boots were too close to the fire, emitting a gentle cloud of steam. He lacked the strength to pull them back.

A few seconds later he was asleep.

Davies jerked out of sleep, instinctively grabbing the hand on his shoulder while his other arm snaked down his body, the fingers groping for the haft of his boot-knife.

'Kikuji, you old devil!' he roared. At the same time he relaxed and stretched.

Kikuji smiled and handed him a mug of strong, unsweetened coffee. Davies took a sip of the scalding liquid and looked at his watch. It was already nearly seven o'clock. He glanced round the dim interior of the hut and saw that everyone else was already up.

He gulped the rest of his coffee and went outside to relieve himself. Their priority was to find out where they were. Kikuji pointed out a couple of hills to the south-east; they bore an astonishing resemblance to the ears of a horse. Correlating these with the map, the two men worked out that they must be within two hours' march of the main highroad — but they didn't know their precise position with regard to the rendezvous point with the two trucks.

Ten minutes later, the whole party was off. In the event, the march to the road took them longer than they had anticipated. It was just after eleven before they hit the rutted red ribbon of the highway.

Davies pulled the men back some twenty metres into the bush and sent out a couple of scouts, one to the north, the other to the south. Here they had a stroke of luck — the southern scout returned in a few minutes with the news that the lorries were about three hundred metres down the road. But the news was not all good: their two trucks were part of a convoy which was being assembled under the watchful eyes of a strong military detachment.

While they waited for the return of the northern scout, Davies and Kikuji investigated the convoy on their own account. They filtered slowly through the thick grass. All the vehicles had pulled off the road into a clearing — which was fortunately on the same side of the road as the mercenaries. Their own two trucks and trailers were positioned at what would obviously be the tail end of the convoy once it was on the move. Their canvas-sheeted sides were hard up against the bush itself.

Two hours later, the two leaders returned with the rest of their squad. Moving with infinite care, they worked through the dense elephant grass until they were next to the blind sides of the lorries. One by one they crept in among the sacks of coffee, five men in one truck and six in the other.

Davies decided against notifying the drivers of their presence: José and Alessandro would behave less suspiciously if they thought they carried nothing except coffee. But he would have to warn them before the border, of course, so they could bribe the customs on the Angolan side.

At three o'clock in the afternoon, the convoy rumbled on to the highroad with an armoured car in the lead. Davies settled himself more comfortably against the sacks, bracing against the swaying of the truck.

His desire, he reflected, had been granted: he was leaving Angola with the unusual courtesy of a military escort, to make sure that he came to no harm from those dangerous guerrillas along the route.

22

'After the pleasant scratching comes unpleasant
   scratching.'

Danish Proverb

The girl was beautiful by any standards — eastern, western
or African. She even earned the highest rating by the most
exacting standards of all — Alexander Dorian's.

The thick-set banker was sitting in a shaded corner of the
bar of the Palace Hotel, Kinshasa. Despite the fifteen hour
journey he had just completed, he felt like a young buck.

The girl was outside by the hotel's pool. The brassy midday sun beat down with merciless ferocity on the tiled mosa-
ics surrounding its blue waters. The tiles were now too hot
to walk on — so no one was in the pool.

Most people were sitting at one of the three poolside bars,
languidly sipping iced drinks in the airless heat. Since this
was Africa, the architects had designed each of the bars as a
typical African hut with an authentically thatched roof; the
conical shape of the thatch offered a coolness which the
Africans had evolved over centuries for their own survival.

The clientele was predominantly male except for one
table where five women were sitting. All of them wore tiny
bikinis. One of them was the girl whom Dorian admired.
On the surface the girls seemed totally engrossed with themselves; they chattered with animation, and there was a lot of
laughter.

But all of them were aware of the watching male eyes
around them — and rejoiced in the fact with the self-

assurance of women who knew exactly what made the world go round.

The whole quintet was attractive, Dorian thought, but the tallest one seemed to have all of the others' best attributes rolled into one delectable body. Her skin colouring was deeper than the others' — so dark that it was almost a blue-black, gleaming with the sheen of youth. Hundreds of tiny beads were woven in her hair, their bright colours contrasting vividly with her complexion. Her hair framed an unusually fine set of features.

Just then the girl laughed, a liquid ripple of sensuous sound which set the beads dancing around her face. As she did so, she glanced towards Dorian, half-hidden in the shade of the interior bar. He smiled and made a small beckoning gesture with his hand. There was an answering flash of perfect white teeth — and an infinitesimal nod.

The girl whispered something to her companions and, gathering up her towel and handbag, walked through the harsh sunlight to join him. Dorian's eyes tracked her movements across the tiles with anticipatory pleasure; her walk was immensely graceful, despite her ultra-high heels. He gained an additional pleasure from the obvious chagrin of a group of Norwegian sailors at the next table. Really, it was a wonder how that microscopic bikini top stayed in place on such a statuesque figure.

She poured herself on to the stool beside him. *'Bonjour, chéri, je m'appelle Albertine . . .'*

Her Belgian French was very nearly flawless. Dorian quickly proposed the business basis of their relationship, the terms of which brought satisfaction to both sides. A waiter in a red and black livery, familiar with the preliminary rituals of these assignations, darted over to take Dorian's order for drinks.

Ten minutes later they left the bar and went up to the banker's air-conditioned suite on the first floor. Dorian remarked on the heat. Albertine took his hand and led him into the shower cubicle, losing her bikini on the way.

*   *   *

Dorian awoke unwillingly from a deep, satisfying sleep. The sun had long gone down. There was a sharp buzzing noise like a demented mosquito in his ears; he eventually tracked it down to the hotel's intercom system, located on the headboard of the huge double bed. Albertine slumbered on beside him.

It was the desk clerk, announcing that there was a visitor for Dorian in reception. The banker's mind rapidly cleared: he issued crisp instructions to the clerk, switched off the intercom and gently woke the girl.

Albertine made a charming *moue* when told she would have to go, but brightened perceptibly when Dorian booked her services for later that night and all of the next day.

The banker quickly showered again while the girl wriggled back into her bikini. She picked up the notes he had left for her and called her goodbyes through the hissing of the shower water.

Albertine left the suite and walked down the corridor to the lift. It arrived a few seconds later. A thin, elderly African, his eyes concealed behind heavily-tinted glasses, walked by her without a glance. That, in Albertine's experience, was an unusual response from men when they saw her in her bikini — or in anything or nothing at all. Curiosity and pique made her look over her shoulder. The African opened Dorian's door and went in without knocking.

That second glance showed her the man's face in profile; and suddenly she realized she knew who it was. It was Holden Roberto, the brother-in-law of Mbutu, the president of Zaire.

For an instant Albertine remained in deep thought by the open door of the lift. *The Swiss pays well . . . but I really have no choice . . .*

She hurried into the lift and descended to the ground floor. She was one of many prostitutes who were allowed — albeit for a percentage of their profits — to operate among the foreign visitors to Kinshasa. But there was another condition attached to this lucrative employment: Albertine's pimp had also contracted to supply the secret

157

police with any interesting scraps of information which came her way. And the president's discredited brother-in-law having a secret meeting with a Swiss banker in Kinshasa was nothing if not interesting.

She changed into her street clothes and phoned her protector. Half-an-hour later the big black man collected her in a battered yellow Mercedes taxi. They drove across the teeming city to the grandiose but decaying building which had once been the Residence of the Belgian colonial administrator. It was now the Kinshasa headquarters of the secret police.

Her pimp ushered her into a large office where she was made to tell her story to two men who sat behind the desk. Both men remained nameless; but they wore the obligatory secret police uniform — mirrored sun-glasses and loud cotton-print shirts with threatening bulges at the waistband.

The two operatives listened intently but, rather to her surprise, asked no questions. Then one of them nodded and her pimp took her outside.

He gripped her arm so tightly that she winced. 'Not a word, you understand? Not a word to anyone.'

Dorian was irritated to find Holden Roberto standing in the middle of the suite's sitting room when he emerged from the bathroom with a large white towel round his waist. He disliked being seen as anything less than his usual dapper, well-polished self — except, of course, by women, in the right time and place.

The banker noticed right away that his business partner was in a state of some excitement. The African was mopping his brow with an enormous white linen handkerchief.

There was a sudden lurch in his stomach as he contemplated the possibility that his visitor brought bad news. Then he saw that Roberto's face was wreathed in smiles.

Dorian was excited himself, but he had his cool, self-contained image to preserve. He kept the African waiting while he retired to his bedroom. When he came out a few minutes later, he was as immaculately well-groomed as ever.

158

Roberto was pacing to and fro across the luxurious lounge.

'Sit down, for heaven's sake,' Dorian said sharply. 'Will you have a drink?'

Dorian poured his guest a large scotch and fixed himself up with a gin and tonic. He settled himself in an armchair and took a long swallow. Finally, the banker allowed himself to put Roberto out of his misery.

'Well, my friend — what's the cause of all this high excitement?'

Roberto snapped open the document case on his lap and passed Dorian a sheaf of flimsy papers. 'These are transcripts of radio messages sent to and from Henrique de Carvalho last night. I got them through a contact at the Zairois listening-post at Sandoa.'

Dorian remained silent as he scanned the messages. But he found it hard to maintain his detached pose when he saw the assessments of the Angolan losses: *forty-five kilos of diamonds and an unknown quantity of foreign currency*. With an effort he kept his voice quiet and even:

'They mention time and again their own casualties — but they appear to have overlooked finding any of ours.'

Roberto nodded. 'There are none — as yet.'

'But I thought there *would* be casualties.' There was a petulant edge to Dorian's tone. 'In fact we banked on it. Your estimate was at least twenty-five per cent. Can we still handle them if they all get out?'

'Don't worry. The plan will be the same.' Roberto ticked off the points, one by one, on his long, thin fingers. 'We meet them in Tshikapa, get the stones in our possession and disarm them. There will be no problem there — they have no reason to distrust us. Then we load them into a VW minibus. I have even arranged for them to be given their flight tickets at that point, which should put them completely off-guard.'

Dorian smiled. 'A nice touch, my dear Roberto.'

'We shall then drive towards Kinshasa in convoy,' the

159

African continued. 'But the minibus will never reach here. At a pre-arranged spot on the route, the Zairois police will let my Range Rover through but ambush the minibus. Most of them will doubtless be given medals for killing all these dangerous foreign mercenaries. (We shall say the whites were heavily-armed, of course.) Meanwhile my people in Tshikapa will . . . er . . . deal with the black elements in the force. It is too sensitive a matter for us to be able to afford witnesses of any colour.'

Dorian nodded, a look of satisfaction on his plump face. He had realized, right at the inception of the plan, that anything other than a twoway split of the proceeds between himself and Roberto was more than bad business: it was sheer stupidity. Furthermore, security alone required the death of the mercenaries and their African comrades — he and Roberto simply couldn't risk the truth about the raid being leaked to the media.

The banker had a third, more personal reason. He had revealed too much of himself — and of the bank's financial dealings — to Davies; and the mercenary had shown himself far too astute for his own good. Dorian had no intention of living with the danger of exposure or blackmail if he could help it.

No, there was only one logical solution: Davies must die.

Neither Dorian nor Roberto had any idea that the Angolan raid which they had instigated had stirred up such an international hornets' nest. And when you stir up hornets, they have a habit of retaliating with stings.

As a consequence the Swiss banker was off his guard. He had had a wonderful night with Albertine; and now he was sitting opposite her in the hotel dining room eating breakfast. He could have had it served in the suite, of course, but it did his ego good to be seen in public with a girl as beautiful as Albertine.

Dorian talked incessantly as he crammed slice after slice of hot buttered toast into his mouth. The success of the raid and his flatteringly frequent exploits with Albertine in the last few hours had combined to put him into a euphoric state of mind. The girl said little in reply — not that Dorian minded: she wasn't paid to talk. If he had been a little less cocksure, he might have noticed that there was an evasive quality about her behaviour.

Her eyes constantly slid sideways to a neighbouring table where four tall, deeply sun-burnt men were sipping coffee and talking quietly. Their faces were tired, and their chins were shadowed with stubble. Albertine's pimp had telephoned before breakfast to warn her about these white *reits* from the deep south.

The secret police had told the pimp to repeat Albertine's story to the South Africans. The white men now knew everything about the meeting between the Swiss banker and the old freedom fighter — including the fact that Dorian had made several references to the disturbances over the border in Angola, when talking to Albertine later that night; his voice had been full of suppressed excitement.

Albertine caught her breath as two of the South Africans pushed back their chairs and made their way across to Dorian's table. The banker had his back to the approaching men. Some flicker in Albertine's eyes made him turn round.

But he was too late: the South Africans had boxed him in. One man stood with his right hand resting negligently in his jacket pocket. The other — the taller one who was their leader — put his hand on Dorian's shoulder. Albertine could see the banker wince as the fingers tightened their grip.

'Good morning, Mr Dorian.' The South African accent was flat and expressionless, but the fingers squeezed harder until the Swiss grunted in pain. 'My name is Jan Reitz.'

23

'The end justifies the means.'
H. Bisenbaum

Yet again, Dorian screamed.

He had screamed so often that the sound came out of his torn and ruptured larynx as a hoarse bubbling. These despairing and unearthly noises were accompanied by a shockingly unnatural arching of his back: his body bent backwards like a bow, and the massive muscles on his neck and shoulders went into violent spasms. Sweat poured from his naked body. Within the last few minutes the muscles of his chest seemed to have developed a life of their own: they twitched and jerked, contorted by irregular waves of cramp.

Reitz' face was drained of emotion — even of interest. He had seen it all before; he read the signs with the practised familiarity of a tradesman who knows his job inside out. He gripped the rubber-insulated handle of the tee-shaped bar and raised it to the off-position.

Dorian flopped back against the bare bedsprings, like a marionette whose strings have been suddenly cut. His cavernous chest heaved as he gasped for air. The hair which covered it was now drenched with sweat. Blood from his wrists and ankles dripped gently on to the concrete floor; the man had been bound to the iron bedstead with thin copper wire and, as usual, his own exertions had done the rest.

The banker's eyes flickered across to the brightly-illuminated dial of the electrical transformer. Two rubber-covered leads ran from it to the bed. Both ended in large crocodile clips. One had been snapped on to the long muscle which lies above the collar-bone, while the other bit into the Swiss's testicles. Reitz had taken care to put the transformer well within Dorian's range of vision. It always helped if they could *see* as well as feel precisely how much voltage he was pumping into them.

Dorian's head lolled back against the bedframe. His eyes were half-closed. He made a huge effort and pulled himself back from unconsciousness.

'I demand . . . to see . . . the Swiss consul.'

Reitz made no answer. He was mildly surprised by Dorian's endurance — they had been at it for over an hour now. The Swiss, presumably, had never had to handle physical pain.

When they had picked him up at the hotel, he had been whisked off to the waiting Land Rover and gagged, blindfolded and handcuffed. Reitz took him to the single-storeyed concrete building inside the perimeter of the airfield, at the far end from the passenger terminal. The building was on loan from the Zairois secret police. Reitz' men had sliced off Dorian's clothes with knives and bound him to the bedstead. Usually men like Dorian started talking when they put on the crocodile clips.

But the Swiss had said nothing beyond demanding to see his consul and proclaiming his innocence. The unnecessary delay irritated the South African. Still, there wasn't long to go.

Reitz persisted with the same three questions, keeping his voice intentionally monotonous to give it a mildly hypnotic effect:

'Where are you meeting them? How many of them are there? When are they due?'

'*I don't know.*' Dorian clung to the idea that any hope of survival must rest on the bedrock of innocence and ignorance. It was his only hope — and no hope at all.

Reitz' suntanned fingers rested lightly on the handle of the transformer. Dorian tried to stare into his captor's amber-coloured eyes, willing him to believe in his innocence.

163

But his eyes would only look at one thing: the hand which stroked the black rubber insulation on the tee-shaped handle.

Suddenly Reitz gripped it and seemed to jerk it downwards. Dorian's body arched itself; and he gave an animal-like screech of anguish.

But this time the white flash of utter madness didn't streak down the red lead from the transformer. Reitz stayed his hand. The anticlimax was too much for Dorian's crumbling will to cope with. His nerve shattered; his bladder emptied; and his bowels relaxed their hold in a final and humiliating gesture of submission.

Reitz looked down on the wreckage of a man spread-eagled on the bed and cruelly illuminated by the blinding tungsten floodlight which shone directly into his eyes. 'Where are you meeting them?' he asked patiently. 'How many of them are there? When are they due?'

And Dorian told him.

Unknown to the banker, there was another witness to his interrogation besides the four South Africans. Holden Roberto was tied to a chair behind the floodlight. The armpits of his pale blue safari suit were stained with dark patches of sweat. If Dorian hadn't told the white men what they wanted to know, the politician knew he would have been next.

He heard the banker's hoarse, whispering voice revealing every detail of their achievements and plans. Then there was silence. Then footsteps.

The African's blindfold was removed and his gag ripped off — with such violence that the sticky tape took much of his beard with it. When the waves of pain receded slightly, he saw the leader of the South Africans standing over him.

'Is there anything you want to add — Kaffir?'

The African shook his head violently, rolling his averted eyes.

Reitz nodded to his colleagues and the four men left the room. Roberto stared at the bizarre scene before him: the circle of light around the pallid bloodstained body of his erstwhile partner, the evil-smelling pool beneath the iron bedframe and the innocent-looking instruments of torture. He could not understand how such a thing could be happening to him — in Zaire, his brother-in-law's country.

'Alexander,' he whispered. 'Alexander . . . can you hear me?'

But there was no reply.

A few minutes later, the white men returned and untied their prisoners. Dorian was given a grey blanket to cover his nudity.

'Please,' the banker croaked, 'may I have water to wash in?'

The request was curtly refused. It was curious, Roberto thought, how the Swiss's obsessive concern with cleanliness and his appearance had surfaced, even at a time like this.

The two prisoners were taken outside into the harsh morning sunlight. Roberto had to support the greatly weakened Dorian; drops of blood followed them across the concrete. They were pushed into the rear seats of a Land Rover with official markings.

Roberto's heart lurched with hope. An African in a dark suit had just come out of the administration block beyond the torture hut. The politician recognized him: it was the chief of the Zairois secret police. He and his wife had dined at Roberto's villa in the mid-1970s; the policeman had even provided the then-head of the FNLA with a personal bodyguard.

The man walked over to the Land Rover. Roberto jerked forward in his seat. One of the South Africans pulled him back, but not before the policeman had looked straight through his old friend as if he wasn't there.

Roberto whimpered. He watched disbelievingly as the policeman cordially shook hands with Reitz and spent a few minutes in conversation with him. He slapped Reitz on the back and strolled away. Why was the first man in his own brother-in-law's secret police force helping a white South African racist instead of a black African politician?

Reitz watched Roberto's reaction out of the corner of his

eye, with quiet enjoyment. The poor sap of a Kaffir didn't know that Mbutu had made a deal with the South Africans. The Zairois president needed Peugeot fighting vehicles, spare parts for his Mirage fighters and the sort of sophisticated spy technology which he couldn't get elsewhere. The South Africans had provided it all — in return for a very good price and some favours now and then. Right now, Roberto was one of the favours.

The South Africans and their prisoners set out on the long road to Tshikapa. The secret police gave them an escort of four Land Rovers crammed with armed men. They drove through the long hot day and made only one stop.

This was on a bridge which spanned another of the river Congo's countless tributaries. Dorian was helped out of the Land Rover by two of the South Africans. Then Reitz climbed out with an automatic pistol in his hand. He put a bullet in the banker's head and pushed the bulky body over the low, concrete parapet into the murky, rain-swollen waters below.

Dorian's request for a wash hadn't been ignored after all.

24

'Eternal vigilance is the price of liberty.'
John Philpot Curran

There was a two man guard at the approach to the camp; and the first good news they had heard for hours was the raucous whistling of an African pop song.

Next they heard the creak of an unoiled bicycle, and the occasional curse from its rider, as its wheels dropped into ruts. The two guards sighed with relief and eased the safety catches on their Kalashnikovs to the off-position.

Kikuji was back.

The last twenty-odd hours had been hell for the mercenaries and their comrades. They had arrived back in Zaire early the previous evening. The truckers had unloaded them in a clearing four kilometres from Tshikapa. The men had melted into the bush at once, for Davies feared that the reception planned for them by Roberto and Dorian might include scouts outside the town itself. They had found a suitable place to make camp. Kikuji had borrowed civilian clothes — a spare shirt and a pair of torn trousers — from José and slipped into town to see what was happening.

The big Nubian suddenly appeared round the bend in the path which the sentries were covering. He was wobbling precariously on a bicycle which was old when Cecil Rhodes was young. Every inch of the bicycle's frame and handlebars was festooned with something — including four fat, squawking chickens. Balanced on top of the rusty handlebars were three wicker baskets, stacked in a column and held in place by Kikuji's chin.

The guards didn't reveal themselves to Kikuji in case he had been followed. Nevertheless they relaxed and chuckled quietly. The white lad pointed to the huge glass carboy, filled with a liquid the colour of milk, which was lashed to the back of Kikuji's bicycle. He nudged his black companion and raised his eyebrows.

The African flashed a smile, tilted back his head and raised a thumb to his mouth — the age-old international sign for alcohol.

Kikuji and his precious cargo were greeted with relief when they reached the camp. The cook seized the chickens with glee; for once there was a broad smile on his usually surly face.

While the long-awaited meal was being prepared on a small, almost smokeless fire, Davies conferred with Kikuji about the situation in Tshikapa. Their faces were sombre, in stark contrast to the cheerful expressions of the rest of the men.

The rendezvous, Kikuji explained in a low voice, turned out to be an old bungalow in its own grounds, right in the centre of town. As far as he could see, it was totally unoccupied — the storm shutters were nailed shut and there was a rusting padlock and chain round the front gates.

'It doesn't make sense.' There was a perplexed frown on Davies' face. 'Dorian and Roberto should be there — even if it's a trap.'

'No one — nothing.' Kikuji shook his head. 'It's crazy, *commandante*.'

But there was another matter to worry Davies — Tippett, the rest of his men and the loot. He had to make the rendezvous with them in the south — and in the next few days. He lit a cigarette and balanced priorities in his mind.

'Kikuji, me old mate,' he said at last. 'Can you get in touch with Alessandro and José? I fancy a trip to the south.'

The two truck-drivers agreed to the thousand kilometre round-trip in return for an even larger bonus than Davies had previously promised them. They broke camp early the following morning, while the stars were still in the sky. Fortunately the two trucks carried mobile fuel reservoirs of forty gallon drums.

The little convoy slipped as silently as possible through the sleeping town of Tshikapa. The drivers put on speed once they reached the broad tarmacked highway which linked Kinshasa in the north with the industrial south of Zaire. The drivers gunned the lorries hard, knowing that the Zairois military traffic police were thin on the ground at this time of the morning; the general opinion was that they were recovering from their previous night's debauchery.

By midday they had clocked up three hundred kilometres, but the drivers now had to slow down — there were too many khaki-coloured Land Rovers with heavy machine guns mounted on their backs; the police had turned up for another day's work.

They took a break in the mid-afternoon. After that Kikuji and another black spelled the weary truckers. Davies wished it was safe for him to drive. Any change of activity would have relieved the boredom. The track of tar and flint seemed to stretch on for ever.

When the lights of Sandoa twinkled out of the darkness ahead, everyone was relieved. The trucks pulled into a two-acre compound surrounded by a low mud wall; the area served as a market and as a parking place for trucks on the transcontinental run. José and Alessandro parked some distance from the other trucks; and they were careful to leave their vehicles pointing towards the exit.

The lorries came to a rocking, hissing halt. The soldiers stayed in the places they had hollowed out among the sacks. The drivers leapt out and soon had a pan of coffee simmering on a fire. Kikuji, whose colour and civilian clothes gave him freedom of movement, sauntered towards the throng of people who mingled around the market stalls and fires at the other end of the compound.

Paraffin Tilley lamps were everywhere, creating puddles of green-white light which acted as magnets for the chattering locals — and for millions of flying insects.

Kikuji returned after several hours, reporting total failure: he had found no trace of the other troops. But some of his news brought a faint grin to Davies' haggard face: the raid, it seemed, was much discussed in the border town — but it had been distorted beyond recognition. It was generally agreed that so much damage could only have been done by the South African forces working with UNITA from southern Angola; at least a battalion must have attacked Henrique de Carvalho.

The African had had the foresight to buy two more sets of civilian clothes. Next day he took two of his men with him when he went to look for the rest of their force.

Davies, meanwhile, grew desperately worried. Time was running out for them, and they had no certainty that Tippett's troop was even alive. Moreover, the terrain around Sandoa was not as favourable to the mercenaries as the dense foliage of the elephant grass around Tshikapa. The open savannahs of the south were covered with knee-high grass which offered little cover. As Davies and his men waited for news, the African sun turned the stationary trucks into slow-burning ovens, increasing the discomfort of the men concealed inside them.

On their third night at Sandoa, their luck changed for the better. Kikuji met one of Tippett's Africans. The rest of his group — except for the ones who had died on the way — were encamped on a small hill to the north of the town, painfully protected by a thicket of low thorn trees.

Davies wasted no time in reuniting his two groups. He was delighted to find that the precious Bergens were intact — but less happy about the physical condition of Tippett and his men.

Tippett explained why during the long drive back to Tshikapa. They had plenty of time to talk because the trucks fell in with a convoy carrying plant and machinery from Zaire's industrial copper belt. The convoy trundled along at a snail's pace; but — because it flew the orange-and-green flags of state ownership — the traffic police stayed clear, neither searching the convoy nor demanding *martarbish*, or bribes, from its drivers.

There were twenty-nine men under Tippett's command

when he was separated from Davies by the river Chiumbe. They had immediately struck hard for the border, with ten minutes of rest for every four hours' march. The country slowly changed from thick grass to marshland; this in turn became swamp, leading down to the next river, the Luembe. This was in spate as well. One of the blacks lost his life while trying to cross. The rest of them had to make a detour upstream, consuming much time and energy, until they found a narrows where they could get across.

By now, Tippett confessed ruefully, they were spurred on less by the fear of pursuit than by a craving to escape the damp, living hell of the swamp. The going became harder. Leeches and bloated ticks clung to their bodies — they even reached the genitals. Only the glowing tips of cigarettes would remove them. Mosquitoes plagued them, and there was the constant fear of the dreaded black flies which carried the Black River Water Blindness.

Davies shivered. He had once seen a man who had been bitten. The tiny fly laid eggs under a human's skin. The eggs hatched into worms which wriggled through the layers of fat. Usually — for some reason only an expert in tropical medicine would know — these parasitic worms aimed for the eyes of their human host. When they got there, the eyes went opaque — and the man was blind.

Their terror, Tippett continued, made them reckless. The group came to a patch of very soft ground which they should have negotiated with great caution. But the three men at point plunged right in — literally, for the ground turned out to be quicksand. All three were sucked down to their deaths. Tippett, who was just behind them, was pulled out just in time by the man behind him. The quicksand's evil-smelling slime was still caked on his trousers.

The quicksand necessitated yet another detour — and this one took half a day. And it led to yet another casualty. Robinson was one of the youngest of the mercenaries — an ox of a lad from Salisbury with the battered face of a boy who loved rugby. On one of their ten minute halts, he had put down his heavy Bergen and sat down. In seconds he was

171

back on his feet, complaining that something had bitten his buttocks.

The ribald laughter of the others died away when Tippett caught sight of a thin black snake zig-zagging away through the grass. Robinson dropped his trousers, revealing two tiny red-ringed puncture marks. Tippett cut a deep cross through the bite, hoping that the flow of blood would take the poison with it.

But Robinson was in a coma within an hour — and dead before sundown.

They buried him in a shallow grave. In a way, Tippett said, maybe it was a blessing: from then on, everyone became far more cautious.

The land began to rise, and they emerged from the swamplands to a featureless savannah. They had spent two days and nights walking on a compass-bearing before they hit the highroad north of Sandoa, at a point close to the hill where they had camped.

'By God, we were desperate,' Tippett concluded. 'We had no medical supplies and precious little food left. If the man we sent out hadn't found you, we'd have been up shit creek without a paddle — without a bloody canoe, if it comes to that.'

Davies grunted. 'We still are, mate. We still are.'

The concealed camp near Tshikapa was reached the next day without any mishap. Kikuji immediately left them on his bicycle: they could do nothing until they had news of what was happening in the town. Without hard information, they couldn't even make plans.

Kikuji took longer to return than they expected. When he came, the big Nubian's shirt was torn and his face was uncharacteristically grim. Davies and Tippett drew him to one side immediately.

The African told them that he had gone straight to the market when he reached Tshikapa. Not only did he need to buy provisions there, but it was also the best place to hear the local gossip.

The market compound was flying with rumours — and heavy with the scent of fear. Kikuji soon learned that a roadblock had been set up just outside the town, on the Kinshasa road. It was not manned by the regular soldiers who usually dealt with smugglers, but by units of the special police, all in civilian clothes.

The military were out in strength as well — but these weren't the soldiers from the town barracks. They had been imported from the capital; they kept a low profile and were equipped with — in Kikuji's words — 'tanks with wheels'.

Men in bright shirts and mirrored sunglasses had combed through the compound where lorries parked. A lot of the drivers had been beaten up.

But perhaps the most disturbing news concerned the bungalow which Roberto had fixed as their meeting-place. While the mercenaries were away, it had been opened up. In the market, they said that someone of the highest importance must be staying there. White bodyguards had been glimpsed around the house — and only a handful of the country's leading men were in a position to have white guards.

Davies was disturbed to hear that the operation was not confined to ground level. Helicopters had made regular patrols over the town and the surrounding bush during the last few days.

The market gossip had an explanation for all this activity: the government must be cracking down on a big smuggling operation. Local police and soldiers weren't trusted by the authorities, because they naturally derived a substantial part of their income from cooperating with the smugglers; this was the reason for the special police and the crack troops from Kinshasa. Kikuji had met a trucker up from Kolwezi who confirmed that similar operations were being mounted in the south.

'We have been lucky, *commandantes*.' Kikuji pulled his heavy lower lip. 'Not clever — lucky.'

Davies nodded. They could have been spotted at so many points during the last few days. He beckoned Sanderson and Manuel and issued a stream of orders designed to increase the camouflage and security of their camp. When the younger men had left them, Tippett returned to the subject which was on all their minds.

'We've got to get out of here — it's becoming a bit too unhealthy. Why don't we head south, as per the original plan, and charter a plane at one of the civil airstrips?'

'*Non bom.*' Kukuji shook his head sorrowfully. 'Mbutu, he has brought the Foreign Legion to the south. No like *martarbish.*'

It was a good point, Davies conceded unwillingly. The Legion handled the internal security in the south and that included the civilian airstrips. They were a very different proposition from the blacks — hard-bitten, well-disciplined combat troops who didn't take bribes. Taking his tired force of mercs down there would be putting their heads in a noose.

'In Kinshasa,' Kikuji said, with the beginnings of a smile on his face, 'everyone take *martarbish*. If we hide until . . .' The African's English failed him.

Tippett supplied the end of the sentence: 'Until the heat dies down. Then we could go to Kinshasa and paper a few palms with greenbacks. Is that what you mean?'

Kikuji nodded vigorously.

Davies considered for a moment. It was really their only chance — though it went against the grain to wait patiently when every man here was a potential millionaire.

The mercenaries took no unnecessary chances. The trucks and their trailers were driven deep into a small grove of trees and heavily camouflaged with branches. During the night, men criss-crossed the area, meticulously removing all traces of the tyre tracks. Then they dispersed to heavily-concealed positions around the grove.

Before dismissing them, Davies made sure that every man realized the position they were in. Their lives had been at risk before, he said, but that was nothing to the danger they were in now. Until they had disposed of the diamonds they were targets for anyone who knew who they were and what they had.

174

'We're in for a long wait,' he concluded. 'Patience is the only game we can play right now — and the name of that game is survival.'

Eight days later, Tippett walked over to where Davies sprawled in the shade of a large tree. Davies was eating an overripe mango. He looked up at his friend, noting the grim set of Tippett's features. He threw away the remains of the fruit and wiped the sticky juice from his thirteen-day-old beard.

'I know what you're going to say,' Davies said. 'It's about time we made a move.'

Tippett nodded. 'Maybe we should wait longer, but the natives are getting restless. They've done the Viking bit, and now they want some of the plunder.'

'All right, mate.' Davies got to his feet and the two men strolled across to the tree whose shade sheltered most of the white soldiers. 'Sanderson, bring in all the sentries. O'Ryan, go and fetch Kikuji's men over here.'

There was a buzz of excitement among the men as Davies spoke. The sullen expressions slipped from their faces. Their enforced idleness in the hide outside Tshikapa was beginning to show. The blacks were happy enough on the whole — content to lie in the sun, eating good regular food and replacing the body fats which had been burned off by the long marches. For the most part, their happy-go-lucky natures had a calming influence on the rest of the men. But unfortunately their influence wasn't strong enough.

It was the white lads who were causing the problems. Their two leaders had anticipated that boredom and inactivity would eventually generate discontent — but had hoped it would take longer than in fact it did. Already there had been two fights — both of which involved O'Ryan. Davies, always a realist, knew that if he wanted to maintain discipline he would have to make a positive move towards getting them out of Africa.

The discontent among the whites had been fanned by the daily trips into Tshikapa made by Kikuji and the other two

175

blacks with civvies. Five days ago, the mysterious whites had left Roberto's bungalow; three days ago, the roadblock on the Kinshasa road had been dismantled. As far as the white lads were concerned, there was no longer any obstacle between them and the capital.

But before Davies could open the meeting, Sanderson brusquely pre-empted him.

'Whatever you're going to say, Davies, you'd better know this first: me and the rest of the lads are leaving today. That's final.'

25

'It is always wise to look ahead, but difficult to look
farther than you can see.'

W. S. Churchill

De Bloom was as tired as death.

The old Afrikaaner absently tapped his leather-bound ink-
blotter with the heavy gold pen. But he wouldn't give up: his
father hadn't given up against those damned British, and nor
would he. He leant back in his hide-upholstered swivel chair
and moodily rasped the back of one horny hand against the
pure white stubble on his chin. From the chair he could stare
through the huge smoked-glass window of his penthouse
office at the panorama of Johannesburg below. He owned
that view, he often felt with some justification, just as he
owned the Picasso, the Van Gogh and the Rembrandt on the
other walls of his office. Usually that thought gave him
pleasure.

But not today.

For ten long days, nothing had given him pleasure. There
had been no news whatsoever of the marauders who had
attacked Henrique de Carvalho. Reitz' capture and interrogation of the Swiss Dorian had not led to the breakthrough
which De Bloom had expected. In the meantime, the old man
had hardly slept and had not left his office.

He had grave doubts about the Angolans, too. It was hard
to believe that such a tiny force of attackers had slaughtered 211 Angolan troops — over two-thirds of the town's
garrison — and escaped with no casualties themselves. It

smelt of treachery — as did the failure to pursue the guerrillas after the attack.

As soon as the De Bloom's man in Henrique de Carvalho reported back, De Bloom himself would fly to Luanda and screw those damned Kaffirs for every cent of recompense he could get.

The telex terminal in the corner of the office gave a preliminary hum and then broke into its staccato chatter. The line printer zipped to and fro across the fast-unreeling scroll of paper.

The old man levered himself upright, holding on to the edge of the desk. He turned his back on the raw twentieth century beauty of the city below. His brain raced ahead of his frail body, producing various hypotheses about the contents of the message. Each hypothesis was melded with the information in his memory. Like a computer, his brain subjected each of them to the open-shut process of logic, appraising the solutions it threw up, and discarding or storing them as appropriate.

De Bloom limped across the Persian carpet to the machine and tore off the message. As he had feared, the telex merely confirmed the gloomy tidings of earlier ones. Angolan casualties had now risen to 216, including civilians. The losses from the mining offices were just as bad as the previous reports had stated. Finally, it had been reconfirmed that a small force of British mercenaries and FNLA soldiers had been responsible. Coetzee concluded with a request to be allowed to join Reitz in Zaire.

Why not? De Bloom shrugged. Coetzee was right: by now the diamonds *must* be in Zaire. He pushed a bell to summon his secretary, and gave the necessary instructions.

When he was alone again, he walked over to the hand-painted map of the world which covered most of one huge wall. It was studded with little flags bearing the De Bloom logo; each one marked one of the company's on going projects or achievements.

This pictorial study of the empire which De Bloom had built was marred by a small map which had been roughly

178

thumb-tacked on to its surface. This was a modern, highly detailed lithoprint of Northern Angola. The heavy brass drawing-pins had scarred De Bloom's empire for ever.

The map was his reference point as he ran through his strategy in his mind.

If the marauders had turned south to Zambia he would have surely heard about it by now. They would either make for Kamapanda, the nearest town to the border, or to the capital Lusaka. De Bloom had every independent air freight operator in both towns securely in his control.

He had covered the south of Zaire, of course, by stationing men in Lubumbashi and Kolwezi; and the Legion was in the area as well. Most of De Bloom's men were based in Kinshasa.

The possibilities whirled in his mind. The mercenaries hadn't turned up at their rendezvous with Roberto and Dorian in Tshikapa. There could only be two explanations: the mercenaries might have smelt a rat somehow, and be lying low; or they might have intended to double-cross Dorian and Roberto from the first.

In either case it came down to the same thing: the mercenaries would try to get out under their own steam. De Bloom tried to put himself in the position of the man who — according to Roberto and Dorian — was their leader. Davies was the name, and the operation so far certainly suggested he was good at his job.

In his place, De Bloom would try to get out via Kinshasa. The other bolt-holes were easier to block; Kinshasa was so big and chaotically-run that it offered a lot of possibilities. Besides, De Bloom thought with a flash of intuition, such a plan might appeal to a man like Davies: the safest place to hide is often the one nearest the light.

De Bloom nodded ponderously, approving his own logic. Yes, his decision to pull Reitz and his men from Tshikapa to Kinshasa had been the right one.

It had to be.

The old Afrikaaner moved with painful slowness to a door in the panelling which led to his small, luxuriously-appointed bathroom. He stripped off his jacket and tie and methodically lathered his face. He shaved with care, guiding the safety razor in and out of wrinkles and over the pouches of sagging skin.

But the routine failed to distract him from the nightmare which had been at the back of his mind for ten long days — what would happen if the stones reached the world diamond markets. He had no illusions about the loyalty of his regular dealers in Europe, America and the Middle East. They knew, only too well, that De Bloom had caused a false scarcity in the commodity to push the price up. They knew that De Blooms had all but closed their own mines because they had enough stocks in their own vaults to last them three decades — as well as lucrative concessions like the Angolan mines.

The old man shuddered at the thought of what so large a parcel of stones would do if they reached London and New York, Tel Aviv and Amsterdam. The price of diamonds would come tumbling down — and would stay there until he was dead and gone.

The razor shook in his hand as he cursed those damned mercenaries. His rage mounted: he cursed the Angolans, first for failing to guard his diamonds, and second for giving up the chase.

The trembling blade sliced sideways into the papery skin beneath the lather. An inch-long strip of blood appeared on De Bloom's throat, widening rapidly.

As he swore with even more vehemence, he felt the pains in his chest. It felt as though there were strings attached to his heart; and someone was tugging the strings with increasing violence. He fumbled in his waistcoat pocket for the phial of capsules. He shook a couple into his palm and hastily swallowed them with water. He waited, slumped against the wall and clasping his chest, praying that the pain would subside.

He couldn't die now, please God — not until he had the diamonds back. And there was so much to do.

Top of the list was the need to make those mercenaries and the Angolans wish they had never been born.

26

'Most men are in a coma when at rest, and mad when they act.'

Epicurus

De Bloom was wrong about one thing: the Angolans were not prepared to give up their forty-five kilos of diamonds and their pound of flesh without a struggle.

But they were in a difficult position. The speed of the mercenaries had taken them by surprise. The mercenaries were now known to be over the border — beyond the reach of Angolan military intervention. The Luandan authorities had no intention of invading Zaire and initiating a major war.

It was a situation which called for guile. The Angolans had mobilized three secret weapons — without telling the South Africans who would have leaked the fact to the Zairois — and sent them over the border.

The three secret weapons were now ensconced in the Palace Hotel, Kinshasa. Their names were D'asser, Rodriguez and Eloi.

The three men had reached Kinshasa three days after the Claymore mines had destroyed the pursuit column which they were leading. Three powerful reasons had encouraged their superiors to select them for the mission. They were highly-trained in all branches of war, including — thanks to Colonel Ghaddafi — the undercover ones. All of them had pressing personal reasons — revenge for the loss of loved ones — to make their mission a success. Finally, they were of Portuguese extraction and only half-heartedly communists: if something went wrong, Luanda would simply deny all knowledge of their presence in Zaire.

Eloi spent most of his time in the bar of the hotel. He posed as a wealthy Portuguese, convalescing after a traffic accident. He let it be known to anyone who would listen that he had money to invest; but he implied that he wasn't looking much further than the neckline of the nearest whore.

His cover was good — so much so that Reitz, who was staying with his men in the same hotel, had no idea of the identity of the fellow guest who so often sat near him in the bar.

Rodriguez and D'asser spent most of their time upstairs. They had taken a room adjacent to the suite where the South Africans were holding Roberto under wraps. They had installed a variety of surveillance devices and were able to keep track of every word and movement in the suite next door.

The Angolans and the South Africans watched and waited. They were at the neck of the bottle through which the fish had to swim.

The days passed sluggishly into weeks.

Eloi was sitting in the hotel lobby, with the international *Herald-Tribune* spread out before him. His lips moved as he mouthed the unfamiliar words. The Libyans had insisted that every self-respecting terrorist (or rather freedom-fighter) needed a good command of English; but Eloi's progress in the subject had disappointed both himself and his instuctors.

He was just beginning to admit to himself that he was bored. They had been here nearly a fortnight now. As the bruises on his head faded, so did the excitement of the chase. His companions, he considered, had a much better deal. At least they got out every day — they had hired a battered Opel and drove out to the airport, where they took it in turns to watch the passengers. But Eloi was stuck in this air-conditioned prison, barred by his duties from investigating

Kinshasa — which was the biggest and most exciting city he had ever seen. Even the hotel's sophisticated attractions — from girls to cocktails — had palled on him. His only diversion was listening to the outpourings of the terrified Roberto in the suite next to theirs.

The young Angolan had reached the point where the high spot in his week was the hotel's weekly dance. They had a band in the poolside bar, and lots of visitors turned up to vary the monotony of the familiar faces around him.

A screech of brakes outside the hotel made him look up. A taxi had pulled up and one of the South Africans was getting out. He was in such a hurry that he forgot to pay the driver. Two other white men were in the lobby, like Eloi with newspapers on their laps. When they saw their comrade's arrival they got up and moved casually but quickly towards him and the lift.

Eloi, his paper crumpled under his arm, followed discreetly, using the main staircase. He let himself into his room and crammed the headphones over his ears. The harsh South African voices were talking excitedly — and therefore quickly. Eloi struggled to follow what they were saying. In the background he could hear sounds which he immediately associated with the cleaning of handguns; bolt actions were snapped back and forwards.

In the corner of his range of vision, the Angolan saw that their automatic telephone recorder had switched itself on: so the De Blooms men had calls to make.

There was a rush of displaced air as the door swung open. D'asser and Rodriguez were back.

Eloi gestured to D'asser who had the best English of the three of them. 'Quick. They've had news.'

As he listened, the first smile of a fortnight spread slowly across D'asser's pockmarked face.

'Start packing,' he told Eloi quietly. He paused to listen again and beckoned Rodriguez over. 'You'd better tank up the car,' he hissed. 'We're going back to N'Gili Airport — the cargo gate. But after that, it could be a long drive home.'

183

27

'Do nothing hastily but the catching of fleas.'
                                    Thomas Hardy

Davies stared at Sanderson for a moment, keeping a tight
rein on his temper. Rage was a luxury he couldn't at present
afford.

'We've been here for eight days now and I understand it's
getting on your nerves.' Davies intentionally kept his voice
low, forcing the men to strain to hear him, and thereby
lowering the temperature of the meeting by a few degrees.
'It's my opinion — and Tippett's — that we should stay
here for at least the same amount of time before we make
our move. As far as we're concerned. it's open season out
there. Everyone's queuing up to put a bullet in us.'

The mouths of the British lads twisted with disappointment; and an angry murmur began to circulate, growing
steadily louder. Sanderson started to get up, his face set and
pale.

Davies waved him back. 'You can have your say in a
moment. I know you all think I'm overreacting. Maybe.
But before you make up your minds, listen to Tippett.
Okay?'

The thickset man squatted down on his haunches. All
eyes were on the tall figure of Tippett by his side.

The explosives expert looked at his audience through narrowed eyes. 'I'm going to tell you about some of our previous jobs — where we've been closer than this to winning,
but blown it in the endgame because we were in too much of

a hurry.' He gave a few persuasive anecdotes from the past and then returned to the present, waggling a long grimy finger to emphasize his points. 'We know that some skul-duggery is on because of the bungalow and all the local Old Bill milling around. We also know that if we get caught carrying firearms here in Zaire, these guys won't fuck around wondering what to do with us. Without our shooters we won't get very far. Once they get a sniff of us, they'll be on to us like a shot — and right now we raise quite a smell. My instinct says: wait a bit longer.'

Tippett squatted down beside Davies, while Kikuji gave a rough translation of his words to his people. After that there was a pause, while the white lads muttered sullenly among themselves. Davies watched them shrewdly: Sanderson and O'Ryan, drawn together by their impatience to get out of Zaire, had become the barrack-room lawyers of the bunch.

Finally Sanderson stood up. 'Well, sir,' he said to Davies. The tension — and perhaps embarrassment — made his Somerset accent more pronounced. 'I seem to be the spokesman for us lads. We just want to say this. You've led us this far okay, no one's denying that. But we think the snags you've run into in the past are colouring your judgment now. Christ, sir — the cops left *five* days ago. We could have gone south to Kolwezi, north to Kisangani, east to Kalemie . . . or dozens of places.' He took a deep breath. 'Please, sir, let's just get home. We've got more than enough money — even without the diamonds.'

The last four words made Davies and Tippett look up sharply. Sanderson pressed home his advantage.

'Look, sir, just pay us off in cash — you keep the dia-monds. Then we'll bugger off and take our own chances.' He nodded across to the group of black soldiers. 'The other lads said they'd see us all right.'

Davies blenched inwardly at the thought of his young white mercenaries trying to survive by themselves in Zaire, even with the dubious help of their black mates. But there was no mistaking their determination. And Sanderson's point about the diamonds was an attractive one. He glanced at Tippett and saw his own feeling of resignation mirrored in his friend's face: they would have to compromise.

The mercenary leader stood up. 'Okay. Against my better judgment, we'll pull out tonight. And you can all have your money now, in case we run into complications.'

Smiles appeared on the men's faces. Davies held up a hand to forestall the storm of excited chatter which was about to burst.

'But I've got one proviso: until we're out of this together, the command structure stays as it is.'

The back of one of the trucks was turned into the operation's pay-office. The whites and then the blacks formed an orderly queue, to be paid one at a time.

Each of the mercenaries had been given half their fee before leaving the UK. Davies gave them the remaining £2,500 apiece and then delighted them with a bonus of twenty-five thousand dollars and five thousand Deutschmarks. The FNLA men were given five thousand escudos and two hundred dollars.

Tippett and Davies still had over three-quarters of the money left. Personal greed wasn't their motive; they knew it would be very expensive to get themselves and their men out of Kinshasa. The diamonds weren't negotiable at this stage.

They repacked the diamonds as efficiently as possible, and managed to cram them all into one Bergen — even leaving room for a layer of dollars on top of the rucksack. One other Bergen was stuffed to capacity with dollars.

The men and equipment were loaded into the two trucks and their trailers. Everyone worked with a will now, with discontent only a memory. Towards evening they left the hide. The little convoy drove slowly through Tshikapa without arousing anyone's interest, and took a road which climbed steeply up to an escarpment overlooking the town.

At the crest of the escarpment Tippett and Davies could tell from Kikuji's tension that here was the spot where the roadblock had been mounted. The danger-point passed in safety and the lorries began to pick up speed.

The steady beat of the engines as the trucks roared through the African night soon had a soporific effect. Soon every man in the back was asleep, with the exception of the sentries which Davies had insisted upon.

The men woke at dawn, their mouths dry and their backs sore from the rough boards. There was a new smell on the air: the stink of a city. They had reached the outskirts of Kinshasa.

Davies peered through the canvas. They were passing through the shanty-town which rimmed the city in all directions, scattering chickens and goats off the road. Everyone else appeared to be still asleep. Behind him, the men were shivering: the thin cotton shirts they wore were no protection against the cool of the African dawn.

The shanty-town gave way to more solid slums. Here and there along the sidewalks, the city's less privileged inhabitants were sleeping, wrapped in old newspapers and polythene.

José and Alessandro took them to the inevitable lorry park which every African city possesses. Davies, Tippett and Kikuji immediately left the others, leaving strict instructions with Sanderson and Manuel about the need to keep a low profile. Tippett and Davies each carried a Bergen.

Kikuji did all the talking. He bought them a couple of shirts which disguised the tops of the white men's uniforms and found them a taxi. They drove across the city which was beginning to bustle with early morning life. Kikuji directed the driver to yet another slum area. Eventually the cab pulled up outside a ten-foot-high fence of corrugated iron which had been painted red some time ago.

The three men waited until the dented Mercedes taxi had vanished around the corner. Kikuji led them to a small side gate set in the fence. He produced a small key and unlocked the heavy padlock which secured it. With a jerk of his head and flash of white teeth, he beckoned the bewildered white men to follow him in.

They were inside what appeared to be a carpenter's yard.

African hardwoods were stacked in neat piles against the fence. In front of them was a large workshop.

There were two low snarls.

The three men looked up. Three huge, beige-coloured mongrels were trotting purposefully towards them.

'Look at the bloody *size* of them, mate,' Tippett said in disbelief. His voice broke off as the dogs' speed increased. Their ears were laid hard back on their scarred, bullet-shaped heads. The great jaws gaped menacingly open.

Kikuji snapped his fingers at the approaching dogs and grinned at his companions' consternation. He called two names and the dogs were instantly transformed from vicious guards to gentle pets. With wagging tails they sniffed happily around the tall negro — and even consented to investigate cautiously the hand which Davies held out to them.

The big Nubian led them out of the sunlit yard into the workshop's darkened interior. He left them there, waiting awkwardly, while he himself vanished into a room at the back.

Ten minutes later he re-emerged with an old, grizzled man who was hastily tucking his shirt into his trousers.

'*Mon grandpère* . . .' Kikuji's arm waved back to Tippett and Davies. 'My good friends.'

Kikuji's grandfather had his grandson's smile. The introductions were soon over. The old man whisked them into his inner room and was soon piling kindling on the glowing embers of the wood-burning stove in there.

Davies and Tippett were given huge breakfasts of freshly-caught fish, sweet, new-baked bread and as many cups of coffee as they could take. While they washed and shaved, Kikuji slipped out into the town to buy them civilian clothes. When these essentials were over, the four of them sat down for a council of war.

'*Mon grandpère*,' Kikuji explained proudly, 'is very clever. He get you out.'

Davies soon realized that the old man was no fool. He suggested several ways of getting them out of the country, all of them fairly practical. He liked one scheme best of all — and so did Davies.

Even dressed as civilians, the old man argued, the white men stood out in Kinshasa. He therefore suggested that he make up some crates in his yard — and ship the whole party out as livestock.

All Davies and Tippett had to do was to find a suitable air freight firm which was capable of getting several crates of valuable livestock to Europe without asking too many questions. Once they were airborne — and out of Zairois airspace, the mercenaries could release themselves from the crates.

Having agreed on a plan, the old man lent Kikuji his ancient Land Rover while he himself began work on the crates. Davies and Tippett stayed concealed in the canvas-covered back as they drove across town. Kikuji visited one contact after another, some at their houses, others at their places of work; he also made a number of telephone calls. Finally he poked his head into the back of the Land Rover.

'Okay!' he said joyfully. 'We go to airport.'

During the drive he threw words over his shoulder, explaining where they were going. The firm he had found was a one-man-band — an owner-pilot who ran a DC3 in and around the central African states, carting anything and everything — as long as the price was right. The man was white.

At the freight entrance of N'Gili Airport, Kikuji made the usual *martarbish* payment to the security guard and drove around the dusty perimeter road until they came to a small group of rust-pitted hangars which the guard had pointed out. As the Land Rover squealed to a halt, a small black mechanic appeared from the nearest hangar, wiping his hands on his filthy overalls.

Kikuji did the talking. The mechanic sullenly directed them to a small brick building to one side of one of the hangars. The three men pushed open the door and went in.

The office was cramped, dirty and chaotically untidy. Its seediness was brilliantly backlit by the hard morning light which streamed through the large window behind the old wooden desk. The desk itself was littered with papers and scarred with the black grooves of cigarette burns.

In the centre of the desk were two feet encased in a pair of suede desert boots which had seen far better days. The owner of the feet was out of sight, tucked behind a three-day-old copy of the *Herald-Tribune*. As the three men in the doorway watched, a large muscular hand clawed its way round the paper and fumbled along the top of the desk.

Davies realized at once that it was searching for the greasy glass, half full of amber liquid, which lay partially concealed by a stack of official forms. He leant forward and noiselessly picked up the glass.

The hand became frantic, trembling slightly, as it explored the empty space where the glass had been. Abruptly, the paper was crumpled to one side, revealing a bony, unshaven face and a ragged shock of grey hair.

The owner of the face and feet uncurled himself from his chair and stood up to his full height of six foot six.

'I suppose you think that's bloody funny,' he snarled, one hand reaching across the desk towards the glass in Davies' hand.

Davies passed him the glass but said nothing. The tall man downed in a single swallow, his Adam's apple bobbing up and down in his scrawny neck.

He slammed down the glass. 'What ya want?' His voice placed him unequivocally and geographically in the land of dingos and kangaroos.

'Are you Simpson?' Davies demanded in a voice devoid of interest in the answer.

'Yeah. What of it?'

Davies pared his reply down to the bare minimum. 'You do charter work. I want to hire you — and your aircraft.'

The Australian's features sharpened as he realized he had the prospect of a charter. 'Where to?' he asked laconically. 'With what? When? Where from? And . . . how much?'

'Nine crates,' Davies snapped back in the same style, 'plus two passengers. Ex-Zaire to Cyprus. No paperwork. Tomorrow. And . . . you tell me.'

Simpson slumped back into his seat. His eyes remained

riveted on Davies' impassive face, but his right hand dragged open the top drawer of his desk. By Davies' side, Tippett stiffened. But Simpson took out not a gun but the remnants of a bottle of whisky. He opened the bottle with his teeth and poured the rest of his breakfast into his glass.

He accomplished all this without a glance at what he was doing; all the time he seemed deeply engrossed in thought. He took a long pull from the tumbler which seemingly lent him eloquence.

'It'll cost you,' he said slowly. 'And in *dollars*, not the monkey money they have around here.' He sniffed. 'Maybe . . . around twenty-five grand.'

Davies nodded. 'Okay. I'll be back with fifteen grand upfront, nine crates and two bodies. When?'

Simpson blinked, perhaps in astonishment that his terms had been so readily accepted. 'I can have all the people straightened out today. You can do it tonight, if you can move that quick.' He took another swallow which drained the glass. 'But I'll need some money to lay around here today.'

That was reasonable, Davies thought: speed, efficiency and discretion all came expensive in Zaire. But could he trust the man?

He pulled out a wad and peeled off fifty one-hundred dollar bills.

'I'd better not come back here and find you pissed, Aussie,' he said coldly. Without another word he turned and left the tiny office with the other two close behind him.

The Australian followed them outside, leaning his stringy frame against the doorpost. 'About nine then . . . Pom.'

Davies looked at the pilot for a long moment and then walked back to the Land Rover. Simpson returned to his office, kicking the door shut behind him. He resisted the temptation to send the mechanic out for a fresh bottle of whisky.

He pulled over the phone but stared at it for a few minutes without lifting the receiver. It must be them, he decided — the ones those mean-eyed South African guys were looking for. Just one phone call and the reward would be his.

Should, not *would.* The Zairois secret police had a slice of the action, and they didn't like other people to get rewards. His most likely reward would be a bullet in the side of his head. Besides, the reward offered didn't match up to the twenty-five grand which the Pom was ready to pay.

He shrugged, pushed the phone to one side and pulled over the stack of official forms. There was a lot of paperwork to get through before this evening. As he worked, he whistled — an old sentimental melody from that long-forgotten time he had spent in Vietnam.

The mechanic slipped away from the open window of the office and sprinted across the tarmac to the phone box near the main terminal building. He fumbled in the pockets of his overalls for the scrap of paper on which the tall South African had written a telephone number.

He dialled the number quickly. As he listened to the ringing at the other end, a broad smile spread over his face. Tonight would be a night to remember — he would be able to afford to wallow in the finest fleshpots of Kinshasa.

28

'When the cock is drunk, he forgets about the hawk.'
Ashanti Proverb

As the aging Land Rover bucked over the ruts at the entrance to the lorry-park, the first thing the three men saw was a crowd of Africans around their trucks.

Kikuji pulled over and braked. From a safe distance, he, Davies and Tippett tried to figure out what had happened during the few hours they had left the men alone.

Drunken voices raised in song — in *English* — wafted across the compound. There was no sign of Kikuji's FNLA troopers. The Africans around the trucks were the usual civilian crowd of market traders, truckers and random passers-by.

'Bloody hell,' said Davies in a tight voice. 'The blacks are out on the town but they brought back some booze for their white mates first.'

The combination of ten days cooped up in the bush and money to spend had proved irresistible.

'Kikuji,' Davies snapped, 'get Alessandro and José. We've got to act *fast*.'

The black nodded. With seeming casualness he strolled over to the lorries. He got up on the toe step of the nearest one and rapped on the window of the cab. A few seconds later the drivers emerged and staggered over to the Land Rover.

Davies watched them dispassionately. They had had no sleep last night, but there was more than weariness in the way they walked; the stupid bastards had been drinking as well.

Shielded by the canvas back of the Land Rover, Davies undid the top of Tippett's rucksack and pulled out a bundle of dollars. He swiftly paid the two shamefaced drivers, and then asked how much they would take for the lorry which held the white men, without its accompanying trailer.

The drivers looked at one another and shrugged. Davies lost patience. He held up the rest of the bundle and raised his eyebrows.

Alessandro, seeing enough dollars to buy several Rolls-Royces, nodded stupidly. Davies thrust the wad in his breast pocket and told him to undo the draw-bar which held the lorry to its trailer.

Under the watchful eyes of Tippett and Davies, the two Portuguese struggled clumsily with the heavy A-shaped bar and the air hoses between the trailer and the truck. The singing had stopped — one of the white lads had seen Davies through a split in the canvas covering the back of the lorry. The crowd of Africans, sensing that the fun was over, drifted regretfully away. Kikuji, meanwhile, had left the compound to buy paint and brushes.

When Kikuji returned, he loaded his purchases into the Land Rover. Davies and Tippett walked over to the truck and climbed into the cab. Davies started the engine and followed the Land Rover out of the compound.

Kikuji led them out of the city and took a minor road which brought them, twenty minutes later, into dense scrubland. When the vehicles were safely off the road, Davies leapt out of the cab and strode to the back of the lorry.

He ripped aside the canvas sheet and stared at the white, befuddled faces inside, their eyes blinking in the sudden light.

'Right,' Davies shouted. 'Everybody out. You've all got a lot of work to do. And if that doesn't sober you up, the toe of my fucking boot will. Now *move!*'

The nine men tumbled over the sacks of coffee beans and

194

leapt awkwardly on to the hard ground beneath — with all the grace, Davies thought, of a flock of sheep going through a gap in a fence.

He grabbed O'Ryan and Brown who happened to be nearest. 'You two,' he snapped, 'will paint the front of the truck — and you'd better make it look good.' He gave them both a shove which sent them sprawling. 'The rest of you drunken cunts will unload this coffee. Then you will strip down the whole of this back end — sides, roof and tail. Now *get moving.*'

In the next two hours, the drunken men burned the alcohol out of their systems, lashed constantly by Davies' tongue. The grey, high-sided lorry vanished: in its place was a gleaming yellow flatbed truck.

Tippett provided the final touch when he replaced the Zairois number plate with a Zambian one he had lifted from the lorry-park while the Portuguese were uncoupling the trailer.

The heavy canvas had now been rolled and folded across the four forty-gallon drums which were lashed against the lorry's headboard. Five of the lads had just finished with the economy-size tin of boot-blacking; their faces and arms were stained a deep mahogany brown. Cotton shirts and straw hats completed their disguise. Their appearance should be good enough to fool anyone who saw them riding on the back of the lorry.

The other four lads were crammed into the lorry's sleeper cab, two to a bunk, with the curtains closed. No one was going to have a comfortable ride, but Davies couldn't care less.

They had achieved the main thing: the lorry looked like the average truck which trundled through that part of Africa; and it bore no resemblance to that grey, high-sided lorry whose description had probably been memorized by every traffic policeman in Kinshasa.

The Land Rover and the truck manoeuvred their way out of the bush. Davies glanced back once, at the jumbled heap of coffee sacks, sectional sides and struts. Beneath that pile

195

were all the group's weapons. The only 'tools' they had were three hand-guns, which Davies, Tippett and Kikuji had concealed under their shirts.

Kikuji led them back to the shanty-town around Kinshasa. He threaded a way through lesser thoroughfares until they reached his grandfather's carpentry yard. Minutes later, the truck and its human cargo was safe inside.

Once in the yard, Davies had a few words with Kikuji about the missing black section of their diminutive army. The big Nubian was obviously worried about their absence, but accepted that the rest of them had to be realistic about it; his men had made their own choice, despite orders, and would have to take the consequences.

On thing worried Davies. If the FNLA men were tortured by the secret police, would they reveal the location of the carpentry yard?

Kikuji shook his head. 'No one know *mon grandpère*. What they not know, they cannot tell.'

Davies sighed with relief and walked over to greet Kikuji's grandfather. The old man's face broke into a gummy, toothless smile. He insisted on shaking hands again with his grandson and the two white leaders. His hand was withered but still firm. With a sideways jerk of his head he indicated the nine crates which stood in a row. The air of the workshop was heavy with the sweet smell of freshly-sawn timber.

Tippett called the lads out of the truck. They gathered round while Davies demonstrated how the crates would be used. Each man would have his own box. The lids would be nailed down in the yard, using short nails for the purpose. Then the crates would be wrapped round with a heavy band of plastic. Everyone would be supplied with a hacksaw blade. Once they were safely airborne — *and only then* — they could poke the saws through the slats of the lids and cut through the plastic. The nails were so short they could simply lever themselves out of the crates.

Sanderson raised a hand. 'There's only nine crates, sir. Are you travelling with us as passengers?'

Then Davies dropped his bombshell.

'No. Tippett and me are making other arrangements. But we'll see you on the plane.'

Davies and Tippett had come to their decision while the lorry was being transformed. Cyprus wasn't the best place to arrive with a rucksack of diamonds. Simpson was expecting to take them on the plane, but the two older men had in mind a slower but safer means of exit which had been suggested by Kikuji's grandfather.

'What will we *do* when we get to Cyprus?' O'Ryan's face was worried. He was the sort of lad who constantly fought against authority but found it difficult to survive without it.

'That's up to you,' said Davies crisply. 'You can take a regular flight home. If you fancy some more fighting, you can always go and sign up with the Phalangists in Beirut.'

'Screw that!' said an anonymous voice from the back of the group. The men lost some of their tension; and there were a few snorts of laughter.

But Davies hadn't finished with them yet. 'Remember, you're not safe yet, not by a long chalk. If they're any more cock-ups like this morning's, we'll wash our hands of you. You can walk home for all I care.' He underlined the warning: 'Remember your black mates? Kikuji reckons they'll all be in custody by the end of the day. Some of them may have been tortured to death already.' Davies looked at Sanderson who failed to meet his eyes. 'Their blood is on the hands of those who didn't stop that drinking bout.'

The yard became very silent. Davies told them curtly that they would be off in a couple of hours. He warned them to empty their bladders and bowels before they left — they could be stuck in the crates for hours. With that he turned on his heel and joined Tippett and the two Africans in the back room.

As they smoked and drank coffee, the old man answered Davies' questions about his younger brother, Kikuji's great uncle. The brother owned a boatyard in Matadi, a town far downstream near the sea. He built large, ocean-going yachts for an American firm which tacked on their own nameplates and sold them on the lucrative transatlantic pleasure market.

197

Yes, the old man confirmed with the suspicion of a wink, his brother was always looking for reliable men to help crew the boats across the Atlantic for delivery in Florida.

Davies and Tippett looked at one another. The prospect of an ocean cruise seemed very attractive after the rigours they had experienced on land.

Kikuji slipped away in the early evening, taking the Land Rover. He drove through the crowded streets to the lorry-park. The remaining lorry and the two trailers were concealed by other trucks. He left the Land Rover and picked his way on foot through the crowded compound.

His heart sank when he realized that there was an impromptu street party in progress around Alessandro's truck. Raucous singing was interspersed with wild whoops. There were several taxis in the vicinity, suggesting that the FNLA men had decided to return in style and share the fun with their white friends. The absence of the latter didn't seem to have put a damper on the proceedings.

The crowd in front of him shifted. The tall Nubian caught a brief glimpse of Manuel, supported by a whore on one side and a cab-driver on the other. Another soldier had upended a bottle over Manuel's open mouth. The flaring light of a nearby Tilley lamp showed the palm spirit cascading down the front of his shirt.

Not all of Kikuji's men were there: probably they had already been picked up. He could do nothing about the rest of them — it was already far too late.

There were men in mirrored sunglasses and bright shirts moving through the crowd towards the truck which was the focus of the party. The circle of secret police was tightening like a noose around the FNLA revellers.

Kikuji walked quickly back to the Land Rover, trying to shrug off his bitterness. One thing was clear: he no longer had any military responsibilities to worry about.

29

'The last hurdle is sometimes the highest.'
Source unknown

The truck pulled out of the carpenter's yard just after eight o'clock. The nine crates were neatly stacked on the back, and covered with a tarpaulin. Tippett and Davies rode with Kikuji in the cab.

Davies fought to control his mounting tension by concentrating on the outside world. The lorry's headlights picked out the glowing eyes of cats and dogs. Pedestrians scurried along the garbage-strewn sidewalks, moving furtively because the darkness around them held knife-wielding muggers. There were no streetlamps in the shanty-town, only the occasional Tilley lamp — huge glow-worms, each surrounded by its complement of black faces and white eyes.

Davies shivered. Beyond those circles of light was the African night — and the African night was always full of unseen dangers.

The stench — from mountains of rubbish, unswept storm drains and the open sewage trenches — was so unbearable that Davies rolled up his window. But the smell remained, whatever he did. It was a relief when the truck reached the more permanent part of the city.

Here, there was rudimentary street-lighting, supplemented by the constant stream of car-lights. Most of the cars were convertibles, with their sound-systems adding an aural dimension to the chaos of Kinshasa. Everyone seemed to be out on the street — either selling pleasure or in search of it.

As the truck pulled up at a small intersection, Davies nudged Tippett in the ribs. 'Know what, mate? In the last hundred yards I've counted fifty-three hookers on my side of the road alone.'

Tippett grinned. 'There must be one hell of a demand.'

The lighting grew even patchier as they neared the airport. Davies breathed a sigh of relief when he saw they were driving along the heavy chain-link fence, topped with barbed wire, which surrounded the perimeter of the airfield. Kikuji pulled up at the end of the queue of vehicles at the cargo entrance.

Once the usual *martarbish* had changed hands, the truck drove down the darkened road which led to Simpson's hangar. Kikuji slowed as the hangar came into view, allowing Tippett and Davies to slip out of the passenger side of the truck and drop on to the grass verge. No one saw them.

The two mercenaries jogged after the truck, angling away from it to bring them behind the hangar. It was just a precaution, Davies told himself: you could never be too sure in this game.

The shining DC3 had been pulled out of the hangar and was waiting on the cracked concrete with its cargo doors wide open. A solitary, fly-encrusted lamp burned over the hangar's doorway.

Simpson and four Africans in blue overalls sauntered out of the hangar. Kikuji handed the Australian his money and explained that the two passengers would not be coming. Davies and Tippett watched from the shadows.

The four cargo-handlers were already at work. They untied the tarpaulin and slid the crates one after the other into the aircraft.

Davies whispered in Tippett's ear: 'We may as well come out. It's on the level and — '

He broke off suddenly. There were running feet inside the hangar. The engine of a Land Rover was started and gunned forward. Five white men burst out of the hangar,

200

three on foot and two in the Land Rover. Three of them flung themselves on Kikuji; the other two — the taller of whom was carrying a handgun and appeared to be giving the orders — pushed Simpson into the plane and climbed in after him. The cargo-handlers melted into the surrounding darkness with a speed which suggested that they had been expecting something like this to happen. The other three men bundled Kikuji into the Land Rover and drove to the front of the DC3.

The old plane's engines coughed into life. The Land Rover moved off, with the plane trundling sedately behind it.

Davies and Tippett wasted no time discussing the situation. Both of them had already drawn their handguns. Now they moved in pursuit of the disappearing aircraft, keeping to the shadows of the grass verge.

Fifty yards later they dived to the ground.

Behind them was the engine of another car, moving quietly and without lights. *Shit!* Davies thought. *The team ahead have got a rear-guard as well.*

But the three men in the hired Opel were nobody's rear-guard. Rodriguez was at the wheel, keeping a safe distance behind the navigational lights on the plane's tail fin. When the plane stopped, he pulled the Opel over onto the grass verge, half-burying it in the knee high grass. He angled the car away from the lights ahead, to minimize the risk of reflections from the Opel's chrome betraying their presence.

D'asser was out of the car at once, straining to see what was happening. He ducked down and spoke through the open window:

'All five of the South Africans are there. They've pulled nine whites out of the plane — plus that black and the pilot. They've taken them into that low building by the plane. I think it's on loan from the secret police.'

'Come on,' said Rodriguez.

The three Angolans walked silently through the grass

201

towards their prey — unaware that they themselves were being tailed. D'asser was mentally computing the odds against them. He knew from their surveillance of the South African's suite that the Zairois secret police hadn't been informed. There were sixteen men in the hut — but only five of them were armed. And the Angolans had surprise on their side.

They had settled their plan of attack in the car. Rodriguez and D'asser worked their way around the sides of the building, while Eloi remained in the shadows at the front. As they had expected, the white racists from the south mounted a guard on the door once they were safely inside with their prisoners.

Eloi stepped forward into the puddle of light which spread out from the doorway. He took a few steps, weaving like a drunk and waving his arms to show that his hands were empty. 'Hey, man, you got a drink? I want to join the party in there.'

The two South Africans moved out of the shelter of the doorway to grab the unarmed Latin. Rodriguez and D'asser seized their victims from behind. Their movements were as synchronized as dancers': one hand gripped a South African's windpipe, to shut off the death-screams, while the other drove a highly-honed knife between the ribs.

It was over in seconds. The blades slid into the hearts of the guards and sliced them open with the efficiency of a butcher's knife. The Angolans removed the knives with brutal tugs. The South Africans slipped to the ground. For and instant they struggled feebly. Then they lay still.

'Bring up the car,' D'asser hissed to Eloi. 'But move the bodies into the shadows first. We're going in.'

The two mercenaries crouched in the grass, trying to make sense of the bewildering scene before them. The tall young Latin was dragging a corpse round the side of the building, leaving a trail of crimson slime. The dead man was white — but Davies and Tippett knew it couldn't be one of their men, because the body wore a light-blue bomber jacket.

202

Christ! Davies realized in a flash — *the men from the car aren't with the other whites. We've got two sets of men after us and the diamonds!*

There was not a second to lose. The mercenaries sprinted across the concrete and took cover behind the aircraft. The tall young man returned and began to drag away a second corpse; Davies recognized the body as that of one of the men who had seized Kikuji.

The Latin reappeared at the front of the building, wiping his hands. Davies stepped into the pool of light around the entrance with his handgun levelled.

The man's dark eyes widened in shock. His hands began to rise above his head.

At that moment Tippett hit him from behind with the butt of his pistol. The Latin slumped to the ground. Tippett clubbed him again to make doubly sure that he was unconscious, and dragged him into the shadows where the corpses lay.

Davies inched open the door. He could see a short brightly-lit corridor. He was just in time to see two men bursting through the door at the end and into the room beyond.

The mercenary beckoned Tippett to follow him. The two Englishmen slipped silently into the corridor. A radio was on in the room at the end, blaring out the Congo version of the Top Twenty. The building's smell was familiar to Davies: he sniffed cautiously. Disinfectant covered something else — blood, perhaps, and urine and faeces.

The stench of fear — this was a place where men were tortured and slaughtered.

Suddenly the raucous music was punctuated by three flat cracks, followed by a tearing sound like splintering furniture. Then there were four more cracks.

Fearing the worst, Tippett and Davies cocked their handguns and burst through the door in a long, lethal dive. They rolled to their feet with their guns covering the men in front of them.

The scene which met them would not have been out of place in Auschwitz, or even the dungeons of the Spanish Inquisition. Eight of the English lads dangled from one of the iron girders which spanned the ceiling. Their wrists had been handcuffed over the beam while they stood on chairs; then the chairs had been kicked away.

The ninth lad was on the floor, his face a mask of agony and his knees a double mess of blood and splintered bone. The face was so contorted that Davies only recognized O'Ryan with difficulty.

The Irishman was writhing on the concrete floor — but his struggles were silent; sticking-plaster had been taped across his mouth.

Along the left-hand wall of the room were two bodies, their limbs jumbled together and tangled with broken chairs. Great gouts of their blood had spurted on to the white-washed wall behind them.

Besides Davies and Tippett, only three men were on their feet in the smoke-filled room. One was a tall white man with slate-grey eyes, the leader of the five in the hangar; he stood at O'Ryan's head, his hands in the air. Facing him were the two swarthy-skinned companions of the tall lad whom Tippett had clubbed outside. Both of them carried handguns.

'Don't even think of moving,' Tippett snapped at them. 'Just drop those guns.'

But Tippett didn't know Rodriguez — or the spur which drove him on towards revenge. The tall man swivelled, bringing up his pistol, his face contorted with a rictus of hate.

Tippett was too quick for him. He pumped a bullet into the Angolan's head. Rodriguez' shot went wild, chipping harmless fragments of brick from the wall. The Angolan fell backwards and joined O'Ryan on the floor.

The shots reverberated round the room. There was a thud as the smaller Angolan, D'asser, dropped his hand-gun. Tippett moved forwards like a striking snake. While Davies covered him, he jammed his pistol into Reitz' ribs and spun him face forwards to the wall. He repeated the exercise with D'asser. Then he kicked each man's legs wide apart and pulled them so their bodies leant against the wall at

204

an angle of almost 45°.

Davies spoke for the first time: 'Where are the pilot and the black?' He emphasized the question with a jab of the pistol barrel which jarred against Reitz' rib-cage.

'They're in the room on the right of the door . . . man.' Reitz' voice held an inflection of derision.

'I'll go and get them.' Tippett left the room. He returned a moment later with the ashen-faced Simpson and the smiling Kikuji. Both were handcuffed, but neither of them had been seriously hurt. That, Davies guessed, would have come later.

Davies frisked the South African and found the keys of the handcuffs and a stiletto knife in his trouser belt. Reitz continued to smile — with all the insufferable disdain of one who believes he belongs to the master race. Davies felt his own anger bubbling up; his face whitened with rage.

Tippett touched his arm. 'Not yet, mate. We need some answers first.' He freed Kikuji and Simpson, and told them to get the eight lads down from their girder.

The first one down was Sanderson. He pulled the sticking-plaster from his mouth, ignoring the pain. 'That South African bastard just shot Jack. Kill him, Tom, kill him — or give me the gun and I'll do it.'

Davies clubbed away the outstretched hand of the over-wrought youngster. 'I'll do what's necessary,' he snapped. 'You help get the rest of the lads down — and behave yourself.'

Davies' controlled voice had the intended effect: Sanderson's hysteria subsided and he meekly took the bunch of keys which Kikuji held out to him.

The big Nubian dropped to his knees beside O'Ryan and released the hands and mouth of the injured lad. Soon his screams were mingling with the Top Twenty. With surprising gentleness, Kikuji split the seams of the Irish-man's trousers and examined what was left of his knees. He glanced up at Davies and a wordless message passed between them.

This lad would never walk again.

Three more of the mercenaries had now been released.

'Get outside,' Davies told them. 'You'll find three bodies — two dead and one alive — round the side of this building. Bring 'em in.'

Davies turned back to the South African. 'Now, cunt,' he said tightly, 'just what the hell are you — ?'

A particularly agonized shriek from O'Ryan momentarily diverted the mercenary's attention. Reitz, who had half-turned when Davies spoke to him, saw his chance and seized it. His arm slashed down in a desperate lunge towards the mercenary's handgun.

Davies sidestepped. Another shot rang out. A new, harsher scream joined O'Ryan's.

Reitz spun round and collapsed, both hands clamped round his shattered knee-cap. Blood spurted through his fingers and profanities through his teeth. His iron will made a supreme effort: he fell silent and glared at Davies with hooded, bloodshot eyes.

'Well, yarpie,' said Davies pleasantly. 'How does it feel when it's done to you?' He could sense the overwhelming hatred in those eyes — and realized that only death would ever assuage it. 'Tell me, what are the South Africans doing in this?'

Reitz remained silent.

Davies kicked the wounded man on his helpless leg. 'Come on, cunt. Answer me. Do you want to lose your other knee?'

When Reitz' gasps subsided, he shook his head. 'All right,' he groaned, 'I'll — '

The three young mercenaries burst back into the room, cutting off what the South African was saying. Brown was in the lead, his face dead-white beneath the freckles.

'Christ, sir, the bloke who was alive has hopped it. A car without lights drove off fast, maybe fifty yards back along the way we came.'

Davies swore beneath his breath and glanced at Tippett. There was no time for interrogations now. They would have to move fast. He nodded at Simpson.

'You still on, Aussie?'

206

The pilot pulled a brown envelope from his pocket. 'Been paid, ain't I?'

Davies unbuttoned the map pocket on his trousers and drew out a slim sheaf of hundred dollar notes. 'Get pissed on me — in Limassol.'

Simpson grinned. 'You betcha. Who's coming for the ride?'

Tippett, Davies and Kikuji quickly organized the evacuation of the building. Reitz was carried outside and handcuffed to the rear of his own Land Rover. D'asser, who had remained silent throughout, was also cuffed, and placed between Tippett and Kikuji.

Minutes later the engines of the DC3 spluttered into life. The control tower gave it clearance and, with the nine young mercenaries on board, it taxied down to the runway. Soon afterwards the silver bird was clawing for height above the twinkling lights of Kinshasa.

The lads began to relax inside the vibrating fuselage. They had not bothered to return to the crates. The last few hours caught up with them: the combination of alcoholic haze, hard work and sheer, unadulterated terror had made them all think twice about on-the-job drinking.

One-by-one they dozed off as the hypnotic noises of the engines dulled their thinking. Soon, only one of them was still awake. O'Ryan moaned softly on the makeshift stretcher: even tiredness and morphine couldn't disguise the face that he would never walk straight again.

Far below, several pairs of eyes were following the DC3 as it climbed higher in the night sky.

Davies and Tippett exchanged glances of relief: the responsibilities of looking after the mercenary kindergarten class were at last off their shoulders. They could get down to the serious business of life now — saving themselves and two rucksacks full of loot.

Many of the inhabitants of Kinshasa and neighbouring Brazzaville watched the lights of the plane. There was hope in their eyes and despair in their hearts. The people in that plane were fortunate enough to be able to leave the country.

Down by the gate to the passenger terminal, someone else watched the DC3, with neither relief nor envy in his heart. Eloi's head was still aching from the blows which the tall Englishman had given him. Nevertheless, there was a smile on his face which widened as the DC3 climbed higher. The smile became a grin — and abruptly broke up as a strangely-girlish giggle burst out of him.

The Libyans would be pleased with him, he thought — especially those instructors with American accents who had taught him his special subject, the art of the booby-trap. There had just been time to install the little grey box on the aircraft, concealed by one of the crates, while the British were busy in the building.

Eloi closed his eyes and visualized the scene within the aircraft. In his imagination he focused on the black dial of the altimeter with its tiny illuminated needle rotating as the DC3 gained height.

He turned his attention, still in his imagination, to the other needle on the little grey box, pre-set for five thousand feet. When the plane reached that height, the time clock inside the box would whirr quietly into action.

Ten minutes later, the bomb would explode, blowing off the entire tail-section of the DC3.

30

'He that plants thorns must never expect to gather
roses.'

Fables of Bidpai

Eloi moved cautiously through the interrogation cell. It now
resembled an abattoir — and it smelled like one as well. He
found the body of Rodriguez but searched in vain for
D'asser.

The tears ran down his face as he emptied Rodriguez' pockets. Eloi was consoled only by his mistaken belief that all the
mercenaries had left in the DC3 — and would be dead in a
few short minutes. The absence of D'asser and Reitz puzzled
him. Maybe Reitz had captured D'asser — or vice versa.
Maybe they had even joined forces. Maybe . . .

Eloi shrugged. There was no clear-cut answer. All he could
do was return to the hotel and wait for D'asser to contact him.

The exaltation of his achievement fell away from him. He
felt as if he had been unjustly deserted by his friends. He stood
up, skidding slightly on the blood-slick beneath his feet, and
walked quickly out of the building to the Opel.

Everything seemed insubstantial — even revenge. Only
two facts remained: he was alone, and in a strange and hostile
country.

The Land Rover bounced along the rutted road from the airport to the city. Davies felt almost buoyant. The lads were out
of the way; their pursuers were out in the open — and had
been given a bloody nose into the bargain. The only problem

was that young Latin who had legged it in the Opel.

Tippett turned round and looked at Davies, who was sitting beside Reitz in the back. 'How's old peg-leg getting on?' he asked with cheerful brutality, nodding at Reitz.

Davies shook the arm of the semi-conscious South African; his wound and the lurching of their vehicle had brought Reitz to the borders of oblivion.

'Wake up, yarpie.' He kept the automatic pistol trained on his prisoner's midriff. 'You still haven't answered my questions.'

Reitz groaned, shaking his head like a punch-drunk boxer. He wriggled in the seat, trying to bring his lean frame into a more comfortable position. He clasped his cuffed hands just above his shattered knee, as if he was trying to hold back the pain from the rest of his body.

Davies prodded him with the gun. 'Come on.'

'Well, Brit . . . I represent De Blooms . . . we have the diamond concession in Angola.' The clipped South African accent spat out the words with difficulty, but Reitz ignored the pain. 'Very, *very* simply — you thick English bastard — we want those diamonds back. They can't be allowed to — '

The Land Rover hit a series of pot-holes and Reitz arched back in his seat. Pain surged up from his leg; the muscles on his neck and along his jawbone stood out like knotted rope. Gradually the worst of the agony ebbed.

The South African gritted his teeth and continued. 'If such a large parcel of stones hit the world market . . . it would ruin diamond prices for the next twenty years.'

Davies shrugged, the movement sending tremors of pain up the man beside him. 'There's not much you can do about it, is there?' He waved his gun towards the small man with the pockmarked face, sandwiched between Tippett and Kikuji. 'And just who the fuck is that? Where does he fit in?'

Reitz relaxed slightly. 'I've never seen the little bastard before tonight. Nor his pal. They don't work for De Blooms, that's for sure.' His eyes travelled back to Davies' face. 'But I tell you this, man.' Pain and hatred sharpened his accent. 'After I've killed you, he'll be next.'

Davies tapped the gun-butt thoughtfully on Reitz' damaged knee. 'I haven't finished with you yet, *Afrikaner*,' he said with a heavy imitation of Reitz' South African accent.

Tippett broke into the tension which spiralled between the two men in the back. 'Are you saying,' he asked Reitz, 'that if we flood the market with that parcel of stones, the price will come plummeting down?'

Reitz nodded wordlessly.

'And when will this happen?' Tippett pressed.

'Right away.' The South African gathered strength. 'You'll knock the bottom out of your own market — you won't make anything like the profit you anticipate. And you'll have another problem. There's a man in Jo'burg who practically owns Africa. You can kill me, but old De Bloom will find a hundred men to put in my place. The local secret police are in our pocket. Your marketing men won't be able to help you — '

'What?' said Davies.

Reitz gave a thin smile, happy to have the opportunity to display the omnipotence of De Blooms. 'Roberto is under arrest. Dorian died . . . under interrogation, you might say.'

Davies and Tippett stared at one another, too stunned to speak.

'Your only option,' continued Reitz, 'is to return the stones. Otherwise De Blooms will squash you out of existence.' A gasp of pain interrupted him. 'And, Brit . . . ' His voice seemed more remote now, closer to unconsciousness. 'You know . . . you can't afford to kill me . . . I'm your only way out.'

Another pot-hole jolted Reitz against the aluminium side of the Land Rover. He shrieked and lost consciousness.

Tippett gave a bitter sigh. 'It seems to me that you and I are just fated not to become rich. Every time we get our hands on a fortune, there always seems to be a fucking good reason to dump it before we can spend it.'

Davies looked up. 'You believe what he said, then?

211

About Dorian and Roberto being captured?'

'We've got to — otherwise he wouldn't even know their names. And it sounds as if Dorian told him everything before he croaked it.'

Davies nodded dumbly. De Bloom's entry had changed the whole picture.

'What I want to know,' Tippett said, 'is who this is.' He stuck his elbow into the little man on the seat beside him.

Davies shrugged. 'Ask him.'

'Please,' said the small man with a sudden turn of his head, 'take me to the Angolan embassy.'

Shit! Davies thought *the man talks English — he will have understood everything.* He reached over the back of the seat and felt in the Angolan's inside pocket. He pulled out a thin green passport.

'He's Angolan all right.' Davies flicked the passport open and struggled to read the name inside by the street-lights. 'His name's . . . D'asser.'

Kikuji slammed on the brakes without warning. Ignoring the honking traffic behind him, he pulled over to the kerb. His cheerful face had turned into a mask of hate.

The African seized D'asser by the throat and shook him like a terrier shakes a rat. All the time he repeated a question, in a language which neither of the Englishmen understood. Eventually he got a reply — a single word:

'D'asser.'

The Nubian gunned the Land Rover away from the kerb and drove to his grandfather's yard. There was no conversation. Tippett and Davies realized that Kikuji had some pressing reason for his behaviour; he would explain it in his own good time.

When they were safe behind the tall red fence, Kikuji leapt out, dragging D'asser behind him. He pulled the small man into the workshop and picked up a roll of wire. He bound D'asser's feet together, spun him on to his stomach and tied the man's cuffed hands to his feet.

Only then did Kikuji turn to his friends. 'He' — he indicated D'asser with a spurt of spittle — 'kill my father . . .

212

my baby sister . . . my mother . . .'

Gradually Davies and Tippett decoded the African's halting words and got an accurate picture of what had happened. D'asser was reputed to have committed more atrocities in the Angolan civil war than anyone else on either side. He had tortured Kikuji's family in an attempt to make his father reveal the whereabouts of his son — then a twenty-year-old buck with the FNLA. When Kikuji's father refused to speak, D'asser had thrown the baby on to a fire.

'I kill D'asser tonight,' said the huge black, 'me and *mon grandpère*. You kill the tall white man too?'

Davies shook his head — with some regret. 'We have to let him go — once we've found a safe place to release him.'

If Kikuji thought this strange, he made no comment. He would no more question the actions of Davies and Tippett than they would his.

The old man appeared in the doorway of the back-room, his smile fading as he saw the two captives on the floor.

Kikuji kicked the Angolan and looked at his grandfather with the light of anticipation in his eyes. 'D'asser,' he said quietly.

The two Brits carried the unconscious Reitz into the back-room and laid him on the old man's bed. Davies examined the wound. It was still bleeding. He bound a tourniquet round Reitz' thigh and found an old blanket to cover him.

He and Tippett sat down at the table with a pot of coffee between them. They ignored the muffled screams behind them: they knew they would have a long wait before Kikuji finished his business with D'asser. Right now their priority was survival — and the hope of snatching some financial gain from the disaster.

It was a long night. Several hours later, Tippett and Davies pulled out the rucksacks from their hiding-place beneath a stack of timber. One Bergen held the rest of the currency, plus about five kilos of what seemed — to the inexperienced eyes of the mercenaries — to be the most promising stones.

The other Bergen, stuffed to the brim with something like forty kilos of diamonds, they would give to Reitz. They would tell the South African that the currency and the other diamonds had been swallowed by the swamp on the border.

It was, they calculated, a chance worth taking. Reitz and De Bloom would be so delighted to have the vast majority of the diamonds back that they would be unlikely to worry about the rest.

The first streaks of dawn were just appearing when Kikuji and his grandfather came into the room. Kikuji gave a tired smile. All he said was:

'It is finished.'

An hour later Kikuji drove the Land Rover out of the yard. In the back were Tippett and Davies, with the blind-folded Reitz squashed between them. Reitz had agreed to call off the Zairois secret police and withdraw the South Africans, in return for the Bergen full of stones. He appeared to believe the Brits' story about losing the rest.

Davies had an uneasy feeling that he hadn't seen the last of Jan Reitz.

Kikuji had come up with the solution of the problem of dumping Reitz in safety. He drove to a seedy hotel in the centre of town. He hired a room on the ground floor. Tippett and Davies helped Reitz inside. They handcuffed him to the iron bedstead and left the rucksack in the flimsy wardrobe.

They took the road west out of Kinshasa. After a couple of kilometres, Kikuji stopped to make a phone call. He telephoned the offices of the official De Bloom representative in Kinshasa, and advised the startled receptionist to pay a visit to room 14 of the Hotel President.

'Mr Reitz is there,' he said. There was a gasp at the other end. 'You know where the hotel is? It's the one just next door to the hospital.'

By midday the Land Rover was two hundred kilometres closer to the town of Matadi and the uncle who made ocean-going yachts. Kikuji hummed an African pop song as he drove, beating time with his left foot.

Tippett rasped the stubble on his chin. 'Think I should grow a beard?' he asked Davies. 'Make me look sort of naval, right?'

Davies shrugged, hardly hearing the question. There was a piece of unfinished business on his mind: Reitz.

THE END

CHICKENHAWK
by Robert Mason

A stunning book about the right stuff in the wrong war.

As a child, Robert Mason dreamed of levitating. As a young man, he dreamed of flying helicopters – and the U.S. Army gave him his chance. They sent him to Vietnam where, between August 1965 and July 1966, he flew more than 1,000 assault missions. In CHICKENHAWK, Robert Mason gives us a devastating bird's-eye-view of that war in all its horror, as he experiences the accelerating terror, the increasingly desperate courage of a man 'acting out the role of a hero long after he realises that the conduct of the war is insane' says the New York Times, 'And we can't stop ourselves from identifying with it.'

'CHICKENHAWK is one bloody, painfully honest and courageous book'
Martin Cruz Smith, author of GORKY PARK

'Compelling . . . a hypnotic narrative'
New York Times

'It will stun readers'
Time Magazine

0 552 12419 2 £2.95

LET A SOLDIER DIE
by William E. Holland

'Whether avenging angels or angels of mercy, helicopters are what made Vietnam's tactics so different from every previous war's . . . LET A SOLDIER DIE is the best and most thought-provoking book so far about a chopper pilot's life over there. Holland's book flies'
C D B Bryan, author of FRIENDLY FIRE and BEAUTIFUL WOMEN, UGLY SCENES

LET A SOLDIER DIE is a searing story of war, of war machines and the men who fly them, and of one brilliant young flier grown old before his time in the valleys of death. Sitting in his helicopter above Vietnam's green fields, the man known to his friends as the Bear never has to touch the people he's killing, or even think of them as human. Never, that is, until the day a group of GIs wander into a fire zone, and find themselves on the wrong end of the awesome fire-power of US gunships.

Bear and his companions have to retrieve the wounded and the dead. Because of that day, Bear begins to hesitate. And in a war where nothing is ever certain, that hesitation can – and eventually does – kill men and women Bear knows, loves and respects.

LET A SOLDIER DIE is a novel that takes the war on its own terms – the sights and sounds, the unending fear, the awful beauty and the enormous and instantaneous cruelty and violence. It is a novel that ranks with the very best war novels of any time, and which will take its place alongside CHICKENHAWK, THE 13TH VALLEY, FIELDS OF FIRE and GOING AFTER CACCIATO as the finest writing to have ever been produced by the Vietnam war.

0 552 12659 4   £2.50

THE FIVE FINGERS
by Gayle Rivers and James Hudson

Seven men – crack special services operatives – code name
THE FIVE FINGERS. Their mission: assassinate eleven
top-ranking Chinese and Vietnamese leaders, including the
notorious General Giap, Chief of Staff.

They were to have no military support, no radio contact with
their despatchers, nothing to rely on but their own considerable expertise in small arms and explosives. They was to be no
capture, no surrender. They were alone in the steamy jungles
of Laos and Vietnam. Once in China, their mission had no
closure. There would be no rescue operation . . .

0 552 10954 1   £1.95

THE WAR MAGICIAN
by David Fisher

More thrilling than fiction – the true story of how Jasper Maskelyne and his Magic Gang altered the course of World War II.

'The outbreak of the 1939 war, foretelling inevitable misery to everyone, meant different things to different people. For me, it involved something very strange and rather alarming – the focusing of my whole imagination and knowledge on how best to mobilize the world of magic against Hitler.'
Jasper Maskelyne

Jasper Maskelyne was drinking a glass of razor blades on a London stage when World War II began. Shortly thereafter he was working before a different audience – Rommel's Afrika Korps – is one of the most extraordinary true adventures to emerge from the war. With a hand-picked group of men known as The Magic Gang, Maskelyne secretly conducted one of the strangest campaigns in the recorded history of warfare.

Using the technique of stage magic, Maskelyne and The Magic Gang confounded Rommel with the most incredible array of illusions and special effects ever produced on a battlefield.

* They hid the Suez Canal. * They moved Alexandria Harbour. * They turned tanks into trucks. * They created an entire army out of shadow, launched a phantom fleet of submarines and a 700-foot battleship. * The greatest trick of all brought the desert campaign to an early, life-saving close.

THE WAR MAGICIAN is the larger-than-life story of an exceptional man and a fascinating re-creation of cirtually unknown events in military history.

0 552 12509 1   £2.95

MERCENARY
by Mike Hoare

Mike Hoare's own story of the Congo Rebellion, an event of unparalleled savagery in the history of Africa.

In July 1964, after four years of uneasy Independence, the Democratic Republic of the Congo was engulfed by an armed rebellion which spread through the country with the speed and ferocity of a bush fire.

The 'Simbas' – the rebel soldiers – doped with heroin, proceeded to strike terror into the hearts of civilians and National Army alike, raping and looting and burning.

Faced with this situation, Moise Tshombe enlisted the aid of Colonel Mike Hoare and his white mercenary soldiers to support the National Army. MERCENARY tells, in horrifying detail, how over a period of eighteen months, Mike Hoare and his men liberated Stanleyville, freed hundreds of European hostages and finally restored law and order to the Congo.

0 552 07935 9   £1.95

THE WILD GEESE
by Daniel Carney

The dramatic, action-packed story of a band of fifty steel-hard mercenaries whose contract takes them into a dangerous Central African state to snatch a deposed black president from the clutches of his country's new ruler . . .

"The story is fast, gripping and exciting. It reflects faithfully the spirit of men who fight for money or adventure."
      Colonel Mike Hoare, Ex-Mercenary Leader

"Extraordinary build-up of tension makes this tale of a mercenary rescue mission one of the rare stay-up-all-night-to-finish kind."
      Glasgow Herald

0 552 10808 1   £1.95

FIREPOWER
by Chris Dempster & Dave Tomkins

THE TRUE STORY OF HOW TWO MEN LOOKING
FOR ADVENTURE ENDED UP IN AFRICA, ALONG-
SIDE A HANDFUL OF MERCENARIES FROM
EUROPE AND AMERICA, FIGHTING A BLOODY
LAST-DITCH STAND AGAINST COMMUNIST
TROOPS AND TANKS

Of the estimated 150 mercenary volunteers who went to
Angola to fight the communists, over 60 remained there – in
shallow graves, or as prisoners to be paraded in front of the
world's television cameras. Chris Dempster and Dave
Tomkins were just two of the men in Colonel Callan's ill-fated
mercenary army.

FIREPOWER is the story of how they came to be fighting in
Angola, and what happened to them when they were there. It
is also a sensational glimpse of today's mercenary scene as
portrayed by two-real life "dogs of war".

0 552 10807 3   £2.95

THE RED AND GREEN LIFE MACHINE
A Diary of the Falklands Field Hospital
by Rick Jolly

"Although several books have already been published about the Falklands War, none gives a livelier or more vivid idea of what it was like to take part."
Duff Hart-Davis, Sunday Telegraph

At Ajax Bay, San Carlos, a makeshift field hospital treated over 600 battle casualties during a 20-day period. This is the personal diary of the hospital's commander – Surgeon Commander Rick Jolly – whose tired and bearded face was a reassuring sight in millions of British homes as he cheerfully stated that, despite the presence of two unexploded bombs in the building 'everyone who reached Ajax Bay alive had gone out alive.'

"Several books about the Falklands war have come my way. With most of them, one tends to skip the occasional page. Rick Jolly's book is different. I felt I could not afford to miss a single line of it. This is a brilliant book."
Liverpool Daily Post

0 552 99068 X   £2.50

OTHER FINE WAR TITLES AVAILABLE
FROM CORGI BOOKS

While every effort is made to keep prices low, it is sometimes necessary to increase prices at short notice. Corgi Books reserve the right to show new retail prices on covers which may differ from those previously advertised in the text or elsewhere.

The prices shown below were correct at the time of going to press.

☐	10808 1	**THE WILD GEESE**	*Daniel Carney*	£1.95
☐	11831 1	**WILD GEESE II**	*Daniel Carney*	£1.75
☐	10807 3	**FIRE POWER**	*Chris Dempster & Dave Tomkins*	£2.95
☐	12509 1	**THE WAR MAGICIAN**	*David Fisher*	£2.95
☐	12686 1	**THE COMMISSAR**	*Sven Hassel*	£1.95
☐	11976 8	**O.G.P.U. PRISON**	*Sven Hassel*	£2.50
☐	11168 6	**COURT MARTIAL**	*Sven Hassel*	£1.95
☐	10400 0	**THE BLOODY ROAD TO DEATH**	*Sven Hassel*	£1.95
☐	09761 6	**BLITZFREEZE**	*Sven Hassel*	£1.95
☐	09178 2	**REIGN OF HELL**	*Sven Hassel*	£1.95
☐	08874 9	**SS GENERAL**	*Sven Hassel*	£1.95
☐	08779 3	**ASSIGNMENT GESTAPO**	*Sven Hassel*	£1.95
☐	10246 6	**A COFFIN FULL OF DREAMS**	*Frisco Hitt*	£1.95
☐	07935 9	**MERCENARY**	*Mike Hoare*	£1.95
☐	12659 4	**LET A SOLDIER DIE**	*William E. Holland*	£2.50
☐	99068 X	**THE RED AND GREEN LIFE MACHINE (B format)**	*Rick Jolly*	£2.50
☐	12419 2	**CHICKENHAWK (B format)**	*Robert C. Mason*	£2.95
☐	08371 2	**THE DIRTY DOZEN**	*E.M. Nathanson*	£2.50
☐	10954 1	**THE FIVE FINGERS**	*G. Rivers & J. Hudson*	£1.95

ORDER FORM

All these books are available at your book shop or newsagent, or can be ordered direct from the publisher. Just tick the titles you want and fill in the form below.

CORGI BOOKS, Cash Sales Department, P.O. Box 11, Falmouth, Cornwall.

Please send cheque or postal order, no currency.

Please allow cost of book(s) plus the following for postage and packing:

U.K. Customers—Allow 55p for the first book, 22p for the second book and 14p for each additional book ordered, to a maximum charge of £1.75.

B.F.P.O. and Eire—Allow 55p for the first book, 22p for the second book plus 14p per copy for the next seven books, thereafter 8p per book.

Overseas Customers—Allow £1.00 for the first book and 25p per copy for each additional book.

NAME (Block Letters) ....

ADDRESS ....

....